W9-BGG-581

A LOOK OF
WILD DESPERATION

...flashed across Kingsley's face and he instantly raised his revolver and fired three quick shots at the approximate location of where the voice was coming from. His companions fired as well in the blur of rearing, spinning horses, their shots crashing into the brush on one side and the timber across the way while they jerked their mounts toward the narrow neck of sand. Bark and wood chips exploded from the log in front of Kincaid's face, and then he was on one knee and raising his Scoff. The first shot caught Kingsley squarely between the shoulder blades...

EASY COMPANY

EASY AT HAT CREEK STATION
COMPANY

JOHN WESLEY HOWARD

A JOVE BOOK

EASY COMPANY AT HAT CREEK STATION

A Jove Book/published by arrangement with
the author

PRINTING HISTORY
Jove edition/November 1982

ISBN: 0-515-06354-1

PRINTED IN THE UNITED STATES OF AMERICA

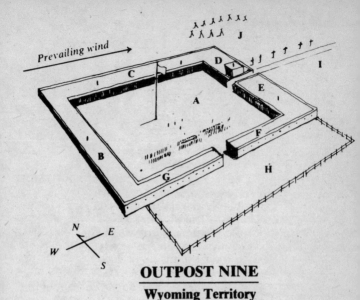

OUTPOST NINE

Wyoming Territory

<u>KEY</u>

A. Parade and flagstaff

B. Officers' quarters ("officers' country")

C. Enlisted men's quarters: barracks, day room, and mess

D. Kitchen, quartermaster supplies, ordnance shop, guardhouse

E. Suttler's store and other shops, tack room, and smithy

F. Stables

G. Quarters for dependents and guests; communal kitchen

H. Paddock

I. Road and telegraph line to regimental headquarters

J. Indian camp occupied by transient "friendlies"

OUTPOST NUMBER NINE
(DETAIL)

Outpost Number Nine is a typical High Plains military outpost of the days following the Battle of the Little Big Horn, and is the home of Easy Company. It is not a "fort"; an official fort is the headquarters of a regiment. However, it resembles a fort in its construction.

The birdseye view shows the general layout and orientation of Outpost Number Nine; features are explained in the Key.

The detail shows a cross-section through the outpost's double walls, which ingeniously combine the functions of fortification and shelter.

The walls are constructed of sod, dug from the prairie on which Outpost Number Nine stands, and are sturdy enough to withstand an assault by anything less than artillery. The roof is of log beams covered by planking, tarpaper, and a top layer of sod. It also provides a parapet from which the outpost's defenders can fire down on an attacking force.

one _____

The town of Douglas, Wyoming Territory, seemed crushed into silent submission by the heat of the midafternoon sun. Its wide main street was abandoned, with the exception of two young boys rolling a hoop in the thick dust, and the numerous horses dozing hip-shot at various hitch rails. The occasional shout or burst of laughter drifting above the bat-wing doors of the three saloons, combined with the distant clang of a blacksmith's hammer, were the only violations of the slumbering silence. Any sense of urgency was lost to total calm, and there was a feeling in the air that all of life's chores had been suspended until the sun finally sank beneath the horizon. But the solitary rider entering the street from the east side of town provided a glaring contrast to the otherwise tranquil setting.

Sitting erect in the saddle, with a gloved left hand grasping reins stretched tightly against the arched neck of his spirited mount, he looked neither right nor left as he guided his horse down the center of the street. The bay gelding walked with a grand display of pride, lifting each hoof sharply and prancing in a partially sideways gait as if impatient with the pressure of the bit in its foam-flecked mouth, which showed pink as its jaw worked against steel in yawning stretches. Its freshly curried hide glistened in the sunlight, and a bold "U.S." brand was emblazoned on one haunch. Sweat-darkened hair along its flanks indicated it had been running hard just moments before.

Controlling his mount with the detached authority of an excellent horseman, the tall rider in the saddle didn't seem to notice the admiring stare of a woman emerging from the General Mercantile as his blue-green eyes remained fixed on some distant object. There was a hard look about his handsome face, and the neatly trimmed mustache trailing just below either corner of his firmly set mouth gave him the appearance of a man who was not given to a great display of patience. The brilliant hue of his crisp blue uniform was accented by the yellow piping down the outer seams of his trouser legs; polished black boots rode high up on either calf. His smartly blocked hat with its crossed-swords emblem was pulled low to his eyes, and upon the shoulders of his tunic were matching straps with twin silver bars displayed on each. A steel saber scabbard hung from one hip and a reverse-holstered Schofield Smith & Wesson was strapped tightly to the other.

As his horse approached the two boys, they allowed their hoop to fall in spiraling rolls to the ground and gazed up at the towering officer with a look of awe written on their smudged faces. He paid them not the slightest attention as his mount passed by and he continued on down the street with his broad shoulders pulled back; a hint of sweat was revealed by the darker blue of his uniform where it touched his spine.

"That's what I'm gonna be when I grow up," one boy said, his voice muted by reverence. "I'm gonna be a sojer jus' like him."

"Hah! Betcha ain't!" the other lad scoffed. "Your ma's gonna have you fetchin' water an' beatin' rugs till yer old an' touched with the gout."

"No she ain't," the first boy replied firmly. "I ain't no sissy momma's boy."

2

"Like heck! Her apron strings is tied 'round you so tight you can't pee 'thout askin' her first."

The redheaded, freckle-faced boy turned on his companion with clenched fists by his sides. "Don't say that no more, Tommy, or I'll sock you an' forget we bin friends."

"Come on, momma's boy," the other lad taunted. "Ain't no kid in Douglas what can whup me!"

The two young boys grappled and fell to the dust in a confusion of bodies and flailing arms, while, farther down the street, the soldier turned his mount and swung down before the Grayson Hotel. He glanced briefly at the scuffling, shouting children fighting some thirty yards away as he looped his reins around the hitching rail, then brushed a fleck of dust from his chest and stepped onto the boardwalk and entered the hotel with long strides.

The desk clerk looked up from the ledger spread before him, adjusted his green eyeshade, and asked, "May I help you?"

"Yes, I believe you can," the officer replied in a deep, controlled voice. "My name is Captain Raymond J. Gann, United States Cavalry. I believe Senator Canfield is expecting me. He is registered, is he not?"

The clerk beamed and tapped the register with the tip of one finger. "He certainly is, Captain. Room fourteen, the best in the house. He asked that you be sent up immediately upon arrival."

Gann nodded without cordiality. "And his daughter? Miss Marla Canfield?"

"Yes she is, sir," the clerk replied, allowing himself a knowing smile. "She has the adjoining room, number sixteen."

Gann's eyes hardened in his rigid face. "A smirk like that would cost one of the men of my command fourteen days in the stockade, mister. It could cost you your life."

"I—I meant nothing by it, sir. Believe me," the clerk said, adjusting his glasses as he straightened and backed away.

The captain's eyes held on him a moment longer, then he turned and walked toward the stairway and took the steps two at a time while pulling the gloves from his hands and tucking them neatly through his belt. His boots echoed loudly as he walked down the polished hallway and paused before room fourteen to rap lightly but firmly on the door.

3

After several seconds' hesitation, an angry voice boomed from within, "Yes? Who is it? By damn, I asked not to be disturbed and I meant exactly that!"

"It's me, Senator. Captain Gann," the officer replied, moving his mouth slightly toward the door.

"Oh! Come in, Captain! By all means, come on in. I've been waiting for you!" the senator called, his voice now warm and inviting.

Gann smiled tightly as his hand went to the latch, then he stepped inside and closed the door quickly behind him while the portly senator crossed the room with a whiskey glass in one hand and the other extended in greeting. There was a florid look about his owlish face, which made the gray muttonchop sideburns along his jaws stand out even more vividly.

"I'm sorry I'm late, Senator," Gann said as his broad hand closed about the senator's fleshy palm. "Army business came up at the last second and I was unavoidably detained."

"Think nothing of it, Raymond, my boy," Canfield rejoined, removing his hand from Gann's grasp and slapping the officer's shoulder with fatherly affection. "Come, let's have a drink," he continued, guiding Gann toward a shelf lined with bottles. "You're a whiskey man like myself, aren't you?"

"Yes I am. I've always preferred a man's drink."

"As well you should," the senator chuckled, pulling the stopper from a cut-glass container and pouring generously. "There was a complimentary bottle of brandy waiting for me when I arrived, but I never drink the damned stuff myself. You're the same sort of man I would have hoped my son to be, if I'd had one."

"Thank you, sir," Gann replied stiffly, accepting the glass and raising it in toast. "To your health, Senator."

Canfield guffawed and his double chin bobbed in merriment. "I am in perfect health, sound of mind and body, and to toast that would be to waste a worthwhile occasion." Now the senator's watery eyes narrowed and he watched Gann closely. "Let's drink to our—shall we say—business venture?"

Gann shrugged with a nod and touched his glass to the senator's. "Fine. To our mutual enterprise."

"I like that—mutual enterprise. You have a way with words, son. You should look into politics once your illustrious career

4

in the military has taken you as far as it can."

Gann smiled and drank as his eyes surveyed the lavishly appointed room. "Perhaps I will, Senator. I have long been an admirer of the finer things in life. My barren quarters back at Fort Laramie certainly don't compare to the elegance of yours here."

"Of course they don't, Raymond," Canfield agreed while retrieving a smoldering cigar from a nearby ashtray, "but look upon your present circumstances as merely another stop along the roadway of life. Cigar? Help yourself; they're in that box on the desk."

Gann took up a cigar, nipped off the end while striking a match, and puffed the smoke to life. "Thank you, sir," he said, exhaling as he spoke. "A good cigar is another one of the finer things I look forward to."

"And which you shall have in due time. Now tell me, how is the construction out at Hat Creek coming along?"

"Fine, Senator. Couldn't be better. If anything, I'd say we are slightly ahead of schedule."

"Excellent!" Canfield clasped his cigar between crooked teeth and spoke with his hands folded behind his back. "I am very much in your debt, Raymond, for what you've done in my behalf with regard to this matter. If it weren't for you, I would never have known a stage station was going to be built there, much less the first such station in all of Wyoming Territory."

"You've helped me a number of times in Washington, sir, when I was there as an adjutant to the general's staff last year," Gann replied with a dismissing shrug. "One hand washes the other, as they say, and I'm honored to have been of some help to you."

"Of some help? My boy, stages are the wave of the future. And whoever is the first one into a highly profitable venture is the one who takes the most out." The senator smiled craftily and added, "Upon your advice, and with some political leverage, I was able to purchase those four sections up there for next to nothing. I'm in on the ground floor, as it were, and I have you to thank. From there I will expand my own stage line and control all of Wyoming. This is no small favor you've done me, son, and you'll be well rewarded."

"Whatever you think is fair, Senator," Gann replied with a tight smile. "But I ask only for your trust and continued friendship. And your silence, I must add, until this project is completed."

"That you have, Captain. A closed mouth catches no flies, as old Ben Franklin used to say, and there are damned few closed mouths in Washington, D.C. Quite frankly, I am surprised that word of this expansion didn't leak out before I could gain controlling interest, and a secret that favors me and my business ventures is a secret forever. The only indication of personal knowledge that I've given of this project, to date, was the appropriation of funds to build the station, and that was completely legitimate, since the construction was to take place anyway."

Canfield puffed his cigar in contemplative silence before adding, "The fact that you, the man responsible for site selection, chose my ground upon which to build is merely coincidence."

"And neither of us can be held responsible, sir. The maps I used to select that particular location were supplied by the government, and I only exercised proper judgment. After all, the site at Hat Creek is ideally suited for this purpose. Since you have already stated that this is your last term in office, and I intend to resign my commission after this tour is up, should anyone become the wiser, we will both be free of any political repercussions."

The senator's eyebrows arched and his glass stopped midway to his lips. "You intend to retire? You've never mentioned that to me before."

"There was no need to, Senator," Gann replied with a reassuring smile. "And besides, the decision was made only recently. I've served my country well, and I feel I've given as much as one man needs to give. It's time I improved my station in life."

"Yes, you certainly have given all that can be asked. I've often wondered why you were wasting your precious God-given talents in such an unrewarding profession." Canfield brushed a long ash from his cigar and squinted up as he did so. "As you know, I hold military men in pretty low regard, generally speaking, and I certainly wouldn't want my daughter

6

marrying one. No offense intended, Captain."

"And none taken, sir," Gann responded, the smile fading from his lips. "Speaking of Miss Canfield, how is she, if I might inquire? Is she at home, or still in Washington?"

"She's fine, just fine, and thank you for asking. No, she isn't either place. She insisted on coming out here with me, but I can't understand what in God's name for. Maybe it's because she doesn't see much of me anymore, what with business, politics, and what not. She has the room adjacent to mine. Would you like to say hello to her?"

"Well, I certainly wouldn't want to disturb her, sir. If she's resting, just give her my regards."

"I imagine she is a little worn out from the trip, but I know she'll be disappointed if she doesn't have the opportunity to say hello personally. I'll tell you what—join us for dinner tonight, on my expense account, of course," he added quickly with a lascivious grin, "and we'll all three have a chance to talk then. She knows nothing of my reason for being here, only that I came on business. We'd best not mention my involvement in this new enterprise."

Gann stubbed his cigar out and placed his empty glass on the table before taking up his hat. "Yes, it's best that we keep it between ourselves for a while. Thank you for the invitation to dinner, but I have some other business matters to tend to while I'm here. I'll be spending the night in Douglas, so perhaps we can have lunch together tomorrow."

"Splendid! I'm a little too tired myself to discuss the Hat Creek Station tonight, so why don't we set aside some time in the morning for a business meeting of our own? I'm going to turn in right after dinner tonight, and I'm sure I'll sleep like a log."

The thin smile crossing Gann's lips might have passed for friendliness, but the cold look in his eyes as he turned away would certainly have failed. "Yes, I'm sure you will, Senator, and I wish you a pleasant night's rest. Good afternoon to you, sir."

"Oh, one more thing, Raymond," Canfield said quickly, crossing the room with one hand pressed to his temple. "You remember those government maps you gave me of the area where we're building?"

"Yes?" Gann replied sharply, with an edge of caution in his voice. "What about them?"

"Funny thing, but when I was back home I took out a map of my own." The senator paused to offer a puffy grin and run his hand through thinning gray hair. "I'm so damned forgetful at times. I couldn't remember where I had left yours. Anyway, later on I compared the two, and on my map the place where you're building is called Sage Creek, but on the government map it's called Hat Creek. That's odd, isn't it?"

Gann shrugged, while watching the senator's reaction closely. "It must be a misprint on your map, sir. Not an uncommon thing. I was with the survey party when the government map was laid out, and I know it to be correct in every detail. Put it from your mind and rely on the official map I gave you. Besides," the captain concluded with an easy smile, "what's in a name? As long as the station is being built on your property, that's all that matters, isn't it?"

"Yes, of course it is. I'm not much good at reading maps anyway, and I even had the territorial boundaries confused when I looked at the two of them." Canfield shook his head in disgust, and the jowls flopped alongside his face. "From now on, I'll leave the map-reading to the men who build, and the moneymaking to men like myself, who invest. But one day I'd like to ride out and take a look at that land I bought, if you would be so kind as to escort me."

A relieved look came into Gann's eyes as he accepted the senator's offered hand. "It would be my pleasure, sir. But for now, I think we'd better hold off for a few days yet. I'd rather have you wait until I have sufficient time to take you on a leisurely tour of your holdings while personally ensuring your safety. As you know, the area is still quite hostile."

"No hurry. No hurry at all. Marla and I will be staying in Douglas until this entire affair is settled. There are banking matters to take care of and such as that," Canfield replied, pumping the captain's hand. "I'm not much of a one for physical conflict, and I would prefer to wait until you can give me your absolute confidence that there is no treachery afoot."

"And when the time comes, I will be more than happy to do that, Senator. Now I must go. Thank you for the drink."

"You're quite welcome, Raymond. One more thing; when

8

you do decide to retire from the military, I would like to have you consider a position with me. It would be small at first, but I'm sure you could rapidly work your way up through the ranks, as it were."

Now the look on Gann's face was one of haughty disdain, but an easy smile hid it from the senator, who had looked down to brush an ash from his vest.

"Thanks, Senator, but I've had all the working up through the ranks I can handle for one lifetime. Whatever I do now, I expect to begin at the top."

Canfield glanced up at the tall officer with a limp, condescending smile. "You know that's quite impossible, my boy. You're unfamiliar with the business world, and I can assure you that promotions aren't handed out as whimsically as they are in the army. One must accept one's position and start from there, just as I did."

"Each bird to his own nest, sir," Gann replied almost acidly as he reached again for the latch, "and I've had my fill of nesting on the ground. Good afternoon to you, sir."

"Ambition is an admirable thing, Captain. May you nest among the highest branches."

"I intend to," was Gann's reply as the door closed behind him.

He hesitated in the hallway for several seconds before pulling a folded slip of paper from inside his tunic and walking quietly toward room sixteen. He glanced once over his shoulder toward the senator's room, knelt, slipped the paper beneath the door, rapped lightly three times, then stood back and watched the note disappear inside. Satisfied that his message had been received, he turned and strode down the hallway.

Hearing the captain descend the stairs, the clerk glanced up nervously from his work and watched with apprehension as Gann approached.

"May I help you, sir?"

"Yes, I would expect that is your reason for being here," Gann snapped, placing his hands spread widely apart on the counter. "I would like a room."

The clerk turned quickly toward the rack of keys behind him and reached for a lower number. "Of course, Captain. These rooms on the first floor are less expensive, but I think you'll find them quite comfortable. Number four should—"

"I don't want any goddamned flop for the night, mister! I want the best sonofabitching room you've got," Gann snarled with hatred burning in his eyes. "Best on the second floor."

As was his habit when nervous, the clerk adjusted his glasses, then tugged his eyeshade down more tightly. "Of course, Captain. I just thought—"

"I don't give a damn what you thought," Gann hissed. "I didn't ask you to think, because I make it a habit not to ask the impossible of any man."

"I—I understand, sir. But I can't give you the best room on the second floor. The senator has taken that for himself."

"I assumed as much. Give me the next best, and make it damned quick!"

"Please forgive me, Captain, but I can't do that either. Miss Canfield is occupying that room. Believe me, if there was any way—"

Gann's hand shot out and his fist closed about the clerk's shirt and dragged the startled man toward the counter. "Give me the best room you have available on the second floor, you little bastard, or I'll drag your ass out in the street and kick your butt from here to the Dakota Territory." Gann glanced at the board, then back at the clerk. "Is number twelve available?"

"Ah . . . yes, sir. It's not quite as nice as the other two, but it is more than adequate."

"I don't want adequate, but I'll take it. My horse is outside. Have him stabled and cared for, and my saddlebags taken to my room. And I'll expect to find a complimentary bottle of brandy up there when I return. Is that understood?"

"Well—I—the rules state that—"

"Stuff your goddamned rules," Gann said, twisting the clerk's shirtfront viciously and splitting a seam. "I'll break your skinny neck right here and now and consider it a service to mankind. Will that brandy be there or not?"

"It—it'll be there, sir," the clerk managed with a frightened smile.

Gann shoved him away, and the clerk sprawled across a rolltop desk behind the counter. "That's better. While I'm here, I'll expect the same treatment the senator gets, and I damned well better not have to mention it again. Is that understood?"

"Understood—understood, sir."

"Good," Gann said. Then, spinning on his heel, he stomped to the doorway, threw the door aside with a bang against the wall, and turned down the boardwalk in the direction of the nearest saloon.

The clerk watched the doorway for a moment in stunned silence, then stood once again, straightened his wrinkled shirt, and let out a slow, wheezing breath.

"God bless the Indian who kills that son of a bitch," he said, just above a whisper.

Feeling the hatred sear his guts like a hot iron pressing against his stomach from within, Gann moved quickly along the boardwalk, brushing past two elderly women without apology, before slowing as he approached Brandon's Saloon. Glancing once at a large roan mount tied to the hitch rail, he nodded his satisfaction, pushed the doors aside, and stepped into the dank-smelling room. The men standing at the bar glanced up as he approached, and several offered nods of greeting to the big, glowering soldier, but Gann ignored them and moved along the bar to stop beside a lone man standing at the end.

His hair was long, stringy, and greasy, and it clung to his shoulders like a dirty mop. A weathered Stetson was tilted forward over his eyes, his lean face bristled with several days growth of whiskers, and a soiled topcoat draped down along his tall, slim frame. One boot was cocked on the footrest, and a Colt .44 was visible where the man's coat had been pulled back for easy access to the weapon. There was the smell about him of a man who hadn't recently subjected himself to bathwater. He didn't look up from the glass he was turning in his finger tips when Gann stopped beside him, but his hatbrim bobbed with the nodding of his head.

"Howdy, Ray. I've been expecting you. How 'bout a drink?"

Impulsively, Gann glanced around before speaking. "Hello, Jarvis. Let's have one at the table, where we can talk."

"Suits me," Jarvis replied, glancing up for the first time with a wave of his hand at the bartender. "A bottle, barkeep, and one more glass."

When the request had been filled, the two men crossed to

11

a table at the back of the room. Jarvis poured generously into both glasses, then kicked a chair back with his boot and sank down to fold his fingertips across his flat stomach.

"You look mighty spiffy in that uniform, Ray," he offered with an appraising glance. "Kinda like you and the army were made for each other."

"We aren't. At one time we were, but we aren't anymore," Gann replied. "You didn't look too bad in one yourself, come to think of it."

"That was a long time ago, Ray," Jarvis said with an easy smile. "A *long* time ago. Must be near two years now since me and the cavalry parted company. Didn't take me long to find out that being a second lieutenant in the officers' ranks wasn't much different from being a low-assed private in the enlisted. Surprised it took you this long to find out the same about being a captain."

"Let's not bullshit each other, Jarvis. I haven't got time for that. You were cashiered out of the army because you were too damned weak to kick ass and take names. Yours was the worst platoon in the whole goddamned U.S. Cavalry, and the only things you did right were drink more whiskey, win more money at poker, and fuck more officer's wives than anybody else in your troop. And where you really put your foot in the shit was when you got caught in the sack with our CO's wife."

Gann had been speaking firmly, and Jarvis's reaction had been that of a cowering animal taking its punishment but waiting to strike. But with Gann's last remark, the tension drained from his face and he chuckled with the return of a memory.

"You might be right, Ray, but—"

"I know damned well I'm right."

"Fine. You're right, as always," Jarvis said with an apologetic shrug. "But since I hated the army anyway, getting thrown out for giving Old Blue Balls' wife a little pleasure was, at least to my warped way of thinking, the perfect way to go. She wasn't that good in the sack, but it was worth every minute of it just for the look on his face when he walked through that door."

Ignoring Jarvis's grin, Gann said, "That might be a fitting conclusion for you, but not for me." His face went hard and his gaze drifted to the far wall. "I'm going out on top. I've been passed over twice for promotions that should have been mine. Sure, I'm a little tough on the troops, but that's the only way to get anything out of the ignorant bastards. That trooper I put in the hospital deserved what he got, but I'm the one who's taking the punishment, not him. The army's changed, and there's no place for a man like me with a milkytoast outfit. Sending me on this construction detail when I should have been promoted to squadron commander was the last straw." His teeth ground in silent anger, and the muscle along his jaw jumped convulsively. "But I'll have the last laugh, and when I'm through, the army brass will be the ones who'll have *their* next promotions to worry about."

Almost instantly, the black hatred faded from Gann's face and he glanced again at Jarvis. "Do you know why I picked you to be part of this deal?"

Jarvis shrugged again as his glass moved toward his lips. "No, not really. But anybody who's got a scheme to do the army a little dirt can count me in. Why?"

"Because you're a schemer, a conniver, a man without morals, and a low-life drifter with enough intelligence to keep his goddamned mouth shut and do the job."

"Pretty impressive credentials, I'd say," Jarvis replied, wiping his mouth with the back of a hand and squinting at Gann with a weak grin.

"Precisely the credentials I was looking for."

Now Jarvis leaned back in his chair, hesitated, then asked, "What's in this deal for me? I mean, besides a split of the take?"

"Whatever I say you can have. The outcome depends on your performance at Farley's Crossing."

"That's a little slim, isn't it, Ray? A promise in return for that many dead men on my hands?"

"I didn't give you a promise, I told you a fact," Gann said sharply. "And if you cross me, you won't have any dead men to worry about, because you'll be dead yourself."

Jarvis raised his hands as a shield. "All right, Ray. Don't get damned testy, for Christ's sake! I'll trust you to treat me right when this is over. Have you talked to the old man yet?"

"Yes. I just left his room. He's in for the whole ride."

"Good. All those pumped-up, greedy old bastards like him

13

are fox-smart and skunk-dumb both at the same time. Did he suspect that map at all?"

Gann took a long drink before offering a reply. "Yes, I guess he did, but I smoothed that over without any problem. As you know, I had two different maps made up, one for him and the other for Lieutenant Ecklehart, my engineering officer out at the site. With regard to the senator, however, the main thing to remember when dealing with people like him is to keep a dollar sign flashing in front of their eyes and they go stone blind to anything else. Even if he did suspect this deal, which I doubt, he won't say anything as long as he doesn't get physically or politically hurt and stands to make a bundle in the process."

"There's nothing I like better than to see some pompous son of a bitch like him fall flat on his ass."

"And that's what's going to happen. Have you got things set up on your end?"

"Sure have. Kingsley and the others are waiting there now. Old French is going to drive that wagon directly to the spot where we want it, and the rest will be like shooting fish in a barrel."

"Good. That should happen two days from now, if they're on schedule, which they should be. Once it's over, you make the split with the others in the cave by the river, then come on back here. Clean yourself up," Gann said, wrinkling his nose in distaste as he surveyed his companion, "buy some new clothes, and deposit our share in the bank under the name of Phillip Bradley. Be sure and let it be known that you're from Texas or somewhere and are interested in sound investments up here. He and the senator are tighter than the cheeks on a baby's ass, and he'll put the two of you in contact with each other. Use your card-playing skills to the hilt with Canfield, and when it's over we'll be major investors in the stage line, our investment money will be clean, and the rest will all be gravy."

Jarvis filled their glasses again and gazed into the bottle as he spoke. "What about the senator?"

"I'll take care of him. He's mine."

"And his daughter?"

"What about her?" Gann asked with an edge to his tone.

14

"You going to marry her?"

"Of course I am. That's part of the deal. That'll be taken care of tonight."

"I kinda like that, Ray," Jarvis said, raising his glass once again. "But there's one thing I'd like to know."

"What's that?"

Jarvis's head swung toward the captain, and there was an expectant grin on his face. "Is there as much satisfaction in sleeping with a senator's daughter as there is with a major's wife?"

"I wouldn't know, Jarvis," Gann replied before allowing a tight smile to cross his lips. "I never had the pleasure with a major's wife. Now let's finish this bottle and run over the details once more, then I've got to go. I've got some work to do tonight."

It was nearly nine o'clock when Gann reentered the lobby and crossed to the stairway with a glance at the clerk's window; to his satisfaction, it was vacant. As he moved down the hallway, he paused before room fourteen and heard loud snoring from within, then he continued on to his room and closed the door behind him. After lighting a lantern, he glanced around the room, noticed the complimentary bottle of brandy that had been placed on the nightstand, and crossed to the washbasin, which he filled with water from a waiting pitcher. He pulled off his tunic and sponged his upper body, face, and hands thoroughly, then toweled off while moving toward his saddlebags, which had been draped over a chair. Rummaging in the bottom of both bags, he found a small vial of cologne, a bar of soap, a shaving brush, and a razor, then returned to the basin, which was situated in front of a small mirror.

While he lathered his face and shaved with long, careful strokes, he admired the lean cut of his muscular body and turned sideways to make certain that his taut stomach muscles had not begun to sag. Satisfied, he toweled his face once more, applied a generous ration of cologne, took up the brandy bottle, and stepped into the hallway again. After three soft tappings on the door, then two more, he stood back and ran the fingers of his free hand through his wavy hair.

Seconds later, the door opened and Marla Canfield stood

15

before him. With the lamplight behind her, her tall, slender body was a curvaceous silhouette beneath the flimsy nightdress she wore, and her blonde hair curled over her right shoulder. Her narrow face was accented by deep blue eyes. Her rich, full lips were now slightly twisted in a tiny, girlish pout. She moved one leg across the other and leaned against the doorframe.

"I've been waiting for you," Marla said in a husky, seductive voice. "It's been a long time."

Gann could smell brandy on her breath, and from the way she stood he knew she was at least half drunk, maybe more. "I'm sorry I'm a little late," he said with an apologetic smile, "but I got tied up with business."

"Business, business. I get so sick of hearing about business." Marla lowered her eyelids and touched a cheek to her folded hands. "I don't want to talk business with you, Raymond. I don't think I want to talk at all. Kiss me?"

Gann leaned forward and pressed his lips to hers, while her hands immediately went around his neck and began stroking his hair. Finally, Gann pulled away and held up the brandy bottle in his hand.

"I've brought something for us. It was a gift from the hotel. 'Complimentary' is the word they use, I think."

Marla glanced at the bottle and tossed her head. "Yes, I know," she said with a sigh. "I had one in my room as well, and they might as well give it away, for all it's worth. Rotgut, nothing more. Come on in. Daddy gave me a bottle of his, and it's superior by far."

She turned and moved across the room, thus avoiding seeing the loathing expression on Gann's face as he stood there, naked to the waist, with a rejected bottle of brandy in his hand. He stepped into the room, closed the door more forcefully than necessary, tossed the bottle onto a chair, and came forward to stand behind Marla as she filled two snifters with brandy. His hands went to her lean stomach, then traced upward to enclose her firm breasts while his lips went to her shoulder and he began kissing a trail to her earlobe.

"You're so beautiful, Marla," he whispered, his hot breath sending a shiver through her body as she tilted her head back with a sharp moan. "So damned beautiful. I want you. I want you to be mine." His tongue made a testing, darting motion against the hollow of her ear. "I want you to be my wife, Marla. I want you to marry me."

"I love you, Ray. At least I think I do," Marla managed with halting words, "but you know how Daddy feels about soldiers. He would never allow us to marry."

"To hell with your father. We'll get married in secret, and he'll never know."

Marla's breathing was coming faster, in short, tortured gasps, as Gann's hand found its way beneath the nightdress and began working downward with caressing strokes. "When, Ray . . . when?"

"Within the next few days, honey. I'll let you know when."

She turned suddenly and her hands went to his hair again and she kissed him hungrily. "Take me, Ray," she whispered as their mouths touched. "Take me now and do the things you do to me."

Gann slowly untied the loose strings at the top of the nightgown, lowered it to her shoulders, and let it fall to the floor. He carried her in his arms to the bed and laid her on the silken spread. She waited for him, eyes closed, unresisting, and he entered her almost viciously. Her moaning cries, pleas, and ecstatic exhortations went unheard as he worked over her, with hatred for a complimentary bottle of brandy emblazoned in his brain.

Outside the door, crouched with one ear pressed against the keyhole, the clerk stood listening. He tried once to peer into the room, failed, and settled for passionate sounds emanating from the room. When the cries and grunts of exertion had died from within, he took a notepad from his pocket, jotted down the time and all that he had managed to hear, then returned the pad to his pocket and yawned widely as he returned to his sanctuary in the broom closet at the end of the hall. Even though he knew he must wait there until Gann left the room in order to make a notation of the time, there was a satisfied look on his face. He had gotten what he came for.

As he pulled the closet door almost shut, leaving an open space of no more than an inch, he smiled and muttered softly to himself, "Maybe I won't need an Indian after all. I'm sure the senator can work out a more painful conclusion to the good captain's career."

two ━━━━━━━━━━━━━━━

"How long, Corporal?"

The telegrapher turned at his desk to look at the tall, broad-shouldered officer standing near the window behind him. "How long until when, sir?"

"How long until you get that damned thing working again?"

"Should be just a few minutes, sir. I think I've found the problem."

"Good. Keep working on it. Half a message isn't much better than half a horse," Lieutenant Matt Kincaid replied, nodding toward the sending device. "From the way things appear, the brass at Fort Laramie seem to have a bit more to say than what I've read so far."

The corporal turned back to his work, and Kincaid leaned on the window ledge to look out across the parade of Outpost Number Nine. Kincaid was a handsome man in an athletic, rugged sort of way, and as executive officer of Easy Company, he was respected as much for his firmness as for his fairness. A graduate of West Point, Class of '69, he had not fought in the Civil War, but was now serving his second Western tour.

As he watched the parade warm in the early sunlight, his mind was given to thoughts about the uncompleted message in his hand, and he found it most curious indeed. He was partial to a direct approach to problems, and he was disturbed by vagueness. What he had read so far of the incoming telegram was the epitome of veiled meanings.

Kincaid's thoughts were interrupted by the rattle of a telegraph key, and he turned back toward the desk to watch the corporal tap out a message and then sit back and wait for a reply. The response was immediate as the key moved with mechanical indifference and the telegrapher glanced up with a smile.

"All squared away, sir. I just sent a test message and we're being received strong and clear."

"Good. Now notify Laramie that we are sending and receiving again, and ask them to repeat their entire message."

"Yessir," the corporal replied, grasping the key between thumb and forefinger to tap out the message.

Within seconds of the end of the transmission, the device began to clatter again while the telegrapher jotted down deciphered words. Kincaid listened to the alien language with open respect, and when the machine finally ceased its clatter and the corporal tore the lengthy message from his pad, the lieutenant shook his head in genuine amazement.

"I never get over that, Corporal."

"What's that, sir?"

"How the hell you can make any sense out of whatever all those *dits* and *dahs* are supposed to mean."

Accepting Kincaid's remark for the compliment it was intended to be, the telegrapher smiled and handed the message to the officer. "It's a matter of practice, sir. Some military messages are hard to make sense out of, and this one is no different. Everything they sent is written down correctly, but good luck with trying to decipher the meaning."

"Thanks. I was afraid of that," Kincaid replied with a tight smile as his fingers closed about the telegram and he turned it to the light. While his eyes skipped over the printed words, the confused look on his face deepened and he read the message a second time before glancing down at the corporal.

"This is it?"

"That's all they sent, sir."

"It figures. Thanks, Corporal. I'd better get this over to the captain," Kincaid said, turning toward the door and then stopping. "What was wrong with that damned thing?"

The corporal offered a knowing smile. "Mostly it's just plain worn out, sir. Like everything else on post, I guess. To be specific, the wire terminals had a thin film of corrosion on them, which made for a bad connection. The plating is shot, and it'll happen more frequently now, I'm sure."

"It would probably spoil us to have anything in good working order around here," Kincaid said. "Perhaps Easy's motto should be, 'Find it, fix it, and then fight with it.' I'm not sure whether the captain will be sending a reply or not, but stand by just in case."

"Yes, sir."

Kincaid stepped into the sunlight and angled toward the orderly room while reading the message a third time as he crossed the parade. The office door stood ajar, and he could see the massive Private Malone standing in front of First Sergeant Ben Cohen's desk as he passed beneath the overhang.

"Good morning, Sergeant," Kincaid offered cordially as he entered the room. "What's Malone been up to this time?" he asked with a nodding glance toward the soldier standing rigidly at attention.

"Good morning, Lieutenant," Cohen replied. "Same old shit, sir. As you recall, Friday was payday, that means passes for the men into town, including Old Ringtail here. Pouring whiskey on an Irish temper is just like pouring gunpowder on a fire. He mixed it up a little bit with the feather merchants, as he calls them, and the result was the usual."

Kincaid couldn't help allowing himself an inward smile as he watched the contrite expression on the huge private's face. Fighting and trouble were familiar complaints against Malone when he got his hands on a bottle of whiskey, but Kincaid secretly admired the Irishman for the soldier he was when sober. Malone would willingly put his life on the line for his comrades, as he had in fact done numerous times in the past, and the inner rage that burned with the white heat of an alcohol-fueled fire concealed his true qualities as a man of tenderness and compassion.

"Well, Malone," Kincaid said, "what have you got to say for yourself, other than that you are totally innocent, and that you were merely defending the good name of Easy Company in particular and the U.S. Mounted Infantry in general?"

It was obvious that Malone was in the throes of a hangover to match his own size as he grimaced painfully and replied, "Sir, you know how it is with some of these civilians. They ain't properly appreciative of the job the army does in protecting their worthless scalps. Anyway, the particular gent they tell me I detoothed—though I'm blamed if I remember much of it—had an awful lot to say about the service for one who's never had a uniform next to his skin. I seem to recollect that he started to get more personal and said something scandalous about my blessed mother, God rest her soul. I reckon I must have blacked out along about that time, sir. I do truly regret that he'll have to live on soup and oatmeal until he can order a new set of choppers from Monkey Wards, sir, but I trust he'll be more careful with his store-bought teeth than he was with the set the Good Lord gave him."

"Let's hope so, Malone," Kincaid said, suppressing a grin. "I suppose you realize that you'll likely be restricted to post for some time to come."

"Just as well, sir," Malone said. "I don't suspicion I'll be welcome in town for a while, anyway."

Kincaid turned to Cohen. "I'm sure you'll be able to find some chores to occupy the private's time while he's on restriction, won't you, Ben?"

Cohen sighed wearily. "He knows 'em all by heart, sir. It's just a matter of pointing him in the right direction."

"Good. Is the captain in?"

"Yes, sir. He's expecting you. Just go on in."

"Thank you, Ben," Kincaid said, moving toward the door, which was slightly ajar. Pausing to rap on the jamb, he stepped inside when the captain acknowledged his presence.

"Just one moment, Matt," the captain said without looking up from the letter he was writing. "I'd like to get this out as

22

quickly as possible, and I've almost got the damned thing done. Have a seat."

"Thank you, sir," Kincaid replied, easing into a chair and crossing his legs comfortably. As he waited while the draft was being completed, he studied the man he had come to admire more than any other officer he had served under since receiving his commission.

Like Kincaid, and mostly due to the obscurity of their assignment, Warner Conway was overdue for promotion, and while he deserved to be a major, he expressed no personal grudge toward those on the promotions board who had passed him over. He had a distinguished service record, including combat command as a lieutenant colonel under General Grant during the Civil War. Born a Virginian, he was a man of breeding and manners, but military to the marrow of his bones. There was a distinguished handsomeness about him, with his full head of hair, graying slightly at the temples, and his physique, lean and firm despite his forty years.

The scratching ceased and Conway read the letter one final time before making a last correction and laying his pen aside. As he folded the letter into equal thirds, he glanced up at Kincaid with an unmistakable twinkle in his eye.

"Somehow I get some pleasure out of pointing out to the paymaster at Regiment that he has overpaid our men on the rare occasion that he does. Usually it's the other way around, or no pay at all, as you are well aware. Is the telegraph working again?" he asked, slipping the letter into an envelope and sealing the flap.

"Yes it is, sir," Kincaid replied with a gesture toward the message in his hand. "But it might as well not be, for all the sense this makes."

"Another one of those, huh, Matt?" Conway observed, leaning back in his chair and touching his fingertips together above his chest.

"Yes, sir. Here, see if you can make any sense out of it."

"No. Read it to me, if you will. That way, it'll be fresh in your mind as well as mine."

"Yes, sir. It starts out with the usual to, from, subject, etcetera, and of course it's directed to you.

23

'You are hereby instructed to send a detachment to Hat Creek, in the northwest quadrant of Nebraska, just beyond the Wyoming territorial border, to inspect and report on the progress of a new stagecoach station currently under construction at the abovementioned location. You are merely to inspect and report. No action is to be taken on your part unless further advised. A cavalry troop under the command of Captain Raymond J. Gann is presently engaged in the actual construction, and we are to be informed of any judgmental errors that might have been made. This is not intended to imply that such errors have in fact transpired. You are assigned to a reconnaissance patrol that is strictly visual reference as to progress and location. This is to be considered a priority assignment and dispatched accordingly.'"

Kincaid looked up from the message and shrugged. "That's it, sir. Make any sense to you?"

Conway pursed his lips in thought and tapped his thumbs against his chin. "Not a hell of a lot. In the first place, Nebraska is technically outside of our command. Second, I've heard talk that there is supposed to be a stage line started from the Dakotas to Cheyenne as soon as the iron bridge being built across the North Platte is completed. But I didn't know anything about a stage station at Hat Creek, wherever in hell that is. Take a look at the map, Matt. See if you can find the exact location they're referring to."

Kincaid rose and crossed to the broad wall map depicting the High Plains region, and traced a finger along boundary lines until he found Hat Creek. "Here it is, sir. About one hundred and four degrees longitude and forty-three degrees latitude. Hat Creek comes out of Dakota, crosses the border into Nebraska, and as the crow flies I'd make it about eighty or ninety miles northeast of Laramie, maybe ten miles from the Wyoming line."

"Fine, Matt. Thank you. Have a seat again and let's see if we can't figure this out. There are some odd-smelling fish in this barrel, if you ask me."

"That's my opinion as well, sir." Kincaid replied, resuming his seat and glancing again at the message in his hand. "I can't understand their wanting a progress report on the construction

24

of the station, but I would think that would be supplied by this Captain Gann."

Conway smiled, lit a cigar, then watched his adjutant through a haze of bluish-white smoke. "Yes, that does seem a little strange, doesn't it? And the wording of that message— it's almost the same as saying, 'There's a rattlesnake ahead of you—don't step on it or kill it, just let it know you know it's there.' I wonder if we're witnessing an old army game here."

"What would that be, sir?"

"I've seen it before, and this has all the earmarks of the same thing. When a valued officer makes a mistake, oftentimes the top brass don't want to upbraid him for his error, they just want him to know that they know he's made one and to correct it before disciplinary action has to be taken. In other words, it's the same as saying, 'I see you and you know I see you, so there's no point in hiding any longer.' According to my interpretation of their meaning, they're almost certain that this Captain Gann has botched things somewhere along the line and they want it corrected without official recognition of the error. That way, everyone looks good and there is no need for the mistake to be a matter of record."

"I can understand that, Captain, and I've seen that same game played myself. But why Easy Company? There are cavalry units equally as close as we are, if not closer."

"That's exactly the point, Matt. Those other units are *cavalry*. We're *mounted infantry*. If Gann has in fact done something that the brass want brought to his attention but not made public knowledge, they wouldn't want another cavalry outfit pointing it out to him. As we both know, there are damned few secrets kept within outfits serving under the same colors."

"Yes, I see your point. Shall I take a detail and head down that way?" Kincaid asked, leaning across to lay the telegram on Conway's desk.

"No, I think not. Obviously they want to keep this as quiet as possible, and an officer pointing out a mistake to another officer might not be the best thing in this case. And besides, I think we'd better cover ourselves as well on this one. According to the tone of this message here," Conway continued, taking up the document and scanning the page, "there is no way a noncom could get drawn into a political trap, but an officer might. I would venture to say that something is definitely wrong, and whatever it is, it's quite apparent that no one is very anxious to take the blame. An enlisted man would be asked to make no decisions beyond what his orders are, but you, myself, or any other officer in this outfit might have to. Perhaps what I'm saying might be misconstrued by some as taking the cowardly approach, but I don't give a damn about that. When everyone else is peeking out from behind the trees, only a fool would charge into the clearing. From what I can see here, we're looking at a simple recon patrol with hidden implications but no real danger beyond the usual."

"That sounds about right, sir. Whom shall we send?"

"Gus Olsen. He's the most savvy noncom we've got, other than Ben. He's an old pro and nobody's going to pull the wool over his eyes, and he knows how to step over cowshit as well as how to walk around it."

"How big a detail do you want to send, Captain, and which men?"

"I'd say five, including Gus. The others should be four of the biggest, toughest soldiers we've got. We can't lose sight of the fact that we're dealing with cavalry here, and there's never been any love lost between us and them."

Kincaid smiled and inclined his head toward the door. "There's a private standing outside right now who is more than qualified, sir. And besides, I think he could use a little time in the saddle."

"He was the first one to come to mind, Matt," Conway agreed while dusting the ash from his cigar. "If it came down to a fight between Malone and a grizzly, I'd have to do some heavy thinking before I placed a wager. Name three more and see if we agree."

Kincaid studied his mind briefly before saying, "Garfield, Winkleman, and Jones."

"Jones? He's a little small, isn't he? Comparatively speaking, I mean."

"He's a little shorter than the other two, sir, but he wouldn't back away from a blood-eyed bull. He's also best friends with the other two, which comes in handy when a man's back needs some cover."

26

"Then it's settled. Find Gus and have him line out his detail, then bring him back here and the three of us will go over the details as to location and objective. If they leave this morning, they should arrive at Hat Creek sometime late tomorrow afternoon."

"Right, sir," Kincaid replied, rising to leave. "I'll find Windy and have him here too. He knows that country better than anyone else."

"Good idea. One more thing, Matt—did you have a chance to see Lieutenant Springer when he was here the other day escorting the paywagon? The two of you were at the Point together, weren't you?"

"Yes we were, sir. Kind of drifted apart since then, but at the time we were damned close friends. I was best man at his wedding, as a matter of fact," Kincaid added with a fond smile of remembrance. "He got himself a beauty when he married Charlene. We had a chance to talk briefly while he was here, and I understand he's got a daughter now, with another child on the way. Ed was telling me that when this tour is up, he's getting out of the military and settling down to a peaceful civilian life—fat and happy behind the counter of a mercantile somewhere. The army is no place to raise kids, he said, and I suppose he's right."

"Yes, I imagine he is," Conway agreed, laying his cigar aside and clasping his hands behind his head. "Since Flora and I have never had any children, I've never been faced with that decision . . ." His voice trailed off wistfully, and then he cleared his throat and went on, "Seemed like a nice fellow, that Lieutenant Springer."

"One of the best, sir," Kincaid agreed. "Luckily, I've never had to make that decision either."

"Well, watch it, Matt," Conway smiled. "I've seen more than one man taken by surprise. In your case, I'd be real careful not to leave any forwarding addresses."

Kincaid smiled back. "Thank you, sir. I do try to stay one step ahead, and I don't intend to get roped until I'm good and ready."

• • •

Nearly half an hour later, Kincaid, Sergeant Olsen, and Windy Mandalian entered the office. Gus Olsen had an unperturbed countenance, and the soft-spoken manners of a Wisconsin-reared farmboy, which he was. He was a big, thickly built man with sloping shoulders and arms that hung like dangling tree limbs by his sides. Scarred from combat in the Civil War and numerous skirmishes later on the frontier, he was the living picture of what a veteran soldier should look like, and the glitter in his deep blue eyes indicated that not one ounce of fight had been taken out of him.

Windy Mandalian, the third man to enter the room, was an entirely different type of individual. Wearing fringed buckskins, with a revolver sagging from one hip and a bowie knife from the other, Mandalian was the embodiment of frontier strength and spirit. His rugged face was dominated by a hawk-like nose, and his dark features and taciturn ways might have labeled him as much of an Indian as those he had fought against for so many years as an army scout. He was known as a fearless, formidable foe on the field of combat, and there were few, either Indian or white, who wished to cast their lot against him.

"Thanks for coming by, men," Conway said, pushing his paperwork aside and taking up his cigar once more. "Did you brief Gus at all, Matt?"

"Yes," Kincaid replied. "He knows his assignment, and all he needs is a final look at the map with Windy here and whatever instructions you wish to give him."

"Good. I've written out specific orders for you to take along, Gus. You are to follow them to the letter, as I'm sure I don't have to point out. You'll be dealing with a cavalry captain named Raymond Gann, and if he orders you to do anything other than that which I have specified, you are to return to the post and I'll take full responsibility for any repercussions that might develop. Is that understood?"

"Yes, sir," Olsen replied in a soft voice, while an easy grin spread across his face. "And from the looks of things, sir, I'm taking most of our discipline problems with me. Am I going to a lynching, sir, or just on recon patrol?"

Conway smiled in return. "I'll admit that's a rather motley crew you've got on your hands, Gus, but I wouldn't want to be one of the boys who comes up against you, if it turns out that way."

"I understand why you're sending them along, sir, and I appreciate that. I've been in the back alley with yellowlegs before, and if I had to pick four men to back me, those are the ones I would have chosen. We're all saddled and ready to go, Captain, anytime you say."

"Fine. How familiar are you with that area around Hat Creek?"

"Not as much as Windy here, but he's given me a pretty good idea of where the best crossings are and what to look for in general. We'll find our objective, sir."

"I'm sure you will. Windy? Give Gus a good briefing on that map over there, will you? While you're doing that, Matt and I'll go over these orders I've written for this patrol, and see if anything has been left out."

"Be glad to, Cap'n," Mandalian replied, hunching away from the wall. "Might even give him the name of a squaw or two I know down that way."

Olsen chuckled and followed Mandalian to the wall map. "Thanks, but no thanks, Windy. I've seen some of your women before."

"Betcha ain't much of a judge of horseflesh either, Gus," the scout retorted.

"Maybe not, Windy, but at least I can tell one from the other."

After Windy had detailed the map for Olsen, Conway handed the sergeant his orders and the four of them passed through the orderly room and onto the sunlit parade. His detail was mounted and waiting, and Olsen turned to salute the officers before swinging up on his saddle.

"See you in a few days, Captain," Olsen said, nudging his horse into a canter and angling toward the main gate with the four burly men riding behind him in two pairs.

"Now if that ain't a pat hand, I've never seen one," Mandalian said laconically. "Four jokers and an ace. If all them fellers' brains was salt and put together in a pile, you wouldn't even have enough to work up the flavor in a steak."

Kincaid and Conway laughed before Matt said, "They're

29

not being sent on this patrol becaue they're geniuses, Windy. They're going along because they know how to handle themselves in a brawl. That doesn't require a whole hell of a lot of brains."

Mandalian squinted at the vanishing patrol and spat to one side. "That a fact? No brains? No wonder they're so damned good at it, then."

As the three of them started toward the orderly room again, they heard a shout from the far side of the parade and turned back.

"Captain Conway! Telegram, sir!"

While they waited for the telegrapher to scurry across the parade, Conway glanced toward Kincaid. "Two telegrams in one day, Matt. Maybe we shouldn't have fixed the damned thing after all."

"I think you're right, Captain. I've never seen one yet that said, 'Congratulations, it's a baby boy.'"

The corporal slowed as he neared Conway, saluted, and handed the message across. "It's from Fort Laramie, sir. They're expecting a reply."

Taking the sheet of paper, Conway turned it right side up and read the short message out loud:

"'Captain Conway: Please reconfirm arrival at and departure from your outpost of paywagon bound from Fort Laramie to Fort McKinney, via Outpost Number Nine. Wagon has not arrived at McKinney and is now one day overdue. U.S. Army regulations require paymaster in charge at each paywagon stop to wire HQ, notifying it of arrival and departure times. Your wire received and acknowledged, but please reconfirm immediately. Yours, Colonel V. Sorensen, paymaster, Fort Laramie.'"

Conway turned and looked at Kincaid and noticed the troubled look in the lieutenant's eyes. "Don't get too concerned just yet, Matt. They did arrive here on time, didn't they?"

"Yes, sir," Kincaid replied firmly. "Four days ago at exactly two o'clock in the afternoon. They left the following morning at daybreak."

"And that would have given them enough time to get to Fort McKinney, wouldn't it?"

"Yes, it should have, unless they broke down or something

else went wrong along the way. I remember Ed's saying that in two nights he would be drinking a cool beer with another old friend of ours up at McKinney.

"Well, let's hope they broke down and nothing more," Conway said with his brow furrowed in concern as he turned back to the telegrapher. "Corporal, send this reply: 'Paywagon arrived and departed on schedule. Will dispatch patrol immediately to investigate.'

"That's all the message we need to send. Put down the dates and times that Lieutenant Kincaid just mentioned."

"Yes, sir."

Again, Conway looked at Kincaid as the corporal trotted back toward the telegraph shack. "Lieutenant Springer means a lot to you, Matt. Why don't you and Windy lead a patrol out this afternoon and see if you can't give him a hand? Probably a broken axle or something."

"Yes, I suppose it's something like that," Kincaid replied in a less-than-confident tone. "They had to cross both the Belle Fourche and Powder rivers. That can be tricky sometimes. Shall I take one squad or two, sir?"

Conway hesitated, then turned away as he gave reply. "Take two, Matt," he said in a lowered voice. "Just in case."

three ————————————

The rhythmic creak of worn leather, the soft jangle of hardware, and the occasional jousting remark drifted across the silent parade as two squads of the First Platoon led their mounts toward the flagpole and away from the stables. The faded blue of well-worn uniforms provided a dull contrast to the glistening flanks of freshly groomed mounts, and the enlisted men walked with that strange, somewhat cocky swagger of men who have faced danger many times before and have no fear of whatever might lie before them. Mixed among the hard, weathered faces of the seasoned veterans was the occasional recruit who bore no scars and whose fresh uniform stood out as a badge of innocence.

Kincaid and Mandalian stood near the flagpole, and with his stirrup hooked over the saddlehorn of his nonregulation stock saddle, the scout was making one final adjustment of his cinch strap while Kincaid tightened the leather thongs holding his bedroll securely in place.

Mandalian worked the cut of tobacco in his cheek, spat, then lowered the stirrup again while turning toward Kincaid and resting one elbow casually on the flank of his big roan.

"Matt, I've been givin' somethin' a lot of thought since the cap'n read us that telegram a while ago, and it's got me plumb disturbed."

Kincaid grinned and patted his bedroll in place. "What's that, Windy? The thinking, or what you've been thinking about?"

"Both. I ain't too fond of either."

"What's on your mind?" Kincaid asked with a chuckle.

"Did you notice anything different about that outfit that was here the other day with the paywagon?"

Kincaid's hands stopped their work and he stared thoughtfully into the distance. "No, not really," he said after a long pause. "Except for the fact that an old friend of mine, Ed Springer, was leading the escort detail. That's not his usual assignment, but somehow he'd drawn it this time. It was his first time out."

"How 'bout the feller drivin' the wagon?"

"The teamster? What about him?"

"It wasn't Sergeant Benjy Harrison."

With the last knot in place, Kincaid leaned his forearms on his saddle and looked across the mount's back at Mandalian. "Windy, old friend, you're going to have to be a little more specific than that. Who is Benjy Harrison?"

"The feller who usually drives the wagon. He's an old pardner from years back and I usually make a point of bein' here if I can to swap a lie or two with him when the paywagon comes in. Well, he wasn't here, and it's the first time he missed since I can remember."

Kincaid searched his mind before saying, "I really can't place him, but then I'm usually so damned busy helping the captain get the payroll straightened out that I don't pay much attention to who's driving the wagon. Did you talk to the other driver?"

"Yup, I did. He was a corporal who called himself by the name of French. Kind of a surly bastard and not much given to jawbonin'. I asked him where Benjy was, and this French said Benjy'd had an accident and couldn't make it, so he'd been assigned to take his place."

"What kind of accident?"

"Said he got drunk, fell down and broke his arm."

"So what's strange about that, Windy?" Kincaid asked with a questioning shrug. "Sounds about normal to me, all things considered."

Mandalian squinted one eye and scratched the bristles along his jaw. "Might be for somebody else, but not Benjy."

"Why?"

"'Cause he was a teetotaler. Never touched a drop in his whole damned life."

A stunned look crossed Kincaid's face. "So this French was flat-out lying?"

"Through his goddamned teeth. I didn't let on that I'd smelled a skunk, and got him to talkin' a bit more. He said that him and Benjy were old friends, drinkin' pals, and that they had been together when it happened."

"Could he have been telling the truth, Windy? I mean, maybe your friend fell off the wagon and decided to have a few snorts."

"Nope, 'cause Benjy never was *on* the wagon in the first place. He just plain didn't drink. He's a straight-up-and-down Seventh Day Adventist and one of God's good little soldiers. He would no more take a drink nor have a smoke than he'd try to piss over the moon."

"I'll be damned. That's interesting," Kincaid said musingly. "All right, so this French was lying. Now the question is, why?"

Mandalian reached for his reins and swung gracefully up before looking down and offering a reply. "I'm afraid that's what we're goin' to find out, Matt. Ain't nobody lies without somethin' bein' in it for 'em. I think we'd best be goin' to see what that is."

"Just a minute, Windy," Kincaid said, seeing Conway crossing the parade in their direction and turning to meet him. "I want to talk to the captain for a second."

"Have a good patrol, Matt," Conway offered when the two officers met midway between the orderly room and the flagpole. "Be sure and tell Lieutenant Springer to wire Laramie the first thing when he gets to McKinney."

"Yes, I'll do that, sir." Kincaid paused, then added, "If he gets there."

"You sound kind of grim, Matt. Why do you say that?"

"It's just a hunch that Windy passed along, sir, and not worth putting any money on right now. But do me one favor— send a message to Laramie and ask why Sergeant Benjamin Harrison wasn't driving the paywagon on this last run. It might be a shot in the dark, but then again, it might lead to something. If they say Harrison has a broken arm, ask if he'd been drinking when the accident happened."

The puzzled look was undisguised on Conway's face, but he nodded in agreement. "It sounds a little strange to me, Matt, but I'll certainly honor your request."

"Thank you, sir. Likely means nothing, but I'll know more about that tomorrow. I'd better be going now, and I'll explain everything to you when I get back."

"Fine. As I said, have a good patrol. I'd send your telegram right now, but as you know, the damned thing is on the fritz again and won't be usable for another couple of hours."

"I know that, and I haven't got that long to wait. See you in a few days, sir," Kincaid concluded, saluting smartly, then striding to his mount and swinging onto the saddle. Moments later the patrol was gone and the heavy gates of Outpost Number Nine closed slowly behind them.

First Lieutenant Ed Springer felt a strange mixture of emotions as he rode at the head of the escort detail with the late-morning sun warm across the broad of his back and a powerful mount between his legs. He had longed to escape his desk chores at Fort Laramie and return to field duty again, and finally his chance had come. With the impending resignation of his commission looming before him, he had felt a strong desire to end his career as it had begun years before—commanding a cavalry unit on patrol.

It had been good to see Matt Kincaid again, he recalled, and in some ways he envied his classmate the assignments he had been selected for. While the majority of Springer's time had been spent in noncombatant, regimental duties, he had heard of his old friend's exploits against the Cheyenne on the Staked Plains, and he had secretly wished for a more active role in establishing a strong military presence on the High Plains. Against his wife's wishes, he had made several requests to his senior officers for transfer to a more challenging duty assignment than liaison officer, but each had been denied. His easy grasp of administrative procedure had made it a natural evolvement of circumstance that he came to be assigned a headquarters billet rather than continuing as a line officer. Not a man readily given to complaint, Springer had accepted his fate and decided to make the best of a bad situation.

But garrison duty had never really suited him, and he had decided to resign his commission long before the birth of his first child. Emily, now three years of age, had been more a catalyst for that decision than the instigating force behind it. And now, riding once more on the open plains with cavalry troopers strung out behind him, he wondered if it was too little, too late, and whether the pleasure he derived from the assignment had been commensurate with his expectations.

In between occasional glances at a folded map taken from his inner breast pocket, his mind returned to the events that had led to this patrol assignment, and he was not entirely clear in his mind as to why he had finally been chosen to get out from behind his desk and once again take to the saddle. He admitted that he had Captain Gann to thank, but he wondered why. He and the captain had long been adversaries—one the hard-bitten combat officer and the other given to interpreting regulations as set forth in huge volumes supplied by the Department of the Army. Theirs had been a tense relationship, mainly on Gann's part, reinforced by Gann's open display of contempt for a "pencil-pushing" officer.

Strangely enough, it had been Gann's personal recommendation in his behalf that had gotten Springer the assignment as commanding officer of the escort detachment, and it had come just shortly before the captain left to begin work on a new stagecoach station somewhere to the north. Springer had been pleased but confused at the time, and he was shocked when Gann came into his office and shook his hand in congratulations. Quite a change, he had mentally observed at the time, for a man who had threatened to kill him if the papers for his potential promotion from captain to major weren't processed correctly. And, even more strange, that had transpired shortly after Gann had been passed over by the promotion board and assigned to a construction detail.

"Lieutenant?" a sergeant asked, riding up beside Springer and jolting him from his reverie.

"Yes, Sergeant?"

"I just spoke with Corporal French, sir, the trooper driving the wagon. He says he's made this trip before, and if so, he's the only one out of all of us who has."

"Yes? Go on."

"He says we'll never make Fort McKinney by nightfall, Lieutenant. According to him, we're about ten miles from the Powder River and he requests permission to talk with you about a way to save some time."

A worried look crossed Springer's face, and he remembered the admonition from Major Blair back at Laramie to stay on schedule at all costs. "We've been doing as well as the mules can handle, Sergeant," Springer said with a hint of self-doubt, "and we've followed the route outlined on the map. I don't see where there's much else we could do. What does he suggest?"

"He wants to talk to you about that, sir. He says the route we're following is the prescribed one, right enough, but nobody else who wants to stay on schedule sticks this closely to it."

"They don't, huh?" Springer asked with a squint at the sun rising toward its zenith. "All right, Sergeant, I'll go back and talk to him. You take the lead."

"Right, sir," the sergeant replied as Springer reined around and rode back to turn in beside the paywagon.

"Sergeant Rawlins said you had something to say to me, Corporal," Springer said as he looked across at the scruffy teamster.

"I do, sir. We ain't gonna make it to McKinney by nightfall, sir, if we stick to this route you're takin'."

"I understand you've made this journey before?"

"Sure have, sir. Up till Benjy took over, it was my job. Know the country like the back of my hand. That's why I was sent with you this time."

"That's admirable, Corporal. And I understand you have a suggestion to make?" Springer asked, unmindful of the slightly haughty tone in his voice.

Corporal French clenched his jaw and concentrated on the reins in his hands momentarily before looking up at Springer with something less than respect in his eyes. "Yes I do, Lieutenant. This time of year the water's low in the Powder. If we was to angle northwest up yonder 'bout a quarter-mile, we could ford the river at Farley's Crossing, and save ourselves maybe half a day's time."

"Is that customary procedure this time of year?"

French smiled craftily. "For the officers who want to get to McKinney before dark, it is. Pardon me for sayin' so, sir, but the fellers that drawed up that map of yours ain't never been out of shoutin' range of Laramie before. The escort officers who make themselves look good on this run turn to Farley's Crossing ever damned time."

Springer leaned back in his saddle and studied the rising ground to the northwest. "And you say if we utilize this Farley's Crossing of yours, we can save several hours of traveling time?"

"Easy, sir." French replied with a yellow-toothed grin.

"All right. Since this is my first time in this situation, I'll trust your advice and ford the Powder at the crossing. However, should any extended delay arise from this decision, I'll hold you responsible. Is that understood?"

French grinned again, even more broadly. "If Farley's Crossing ain't to your likin', sir, I'll gladly take full responsibility."

Springer stared at the corporal for several seconds, then made his decision. "We'll turn to Farley's Crossing. You pass the word along as to where we turn."

"Yes, sir."

As Springer returned to the head of the column once more, he felt a certain sense of relief. Having signed for an extremely large sum of money, he was glad to think they would be within the safety of Fort McKinney's walls before nightfall. And there were other matters on his mind, as well, that fueled his desire to speed the journey to Fort McKinney, the foremost of which was the knowledge that there would be a telegram from his wife awaiting him upon arrival. In the thrill of this new, though brief assignment, he had forgotten how deeply separation from her affected him, and pangs of regret had begun to creep into his mind with the memory of his brusque, even curt dismissal of her objections to his going on patrol once more. His thoughtless statement about being a man and a soldier first, a husband second, had haunted him from the very moment he swung into the saddle back at Laramie, and now he could feel her eyes upon his back in response to his refusal to turn and acknowledge her wave of farewell.

Even though he had mentally forced himself to revel in the pleasure of a field command, it had been a secret disappointment to him, and now he only wished to have the thankless task done with so he could settle once more in the chair behind his desk and await the processing of his resignation papers. He felt he had hidden his lack of enthusiasm for command from his men, and from Matt Kincaid as well, but there was no way he could conceal from himself the sense of emptiness that comes with dreams gone awry. It was not the same and never could be again; his daughter and his pregnant wife were the principal preoccupations of his mind, and he longed for some contact with them, even if only through the means of a simple telegram. Perhaps this last assignment was for the best, he allowed, for now he could reject unsettling thoughts about a disappointing military career and settle down to the most important project of his life—the raising of his family.

"Lieutenant," a private said, coming up from the rear. "Corporal French says we turn to the northwest just by that washout up ahead on the right."

"Thank you, Trooper," Springer replied somewhat coldly in response to the distastefulness of being told proper direction from an enlisted man. "Inform the corporal that his instructions have been received."

"I will, sir," the trooper responded, turning his mount's head and retreating toward the wagon once again.

Since they were heading due west at the time, Springer cut away from the established route at a forty-five-degree angle to the northwest beside the washout, and led his command across the trackless, open plains in the direction of some flat-topped buttes he could see breaking the horizon in the distance. After another two hours had passed by, he could detect the sound of rushing water and glimpse the tops of cottonwood trees dotting the prairie in a ragged line that approximated the course of the Powder River.

But the buttes held the most concern for him, and he studied them carefully as the unit drew near. The closer they came, the more he realized that these were bluffs breasting the river on either side, and not the isolated land formations he had originally thought. When he raised his hand to halt the columns fifty yards shy of the nearest bluff, he rode forward alone to gaze down at the trail, and an unsettled feeling touched the corners of his mind. He was aware that the route detailed on the map had been selected specifically for the paywagon to avoid any geographic obstacles and utilize terrain that was free from the possibility of ambush. What lay before them at that moment, however, was a long, narrow trail cutting down through the bluffs, crossing the river with limited visibility in either direction, and then winding upward once more to the prairie floor on the opposite side. The walls of the bluffs were ragged columns worn into the earth through centuries of erosion, with outcroppings of rock protruding here and there, flanked by dark indentations that received no sunlight even at midday.

Taking the map from his pocket once again, Springer traced the river's route to Baker Flats, the intended crossing for the paywagon, and his heart sank as he calculated the distance in terms of the amount of time it would take to retrace their course of travel and cross the Powder in the designated location. To do so would require an additional four or even five hours of travel, and they would be losing valuable time rather than gaining it, as had been the original objective.

Springer turned to look at Corporal French, who was watching him with cold detachment, then reined his mount around and rode back to the paywagon.

"What's the meaning of this, Corporal?" he demanded.

"The meaning, sir? I don't understand," French replied.

"This crossing is not fit for our purposes. We will be entirely vulnerable to surprise attack from the moment we enter the trail on this side until we get to the top on the other side." Springer watched the corporal closely. "I believe you knew that."

"I knew what the crossing looked like, I'll admit that. But you never asked me for a description, if you remember rightly, sir. You only wanted to know how much time we could save, and I told you what you wanted to know."

Knowing the soldier was right, Springer took a moment to study his mind before speaking again. "You say this crossing

41

has been utilized by other escort officers in the past?"

"Yup, sure has, sir. And I've been with 'em most times when they did."

"And the wagon was able to negotiate it with no problem?"

"Nary a hitch, sir. This old bastard," he said, kicking a side board with the toe of his boot, "was built for rough goin'. She's made 'er before, and she'll make 'er again." French squinted up at Springer and added in a slightly challenging tone, "That is, she's made it for officers who had enough guts to put their trust in her, sir."

The corporal's inflection did not escape Springer, and he gazed again in the direction of the cutback. "This is not a matter of guts, Corporal, it's a matter of good judgment, and I'll thank you to keep your opinions, implied or otherwise, to yourself. How long do you estimate it would take us to get back to Baker Flats?"

"Five, maybe six hours. Be near dark by then," French replied before nodding in their proposed direction of travel. "'Bout the same time it'd take us to get to McKinney from where we are now, if we cross here. From Baker Flats to the fort is that much time again, maybe longer."

"It doesn't look like we have a hell of a lot of choice now," Springer said with a weary sigh. "But I'll tell you this—if I'd had any idea we would come up against something like this, I never would have given my approval in the first place."

"It's a little bit late for that kind of reasonin', isn't it, sir?" French asked with a lazy grin. "You wanted to save some time and I told you how the other officers do it. Ain't never been one of 'em afraid to use Farley's Crossing before, but that's up to you. I didn't build the damned thing, I just put my team through it better'n most others can. Anything else that has to do with whether we cross here or not is your decision to make, not mine, Lieutenant."

"I'm aware of that, Corporal," Springer snapped. "We'll cross here. Sergeant!"

Rawlins instantly spun his horse around and came back from his position at the head of the detachment. "Yes, sir?"

"We will be fording the Powder here at Farley's Crossing. I want one squad to the front and one to the rear of the pay-wagon. Pass the word along that I want all eyes kept sharp, and that we'll go down in pairs spaced five yards apart. Should anything go wrong, I want it remembered that our first responsibility is to protect the payroll and other government property."

"Yes, sir, I'll pass that along. May I ask you one question, sir?"

"Of course, but make it quick. We're losing valuable time as it is."

"Wouldn't we be better off to sacrifice a little time in the interest of security and turn back toward Baker Flats? What we've got ahead of us is a perfect place for an ambush, sir."

Springer studied the proposal momentarily before shaking his head. "No, I think not, Sergeant. As I said, our first responsibility is to protect the payroll, and that can be accomplished most effectively by getting to Fort McKinney before nightfall. Now let's get on with it."

"Yes, sir," Rawlins said. "We'll be ready to move out in two minutes."

While Rawlins passed among the troops, Springer went again to the narrow trail and studied the lay of the land until the sergeant came up beside him once more.

"All set, sir. Whenever you're ready, sir," Rawlins said with something less than enthusiasm. Then, as if deciding to take a chance on incurring the lieutenant's wrath, he added softly, "Have you noticed the birds, sir?"

"Birds? What birds?"

"Those birds, sir," the sergeant replied, pointing toward the canyon with a gloved hand.

Springer's eyes followed and he saw several swallows soaring and then diving along the bluff with shrieks of irritation, and he wondered momentarily why he hadn't noticed them before.

"What about the birds, Sergeant? They're probably just hunting for food," Springer replied with a hint of irritation.

"Could be, sir, but I doubt it. They nest at midday and hunt during the morning and evening. Something's got them upset, sir." Rawlins paused, then added wit a squinting surveillance of the bluffs, "Something we can't see, but something that's there, right enough."

Springer glanced at the swirling birds once more before

dismissing them from his mind. "Let's go. We've got a payroll to deliver," he said, urging his mount forward and entering the trail with the sergeant by his side.

Jay Jarvis lay upon his stomach in a darkened cave some thirty yards above the Powder River and overlooking Farley's Crossing below. Extra rounds of ammunition were neatly stacked beside the rifle positioned before him, and his eyes were fixed on the trail leading down to the water, as they had been since early morning. A sense of impatience passed through him, and he rolled onto one side to call softly to the three men off to his left.

"You boys see anything yet?"

"Nothin', Jay," the nearest man replied. "They should be here soon if they're comin' at all."

"Yeah, I know. I'm tired of waiting, and those goddamned squawking birds are about to drive me insane."

A quiet chuckle of agreement was the only reply, and Jarvis turned onto his back and studied an object of irritation just to the rear and slightly above where he lay. It was a mud nest attached to the cave wall through the painstaking labors of a mother swallow, and from its rounded opening at the top, two tiny, baldish heads could be seen bobbing up and down. Infantile screeches came from strangely enlarged mouths. Ravenous with hunger and frightened by the overly lengthy absence of their mother, they alternately squawked and peeped, with one taking the place of the other when fatigue set in.

Jarvis watched the chicks momentarily before crawling forward on hands and knees and reaching up to take one bird from the nest and cup it in his hands. Even more frightened now, the tiny creature wobbled across his palm on outsized feet, with neck outstretched and bulging eyes yet closed in infancy while its wailing song of despair continued unabaited and increased in desperation.

Jarvis studied the tiny creature intently, and it slowly evolved into the symbol of all his inner rage and frustration. Its helplessness, the pitiful wailings going unheard, its abandonment by its parents, and its almost uncontrollable fear in the face of danger were scars painfully burned into his own soul. He resented the hatchling for all that it represented.

44

A glazed, distant look came into Jarvis's eyes, as though his mind had gone to some distant, horrid memory.

"It is not worth it, little bird," he whispered in a coarse voice as his hand began to close into a fist. "I am your friend and I am doing you a favor. It isn't worth it." The fingers tightened into a crushing grip, and the squawking decreased to a tiny peep and then nothing, but Jarivis's fingers squeezed more tightly. "If you could talk, you would thank me," he said. The muscles jumped alongside his jaw with the clenching of his teeth, and his white-knuckled hand quivered before his face. He threw the tiny bird against the wall of the cave, then reached up frantically for the second chick. Snatching its head from its body, he threw it down beside its nestmate.

Jarvis lay back, panting as though he'd completed some arduous physical labor. He wiped his hands on his shirtfront with desperate, clawing strokes that might have suggested they were entirely covered with blood.

"What the hell's going on over there, Jay?" a gruff voice asked from somewhere in the gloom. "Everybody's going to have to be goddamned quiet if we're going to pull this thing off, and that includes you."

Jarvis turned back onto his stomach and crawled forward to lie down behind his rifle again. "Sure, Harvey. Sorry. I— I thought there was a snake behind me, and I tried to kill it."

"If there was a snake in here, it would already have bit you if it had a mind to. Where the hell is that goddamned paywagon? It should have been here by now, according to Gann."

"Maybe it ain't comin', Harv," another man said suspiciously. "Don't it seem a little strange to you that an army captain would lay an ambush for his own kind? Maybe we've been made to look the fool on this one."

Jarvis had recovered his composure sufficiently to regain command, and he spoke in an authoritative tone. "I don't want to hear that kind of talk from any of you, dammit!" he hissed. "Gann hates the army worse than any man here, and he'll stop at nothing to get his revenge. You'd all be better off not to forget that. Ray's been planning this operation for a long time now, and he made all the arrangements himself before he left Laramie. That's a green-apple detachment escorting the paywagon, with the exception of a Sergeant Rawlins, and the lieutenant in command is a pencil-pusher who hasn't smelled gunpowder since his last weapons qualification. French is the key to it, and he knows damned well how to handle a green officer. They'll be here as planned. Kingsley and the others are across the river diagonally from us, and we'll have that detachment under a crossfire the second the first horse sets foot on the opposite bank. Now don't tell me Ray would have gone to all this work, setting things up the way they are, if he wasn't damned determined to see it come out his way. There's only one thing any of you have to remember, and don't forget it— nobody, not a single one of them, comes out of this alive. Now let's everybody shut up and get ready for the job we're being paid damned well to do."

"Jay's right," a man named Kushing threw in. "There ain't one of us here that wasn't thrown out of the army for some reason or other, and that's why we were all brought in on this thing. Why should we give a damn what Gann's reasons are for setting up this ambush? Him and Jarvis here get fifty per-cent, which'll be more than any of us will ever see again the rest of our lives. This is our one big chance, so let's not louse it up, and besides that, it's our one last chance to get back at the army for what they did to us. Aim good, boys, and just fill your front sight with blue and remember the officer you hated most when you pull that goddamned trigger."

"Thanks, Kush," Jarvis said. "You make good sense when—"

"Ssshhhhhh!" The sound came from Harvey, who had one finger pressed to his lips and the other hand pointing toward the trail below. "Looks like we've got company coming."

All eyes shifted to the far bank, and they saw Lieutenant Springer pause and consider the trail, then study his map and turn back in the direction from which he had come. Nearly five minutes passed, and the man called Harvey glanced toward Jarvis.

"What do you think, Jay? Maybe he ain't as dumb as we thought he was. Think he turned back?"

"No, I don't think so. He came this way to save time, and he'd lose more than half a day if he went back now. Most likely he was just having a little look-see. Wait—here he comes again now," Jarvis said, lowering his cheek to the rifle stock.

46

"Get ready, boys, the turkey-shoot is about to begin."

The cavalry mounts hesitated at the lip of the trail, and then started down the steep incline with front legs braced against their own weight. Blue uniforms contrasted with the dull reddish brown of the cutbank, and sunlight sparkled off the crystal-clear water below. There was an eerie silence as the first squad worked its way down the softened earth of trail.

Next the wagon clattered over the crest, with the teamster up on the seat shouting curses and commands to his team of mules, who balked in their traces at the increased weight from behind and the steepness of the trail before them. Once the wagon was committed, the team settled down to a balky descent toward the river, and by the time the front legs of Springer's horse touched the water, the second squad was also working its way down the trail. There was the look about them of a funeral procession, so silently and steadily did they move.

With Sergeant Rawlins by his side, Springer urged his mount into the rapidly flowing river, and by midstream the water had risen to his stirrups, but no deeper. There was a soft quietness about the gurgling sound of water flowing over rocks, birds calling in the azure sky, and the reassuring warmth of an abundant sun. Springer turned once in his saddle to glance rearward, and he saw the wagon maintaining its steady forward progress. The entire detachment was now fording the river. Turning forward again, he studied the trail leading up from the river on the far side, and he relaxed slightly in the knowledge that there were but ten yards to go and the river crossing would have been successfully negotiated.

He turned toward Sergeant Rawlins, whose eyes constantly swept across the bluffs above them, and offered an easy smile. "Now that wasn't so bad, was it, Sergeant? I'd say we made it with little difficulty and saved ourselves several hours' traveling time in the process."

Rawlins held his reply until his horse's hooves touched the opposite bank and he glanced forward to guide his mount clear of the river. "We're not out this yet, Lieutenant, and won't be until we're back on open ground again. There's just too damned many places—"

Sergeant Rawlins never finished his sentence, as a rifle exploded above them and the first bullet ripped into his chest,

47

sending him sprawling sideways against Springer's mount before he toppled backward into the river. Instantly, seven more rifles opened fire and other troopers went down, some riding dead mounts into the water. A slug tore a searing hole in Springer's thigh, nearly toppling him from the saddle.

"Return fire!" he screamed, freeing his Scoff from its holster with one hand while trying to control his plunging mount with the other. The order was as unneccessary as it was futile, since the remaining cavalrymen had already begun to shoot at unseen targets identified only by puffs of smoke drifting along the walls of the bluffs. The staccato fire of dozens of weapons exploding at once filled Farley's Crossing with a deafening roar, and the water turned crimson as it continued its untroubled course downstream, carrying dead soldiers and slain mounts along on its swift current.

"Get that goddamned wagon up here and make a run for it!" Springer screamed, jerking his mount around and waving his Scoff at the teamster, who, it seemed to the lieutenant, was making little effort to encourage his team to a faster place.

Corporal French stared at him coldly and held the reins firmly in his hands, as if trying to keep the team from running, rather than attempting an escape.

A horrifying realization swept through Springer's mind as he saw more of his troopers spilling into the water. Not a single shot had struck the teamster, who made a perfect target, perched as he was on the seat of the wagon.

"You're in on it, you traitorous son of a bitch!" he screamed as he raised the Scoff in his hand. "You miserable bastard! You're in on—"

The words died in his mouth as a slug ripped into his stomach and he pitched backward over the rump of his mount, rolled down the bank, and slid slowly into the water up to his waist. The few troopers still mounted wheeled their horses and made a break for the shore, but they were all cut down, with the exception of one private who managed to make it twenty yards up the trail before his horse was shot out from under him. Leaping clear, he ran for the shelter of the nearest boulder, but a bullet slammed into his spine and he lurched forward in a staggering death waltz before slumping to the ground.

Then there was silence once again, and the paywagon clattered from the streambed and continued on its course up the trail leading away from the river. Corporal French never looked back at the carnage behind him.

four

Sergeant Gus Olsen had felt, prior to the patrol he was presently engaged upon, that he had been exposed to just about anything the army could throw at him in the way of unusual situations. He had not anticipated, however, the possibility of leading a detachment such as the one that now trailed closely behind him. Privates Malone, Garfield, Winkleman, and Jones were to military discipline what Benedict Arnold had been to patriotism. With the exception of their uniforms, they had absolutely no military bearing once they were outside the post walls, and they were much like a team of strong-willed horses kept in check only through the concerted effort of the unfortunate individual holding the reins.

Often on spring mornings he had seen young grizzlies cavorting in the welcome sunshine on the eastern slopes of the Rockies, and he couldn't help but mentally equate the four men behind him to those massive beasts—somewhat innocent in their ways, playful, unmindful of their own strength, and born with a streak of meanness that manifested itself the moment conflict arose. The previous night's bivouac had proven this analogy to be true, and even when they roughhoused with each other, which seemed to be a never-ending ritual, there was always a tacit understanding of the fine line that distinguished sport from war. Whether it be knuckle-twisting, arm-wrestling or a brief sparring session, there seemed to be an invisible barricade in each of their minds that none of them chose to cross. It was like a test of wills in which there could be no clear-cut winner, and the man bested in one contest would surely be the victor in another.

When a hard, cuffing slap across the cheek brought a flush to the skin, it was invariably met by a matching blow of equal force, but never allowed to go beyond a one-for-one basis. There was no baiting, no verbal abuse, and when the sparring ended there was coarse laughter and the embrace of powerful arms locked about each other's shoulders. Among themselves they had apparently established an unspoken code of conduct, a task at which the army, for all its rules and regulations, had proven a miserable failure. It was as though their innate brute strength were an arsenal of weapons to be tested in constant readiness, but never utilized in full measure unless upon a mutual enemy.

Through listening to their relentless banter for the previous day and a half, Olsen had come to realize that each of the four possessed keen wit, and even though each man took his abuse in turn, no individual was singled out for group harassment. Their intelligence had been discounted by many, but the sergeant had begun to wonder whether the four perennial privates were victims of their inability to *accept* being ordered about or of their inability to *understand* the orders, the latter being the usual assumption. When left to their own devices, they were instantly obedient to Olsen's wishes, and even seemed to desire his approval for their actions, which Olsen readily gave. How different that was, he had cause to observe many times, from the situation back at Outpost Number Nine when a shavetail lieutenant attempted to force his will upon any of the four men.

If there was any one distinguishing trait among them, the

smallest of the group, Denton Jones, would have been its embodiment. While payday for the others meant whiskey, women, and fighting, in that order, Jones had one priority he placed above all else: cigars. When the four of them hit town, on the rare occasions when one of the group wasn't on restriction for some violation or other, the first thing Jones did with his meager salary was to buy a month's worth of cigars. Then he cast the remainder of his fortunes to the wind. But, knowing he would surely wind up on restriction, the bull-necked, thick-shouldered little man was content in the knowledge that he could serve his punishment cycle in the company of a cigar that was as much a part of his features as was his nose.

Without apparent consent from the others, Private Winkleman seemed to be the group leader, a wheelhorse of sorts, and the others keyed their behavior to his actions and reactions. It was rumored that Winkleman had once risen to the rank of sergeant during the Civil War, and it might have been that one fleeting experience of the responsibility of rank that made him a natural leader for his misfit companions. Taking note of that fact, Olsen directed most of his communications with the detachment through Winkleman, that communication coming more in the form of suggestion than direct order. Olsen was a firm believer in the old adage "You can lead a mule a lot farther than you can drag it," and while he would not compromise his position as platoon sergeant, he did manage to develop a working rapport with the men serving under him.

It was late afternoon on the second day when Olsen stopped the detachment atop a low, rolling knoll and pulled from his pocket the hand-drawn map that Mandalian had provided him. He studied the angle of the sun, mentally calculated the distance they had traveled since crossing the Niobrara River, then rose on his stirrups and glanced around at the featureless landscape.

"Well, men," he said finally, relaxing on the seat of the saddle once more, "welcome to Nebraska."

Winkleman urged his mount forward and stopped beside the sergeant while giving the surrounding terrain a vacant appraisal. "Sure is a world of difference, ain't there, Sarge? Ain't no man alive that could confuse Nebraska for Wyoming Territory."

Olsen allowed a slight grin to touch the corners of his mouth. "Be a damned fool if he did, as obvious as the difference is."

Jones rolled the cigar between his lips, then took it between the thick stumps of two fingers and spat to one side. "Can't imagine some dumb bastard livin' over here in Nebraska when Wyoming's got it beat hands down."

"The way I've got it figured," Olsen observed, checking the map once more and taking his bearings a second time, "we should be about five miles from Hat Creek, maybe a little more. If we get a move on now, we might be able to make it in time to line up for a little of that good cavalry grub this evening."

"Yellowlegs don't line up for grub, Sarge," Jones observed, clamping the cigar in his jaw again. "They just crawl to the trough on their hands and knees."

A low round of approving chuckles met the smaller man's remark, while Olsen replaced the map in his pocket. "Let's save our opinion of the cavalry for when it'll do the most good, Jones, and then only if it comes to that. We were sent up here by Captain Conway for a specific purpose, which doesn't include baiting cavalrymen. If there's going to be any bad blood between us, let it begin with them."

"Sure, Sarge," Malone said, "but do you think for one lonely goddamned minute that a bunch of yellowlegs are going to appreciate mounted infantry being sent to make sure they remembered to wipe their ass this mornin'? We're going to be just about as welcome as flies in the soup."

Olsen was firm in his reply. "Be that as it may, we're not going to make the captain look bad by starting any trouble. He's aware of what we might be up against, and this detail was hand-picked for that purpose. But we're acting under orders, and so is he, and if they're carried out to the letter, any trouble that might arise will be on the backs of the cavalry. When we find 'em, let's just keep our mouths shut and do our job. If we're pushed too far, we'll fight back, but not until we've tried our best to accomplish our objective." The sergeant turned and looked at each man in turn. "Is that understood?"

There was momentary hesitation before Winkleman nodded and the other three complied as well. "We're with you all the way, Sarge," the burly private replied. "Let's get on with it."

"All right. The way it looks to me, Hat Creek drains to the north and empties into the Cheyenne River, well into Dakota

Territory. It's my guess they would be building the station at the headwaters, which is where we're going now, to have a fresh water supply and to avoid an unnecessary crossing. We'll start looking there."

Jones couldn't resist one final remark. "Knowing the cavalry like I do, Sarge, the most likely place to find that station is the least likely place to start lookin'."

"We've got to start somewhere, Jones. Let's hope we find it by nightfall."

The first indication of Hat Creek's location was a line of cottonwood trees following a zigzag course toward the horizon, and as they approached, the ground turned spongey and the grass flourished in tufted clumps that would indicate the presence of a plentiful water supply, especially during the wet months of winter. Waterfowl winged down in precise formations to alight on a small marsh reduced in size with the lateness of spring, and tules and rushes sprouted in the mud left behind by the receding water.

"This must be the source," Olsen said, skirting the bog and staying to high ground while angling toward the stream. "Must be an artesian spring under there somewhere that feeds the creek year 'round." He rose on his stirrups once again to gain a better view, and searched the surrounding plains. "Don't see any sign of a station being built around here anywhere, but this place fits the description Windy gave me back at the outpost."

"If anybody would know where to find the headwaters of Hat Creek, he'd be the man, Sarge. Looks like we've got about two hours of light left," Malone said, glancing toward the lowering sun. "Could be they found a better place a little farther north."

"Yes, they might have. We'll work our way in that direction and if we don't find it by nightfall, we'll make camp and keep looking in the morning. Couldn't be more than twenty, maybe thirty miles from Dakota Territory now, so if we don't find it by noon tomorrow, we're out of luck."

"What then, if we don't?" Garfield asked.

"We'll work our way toward the west. They're supposed to be just across the Wyoming line, which should rule out anything to the east of Hat Creek. Likely we'll find it along the creek here somewhere."

"There's a whole lot of ground around here for those yel-lowlegs to get lost in, Sarge," Jones said. "I 'spect they'll use every damned inch of it for that purpose."

Malone grinned and slapped his smaller counterpart between the shoulder blades. "It's a little like chasin' the girls back in town. A time or two 'round the bed makes catching 'em that much sweeter."

"A dog wouldn't chase some of the women I've seen you with, Malone, much less try and catch 'em."

"Jealousy is the poison of a bitter heart," Malone retorted in his typically unflappable way. "Beauty, as the bards would say, is only skin deep."

"Yeah," Jones replied, taking up his reins and following Olsen, who had moved out in the direction of the stream. "But ugly goes all the way to the bone."

By the time it became too dark to see, the patrol had covered another eight miles along the winding course of Hat Creek without finding the station that was supposedly under construc-tion. What had once been a mere trickle was now a full-flowing stream many yards across in some places and narrowing in others to a deep trench carved into the prairie floor. With Malone and Garfield taking up sentry positions for the first guard mount, the other three built a small fire and prepared a meager evening meal in a depression well away from the stream. It was standard practice to build cookfires in the con-cealment of draws, in order to keep the firelight from acting as a beacon to attract bands of Indians.

When the coffee finally boiled, Olsen splashed some cold water into the pot to settle the grounds, then filled three cups before settling back with a steaming mug cupped in his hands. As was typical of the High Plains, the night had turned cold suddenly with the disappearance of the sun, and the soldiers huddled close to the fire to draw in its limited warmth.

"Damned strange," Winkleman said around a mouthful of cold biscuit, "that we haven't cut their trail. Didn't you say there was a whole damned platoon of 'em supposed to be around here somewhere, Sarge?"

"Yes, that's what the wire said. A captain named Gann is supposed to be in command."

"Probably wouldn't make a pimple on a private's ass in the

mounted infantry," Jones observed dourly as he retrieved a glowing stick from the fire and touched it to his cigar.

Olsen watched Jones closely. "You've really got a case of the red ass at those cavalry types, don't you, Jones? Aside from the obvious rivalry bullshit, what's your problem?"

Jones puffed his cigar in silent concentration until he was satisfied with the plume of smoke, then he tossed the firebrand down onto the coals and spoke without taking his eyes from the blaze. "I've got my reasons, Sarge. First off, I don't like some blowhard son of a bitch who ain't got enough guts to get off his horse and fight like soldiers are supposed to. Second, I don't like their goddamned smartassed attitude like they were better than everybody else in this man's army. And in the third place," he continued in a lowered voice, "my wife ran off with one of the sons of bitches about ten years ago."

Winkleman glanced up in a surprise. "Hell, Jonesy, I didn't know you were ever married."

"I don't brag about it a helluva lot."

"What happened?"

Jones shrugged dismissingly. "Same old shit, I suppose. She was a real pretty gal, and I loved her in my own way. Too damned much, I guess, and it seems I was a little too rough around the edges for her. She met up with some young second lieutenant who was prancin' around her in his uniform like a turkey come a-courtin' with its tail feathers spread. I was in the field at the time, and when I got back to the fort, word came to me that she had slipped 'tween the sheets with him a time or two." Jones's eyes went hard and he continued to stare into the coals. "Never was much for hittin' women, but the same don't apply to smartassed shavetails. Broke his jaw and one arm. Had me a witness who said he'd attacked me, and since it happened late at night, nobody could prove different. Got transferred, and when that hitch was up I joined the mounted infantry."

"You mean you used to be a yellowleg?" Winkleman asked.

"Yup. Could say there ain't any real love lost 'tween me and them."

Olsen watched Jones in silence for long moments before saying, "Does the captain know about this?"

"Nope. If he did, he wouldn't have sent me on this detail,

Sarge." Jones's head turned slowly toward Olsen. "Is he gonna know about it when we get back?"

"No he won't, Jones. What you told us was man-to-man, and it'll stay that way as far as I'm concerned," Olsen replied, reaching for the coffeepot again. "Damn, it gets cold when the sun goes down, don't it?"

The two privates knew the subject had been dismissed, and Jones rose, taking up his rifle as he moved into the darkness. "Sure does, Sarge," he said without looking back. "Think I'll relieve Malone. If we let his big ass stiffen up on us, we'll never get him thawed out by morning."

After Jones had gone, Winkleman glanced across at Olsen. "Kind of a shitty thing to happen to a feller, wouldn't you say, Sarge?"

"Yeah, but he isn't the first and he won't be the last. I agree with you, Wink—we should have seen some sign of that cavalry outfit by now."

Even though he was reluctant to let the subject drop, Winkleman sighed and held his coffee cup across for a refill. "Sure as hell is, but—" He paused to stare at Olsen. "What the hell happened to the crickets?"

The first shot exploded in the night with an orange belch of flame, shattering the calm with echoing reverberations, while several more rifles opened fire from somewhere along the creek.

Instantly, Olsen slammed his boot sideways into the fire, sending a shower of sparks rising into the ink-black sky and spewing coals and burning twigs across the grass.

"They're behind us! Down by the creek! Let's get away from this goddamned fire!" Olsen yelled, snatching up his rifle and diving away in a tumbling roll as two shots ricocheted off the ring of rocks.

"Don't take me long to look at a horseshoe!" Winkleman retorted, rolling away in the opposite direction as a bullet slammed into the coffeepot with a clang, spilling coffee onto the coals in a hiss of steam.

Three Springfields returned fire from above them, and as Olsen worked into position to aim his weapon, he counted the shots and knew that none of his men had been killed. He waited until the next muzzle flash erupted in the darkness and squeezed the trigger in the same instant, and heard a sharp cry of pain as he rolled once more to avoid an incoming round, which he knew would be aimed at his position. A slug splatted against the hard earth in the exact spot where he had been lying seconds before. The veteran sergeant smiled in the darkness as he slid another round home.

Using the muzzle flashes along the creek as a counting device, he determined that they were under fire from a force of maybe six attackers. He had no doubt that they had been jumped by a small Indian party, and a tingle ran down his spine as he glanced over his shoulder into the darkness to the rear. If there were six of them along the creek, then there would surely be six or more who had circled around behind them and who would be moving forward even at that moment under the diversionary fire of their companions beside the stream.

"Winkleman! Jones! Keep 'em pinned down along the creek! Malone, you and Garfield cover the rear with me! Scoffs out and ready!" Olsen shouted, easing his revolver from its holster and listening intently to the silence that came between their spaced shots. He had not long to wait. Off to his right, four shots were fired in rapid succession, and he could hear the familiar blast of Schofield Smith & Wessons. Then he caught a flash of movement directly in front of him. The warrior who had sprung up to run forward was caught full in the chest by Olsen's slug, and he spun in a twisting arc as he fell to the ground. A spray of dirt splashed against the sergeant's face and he rolled onto his back and fired in one motion. His second shot caught an Indian squarely in the stomach, and the brave stumbled forward to collapse across Olsen's legs. Olsen fired one more round into the apparently lifeless form as he kicked and scrambled away to see a crouched-over warrior running toward where he assumed Winkleman lay. Aiming as carefully as he could, Olsen squeezed off another round and saw the warrior hesitate as if suspended in midair by invisible wires, before his rifle fell with a clatter onto the ring of fire rocks and he tumbled into the burning coals.

"Thanks, Sarge," Winkleman said calmly after firing another shot. "That son of a bitch had me sure as hell!"

Almost as quickly as it had begun, the fight ended and silence closed about them as they lay in their positions and waited for a second assault. Nearly ten minutes passed before Olsen heard an owl hoot from its perch in a cottonwood tree along the creek, and the first tentative chirping of crickets again rose along the stream. He lay there upon the cold, damp ground for another five minutes until the buzzing of night creatures again returned full measure, then he rose to one knee with the Scoff cocked and ready before him.

"Anybody hit?" Olsen asked, rising cautiously in a crouched position.

"Not here," Winkleman shouted back.

"I took a little burn along the ribcage," Garfield said from somewhere in the darkness. "Got a little wet in my eyes, but nothin' more than that?"

"Jones?"

"Them bastards couldn't hit a bull's ass with a banjo, Sarge."

"Malone?"

No response, and Olsen cocked his ear in the direction where he thought the big Irishman had been.

"Malone? You all right?"

Then he heard a scuffling sound followed by a muffled scream and he instantly swung his weapon in that direction. There was a sharp crack, like the sound of wood breaking under impact, and then silence again.

"Malone?"

"I'd be pleased to talk with you, Sarge," came the panted reply, "but not with some heathen savage hangin' on my back. He's wearin' his own knife for a bellybutton now, and his rifle looks a tad better across his head than it did in his hands. Once I get the stink of him off me, I'll be fine as frog hair."

"Good. Did they run the horses off?"

"This fellow over here was tryin' to, but they're still on their picket ropes. A mite upset they are, but they're still here."

"Good work, Malone. It looks like they've been turned away this time, and I don't think they'll be back, but you never know. We'll forget the fire for tonight and stand guard in shifts of two and three. Winkleman and Jones and I will take the first shift," Olsen said, moving toward the dying embers of the fire once more.

For the first time that night, the cloud cover had broken and a silvery moon illuminated the soldiers moving toward their respective positions.

"They shot a hole in our goddamned coffeepot," Winkleman said in disgust while retrieving it from the coals and holding it up for Olsen to see as he came near. "Now if that ain't a downright miserable thing to do."

"I don't think that was their intended target, Wink," Olsen replied, bending over to drag the dead warrior from the fire bed and turn him onto his back. "Looks like we came up against a Sioux war party, or at least a band of young hotheads who don't like the answers, so they don't ask the questions. I wonder if they might have mistaken us for that construction gang. I don't imagine their people are too happy with any construction going on around here, after what happened to them in the Black Hills."

"Custer wasn't exactly tickled about what went on in the Black Hills either, was he, Sarge?"

"From all accounts I've heard, he bought the farm with his own money," Olsen replied.

"Well, there is a bright side, Sergeant."

Olsen looked up from the dead warrior. "Oh? If there is, I'd like to hear it."

"If those Indians were looking for the construction platoon and picked us instead, then we aren't the only dumb ones around here."

A hint of irritation crossed Olsen's face as he stood and looked at the private. "Get to the point, Winkleman, for God's sake."

Winkleman grinned and shrugged his shoulders. "I'd say they're not having much more luck than we are in finding 'em, and they live around these parts to boot."

"Yeah," Olsen replied as he turned away and walked toward the distant rise. "That's real comforting."

Jarvis lifted his eye from his gunsight and watched the smoke drift lazily from his gun barrel as he stared out over the carnage below. He was experiencing mixed emotions. There had been a certain thrill about carrying out a successful ambush, but somehow he didn't like the idea of shooting men from their saddles in such a way that they had no chance to defend themselves. Somehow it reminded him of the hatchlings lying dead in the back of the cave, and he felt a desperate urge to quit the crossing and breath long and deeply of fresh, clean air.

"Nice shooting, boys," he said offhandedly, rising and stepping to the mouth of the cave. He waved his rifle across his chest three times in an all-clear signal, then waited while Kingsley and his men slowly emerged from the crevices across the draw and began to work their way down the bluff walls. Turning toward the north, Jarvis fired three quick rounds from his Spencer, followed by two more, before lowering the rifle across his waist and waiting until two handlers began moving down with saddle mounts on lead.

The three men in the cave were filing past him, and the man named Kushing paused to lay a hand on Jarvis's forearm. "That was good work you did on that sergeant, Jay. Poor bastard didn't know what hit him."

Jarvis nodded numbly and looked away, but Kushing wasn't finished. "Who got that lieutenant? I took two shots at him and missed both times."

"I don't know, Phil. Hard to say, I guess."

"Don't matter anyway" Kushing replied, brushing past and grasping a rock to lower himself down. "The son of a bitch is dead, and that's all that matters in my book." He worked his way downward three steps, then stopped and looked up at Jarvis. "You comin', Jay? We've done all the damage we can do here for one day."

"Yeah. Yeah, I'll be right down. Get my horse for me, will you, Kush? I left something back here in the cave."

Kushing studied Jarvis in momentary silence before nodding. "Sure, Jay. I'll get it for you. Don't be too long. We've got some money to split up, and you're the man who's supposed to count it out."

"I won't be, Phil. Just a couple of minutes."

After Kushing had gone, Jarvis walked back into the cave as if he were entering a crypt. He stopped beside the swallow's nest and gently reached up to touch its rough outer edge. His eyes went to the far wall and then down to the floor of the cave, but the two tiny birds were lost in the darkness. Jarvis felt cowardice well up within his chest and he closed his eyes briefly. It was there again, that exhausting sensation of survival and the flooding nausea of fear. Alone in the darkness of the abandoned cave, he could smell death about him, and his mind's ear could hear the wailings of families whose men would never return home.

He covered his ears with his hands, but the sound would not diminish, and he remembered the laughing of the children at the orphanage the first time he had been left alone on the playground. Eyes rolling in terror, he sought to drive the sound from his mind. He wanted to smash something, and he slammed the butt of his rifle against the nest and sent it crumbling to the floor. He smashed the floor of the cave several times with the buttplate of his rifle, then, gasping for breath, he leaned against the wall and breathed deeply several times with his head pressed against the rocks and his face twisted in a tortured grimace.

Finally he jerked forward with a start in response to a stern call from below. "Jarvis! What the hell ya doin' up there? Get on down here!"

"I'm comin', Harvey. Be right down," Jarvis mumbled, taking one step forward and then another. But when his boot came down the second time, he stopped abruptly at the cushioned feeling of something being squashed beneath his foot. Jarvis knelt and felt along the floor until his fingers closed around one of the birds, which he picked up gingerly and held before sightless eyes. The tiny creature was cold and stiff, but it felt warm to his hands, and a beautiful woman swam before his vision. She had long blonde hair, her body was as firm and tight as the hatchling's, and the memory of how her skin had felt beneath his fingertips was similar to that of the infant swallow now lying on his palm.

"Marla," Jarvis said softly. "I'm sorry, Marla." His finger trailed lightly over the sparrow's body and his mind was lost to a world of memory. "I would never hurt you, Marla, and I won't let Ray hurt you, either. You will be mine, Marla. We—we'll go away. Go away somewhere where nobody gets hurt and nobody cries anymore. Just you and me, Marla. I've got it figured out. Just you and—"

"Jay, goddammit! Get your ass down from there and let's get the hell away from here!"

Jarvis' head snapped up at the sound of Harvey's voice, and he dropped the bird, wiped his hands frantically on his pants, then took up his rifle again and walked to the front of the cave.

"I found it, Harvey!" he called, taking his knife from the sheath attached to his belt and waving it for those below to see. "I lost my knife, but I found it again! Be right down!"

By the time he reached the trail, Jarvis had regained his composure, and he walked up to the men waiting beside the paywagon and offered a casual smile while patting the knife by his side. "It's my favorite knife," he said simply. "I'd hate to lose it."

Harvey studied him closely. "Is that knife anything like that snake you tried to kill, Jay?" he asked softly.

"Don't know what you're talkin' about," Jarvis said offhandedly as he brushed past Harvey and approached the paywagon. "You did a hell of a job, French," he observed, looking up at the teamster. "Brought 'em right to us, like you said you would."

"Guess them lieutenant's bars kinda blinded old Springer," French said with a wide grin. "Happens every time."

"Yes, I suppose so. It happens to a lot of us. Do you remember where the rendezvous point is?"

"Shore do, right enough, Jay. That big old cave on the south bank of the Powder, just this side of the switchback. It's sandy there, and I'll go upstream and take the wagon inside along the bank. Tracks'll be washed out by mornin'."

"Good, French," Jarvis said, patting the teamster's knee while turning to Kingsley. "Jim, you take your boys and escort the wagon to the washout French was talking about. Me and the others will make sure there isn't anybody left to tell something that shouldn't be told."

"All right, Jay. It'll be dark soon, and we've got some supplies stashed there like you told us to." Kingsley grinned and wiped his mouth with the back of a hand in anticipation. "Even got a few jugs of good whiskey there for a victory celebration. We'll count out the money, and in the mornin' each of us'll go his separate way."

Jarvis smiled with the nodding of his head. "That's good, Jim, damned good, but I think I'll be moving out with my cut tonight. I've got a long ways to go and damned little time to get there. I told Gann I'd be back in Douglas within two days,

64

and he isn't a real patient man, if you know what I mean."

"I know what you mean for damned sure," Kingsley said with an understanding smile. "You just do what you have to here, and we'll be waitin' for you at the washout when you get there."

Jarvis's eyes narrowed and he looked Kingsley straight in the eye. "Make damned sure you are, Jim. All right?"

"Hey, what do you mean by that?" Kingsley asked, holding his hands up in mock defense. "We're in on this thing together. I'll be there like I told you I would."

"Like I said, Jim," Jarvis said evenly before turning toward the bodies scattered along the riverbank, "just make sure you are."

five ━━━━━━━━━━━━━━━━━

Windy Mandalian had been ranging far ahead of the search party for most of the day, and now, as he returned, the westering sun cast a long shadow in front of his horse. The scout reined in beside Matt Kincaid and scratched the back of his head as he looked back in the direction from which he had come.

"They're stickin' pretty close to the trail, Matt," he said while working the cut-plug in his cheek and pursing his lips to spit. "We're about three hours out from Baker Flats right now, and if we don't find 'em there, I'd say they made it all the way to McKinney."

"Since we didn't find them at the Belle Fourche crossing, Windy," Kincaid said with a hint of expectation in his tone, "let's hope they just had some kind of minor breakdown and are now safely at the fort. If anything major had gone wrong, we should have caught up with them by now. What would you guess—shouldn't we be gaining on them at the rate of about three, maybe four miles an hour?"

"Should be about that, what with them having the paywagon to deal with," Mandalian allowed as a stream of tobacco squirted from his lips. "It'll be dark just about the time we reach Baker Flats, and if they aren't there, then that means they pushed on to get to McKinney tonight. That wagon's leaving a trail a blind man could follow, and I'm damned sure we haven't passed 'em up anywhere along the way."

"I agree, Windy. There isn't anywhere else they could cross the Powder except for Baker Flats, is there?"

Mandalian squinted toward the lowering sun. "Not if they've got any sense, they wouldn't. Did you say this was the first time Lieutenant Springer was assigned to the escort detail?"

"Yes it was. Come to think of it, nobody besides the teamster had ever made the trip before, according to Ed."

"Ain't that a mite unusual?"

"No, not at all. Cavalry outfits pride themselves on being highly mobile and completely flexible. Any officer in the outfit is supposed to be able to do any job he might be assigned, and that includes escort duty for the paywagon. Why do you ask?"

"Because there is one other place they could cross the Powder in this area, and that's called Farley's Crossing. If a man was green to the lay of the land around these parts, but put his trust in a map, he might find Farley's to his likin' as a means to save time. You can save a few hours, sure enough, but that ain't reason enough to take the risk."

"Risk? What kind of risk?"

"With a wagon like they've got, they could ford the river at Farley's, but that'd set 'em up for a perfect ambush. High bluffs on both sides, and no visibility once you're committed to the crossing. Only a fool would take the kind of chance just to save a few hours."

"I'll admit that Ed is a little rusty after all those years behind a desk, but I wouldn't rate him a fool by any means. Impatient perhaps, but not a fool. I think he wants to prove something on this assignment, something like wanting to demonstrate to himself and his superiors that he's made of better stuff than they think he is. I kind of sensed that when I talked with him the other day."

"Could be sometimes that's worse than bein' a fool, Matt," Mandalian allowed with a sorrowful shake of his head. "The prairie has a way of swallowin' up a man who doesn't give her the respect she deserves."

"I know. How far is it to the turnoff to this Farley's Crossing you mentioned?"

"No more'n a mile." Mandalian said, taking in Kincaid's concerned look. "Don't get too edgy, Matt. Even if they did take the trail to Farley's Crossing, they might be all right."

"Could be," Kincaid responded with a helpless shrug. "But that business about this teamster named French keeps rattling through my brain. He flat-out lied, and I'm damned if I can figure out the reason why."

"Let's hope he was one of the kind that doesn't need a reason, Matt. Think I'll ride on up ahead now and take another little look around."

"All right, Windy. We'll stay on the same trail we're following."

"Keep your nose to the wind," Mandalian replied, galloping ahead of the column once again.

No more than fifteen minutes had passed before Kincaid saw the scout's horse standing in the matted trail left by the wagon, and he urged his mount forward to meet Windy, who was kneeling in the tall grass.

"What have you got, Windy?" Kincaid asked, stepping down beside the buckskin-clad scout. "Have you found something?"

"I'm afraid I have, Matt," Mandalian replied, rising with a last hesitant look at the beaten-down grass. "They quartered off here. Must've decided to have a go at Farley's Crossing."

"Why would he do that, Windy?"

"That's what I've been tryin' to figure out. According to the sign here, they stopped for a while and I imagine they were havin' a confab of some kind or other. I followed the track for a quarter of a mile or so, and they're definitely headed for Farley's. I don't like the cut of it, Matt."

"I don't either. Let's pick up the pace a little bit, Windy. I doubt it, but maybe at a gallop we can catch them before it's too late."

Mandalian grasped his saddlehorn and leaped onto the roan's

back in one fluid motion. Tugging his hat down snugly, he said, "It doesn't look good, Matt. The army hasn't used Farley's Crossing for several years now because of the risk of ambush, and it damned sure shouldn't be used when a payroll of that size is at stake. About the only people who do use it are buff hunters, homesteaders, and other folks who are a little slack in the brain."

"I guess it's too late to say what should and shouldn't be done," Kincaid said, speaking loudly enough to be heard over the drumming hoofbeats of galloping horses. "I can't get that damned Corporal French out of my mind. Even though this crossing was shown on the map he had, I doubt that Ed would have elected to use it without some encouragement from another, more experienced person."

"I ain't much of one for readin' the Bible, Matt," Windy said, "but I did hear about a feller named Judas."

Kincaid nodded but offered no reply, and attempted to concentrate on the positive aspects of the situation. The paywagon had not been found, therefore it was continuing onward unmolested as verified by the tracks ahead of them. While he had seemed slightly impatient and a little on edge, Lieutenant Springer was an intelligent man, and it could only be assumed that the choices he made were well thought out and generally correct. There had been no robbery of an army paywagon in quite some time, so it could further be assumed that there were no known outlaw gangs working in the area, or at least none who were after army payrolls. The detachment had the advantage of daylight on its side, and two squads of cavalry troopers would be a fairly formidable challenge for anyone.

And so it went for nearly two miles, with the positive assessments of the situation revolving in Kincaid's mind like the paddles on a waterwheel dipping into a pool of thought, surfacing, and then going under once more. With each revolution, though, the man named French came closer to the forefront of Kincaid's musings. Why had he lied about something as innocuous as being assigned teamster duty in place of the regular driver? Kincaid was about to review the entire scenario one more time when he was jolted from his reflections by the voice of Windy Mandalian.

"Look, Matt. Over there, just past that draw. See them?"

Kincaid looked in the direction indicated, and saw three horses standing droop-headed in the warm sunlight, while a forth stood some distance away, obviously favoring its left front leg. His heart sank when he recognized them as army bays, and even from that distance he could discern the McClellan saddles and the cavalry saddle blankets with their bright blue field and yellow trim.

"Yes, I see them," Kincaid said grimly as he raised his hand and slowed the detachment from a steady gallop to a conservative walk. "It looks like that one on the far left has been shot or broke its leg somehow," he observed, turning in the saddle and looking back toward the ranks. "Corporal! Take two men and go out and collect those mounts. Go easy and don't spook them."

"Yes, sir."

As the three soldiers maneuvered their horses toward the abandoned stock, Kincaid glanced first toward the cottonwood trees dotting the path of the distant river, then across at Mandalian.

"We must be pretty close to the river, eh, Windy?" he said, the words sounding empty and hollow to his ears.

"Yup. No more'n half a mile."

"Those mounts—you think it was an ambush?"

"That'd be my guess. They wouldn't stray and be forgotten if there was another horse left to round 'em up with." Mandalian hesitated before adding, "And somebody left to ride that horse."

Kincaid nodded and directed his attention to the three mounts being led, stretch-necked, at an easy canter, and the fourth being brought along at a slow, hobbling pace.

"Take them to the rear, Corporal," he said as the first two soldiers neared. "We'll bring them in with us."

"Yes, sir."

A private came up last with the lame horse, and the scout slipped from his saddle to examine the injured leg. His fingers probed expertly over the swollen flesh and blood-matted hair before he turned to look at Kincaid over his shoulder. "It's been shot, Matt. Three, maybe four hours ago. The leg's broken just above the knee joint."

Kincaid nodded but allowed no expression to cross his face. "From the look of its other legs, it's been in fairly deep water.

Isn't that grass seed hanging from its underbelly?"

"Yeah, it is. This old feller's been in water damned near up to his asshole, then went through some tall grass. He's been in the Powder River all right." Mandalian straightened and patted the horse's withers with one hand while reaching for his bowie knife with the other. "Take the saddle off, Private, and load it onto one of the other horses. Then when I'm done, come back and get the bridle."

"Sure, Windy," the soldier replied, jumping from his mount and stripping the saddle from the horse's back. "He ain't gonna make it, is he?" the young private said with a single stroke of his hand along the bay's neck.

"No, son, he's gone his last mile. I'm gonna have to put him out of his misery with this, 'cause we can't risk a shot right now. Better get a move on if you haven't got the stomach to watch."

"You bet, Windy. I'm gone," the soldier replied, dangling the saddle over his shoulder and leading his mount toward the rear of the column.

Mandalian turned to the horse and stroked its neck while speaking in a low, soothing voice. "Easy, fella. Easy, now. This ain't gonna hurt near as much as that leg you're carryin' around. I hate to do it, but—" With one deft stroke the scout slipped the razor-sharp blade into the horse's throat just below the left ear and, with a twist of his wrist, carried the thrust to the other side of the neck, severing the jugular vein and windpipe in the same instant. The horse attempted to rear, stumbled, and fell onto one side and lay there on the grass, with its life's blood gushing from its throat. In less than a minute the trembling ceased in its legs and the animal lay still.

Windy stooped to wipe his knifeblade clean on a tuft of grass while the private returned to remove the bridle, then he sheathed the knife and slowly climbed back onto his saddle.

"It's harder to kill a horse that doesn't deserve it than to kill a man who does. Maybe I'll get a chance at the feller who did that to him before the day's out."

"I hope you do, Windy. I hope we all do. Since you've been to this crossing before and I haven't, how do you suggest we approach the river?"

Mandalian studied the question as he gazed at the terrain

ahead. "First of all, there ain't any 'we' in what I suggest. Let me go on ahead alone and have a little look-see around. There's only one approach to the river from here, and we could get ambushed just as quick as Springer did, if that's what happened to him for a fact."

"All right. How long will you need?"

"Half an hour. Give me that much time, then follow the wagon tracks to the trail's edge. If there's any danger, I'll be back before then."

"Good. See you in half an hour, and be damned careful."

The scout allowed a weak grin as his horse moved forward. "Careful is for dancin' with the ladies, Matt. I've kinda got a hankerin' to step on some toes about now."

It was an impatient Matt Kincaid who waited out the prescribed half hour, and when the time had finally passed, he led the detachment toward the bluffs at a slow, wary canter. Just where the trail broke over the edge and led down to the river, he saw Windy waiting for them and noticed the water-darkened, deep brown of the scout's buckskin leggings. The look in the scout's eyes told Kincaid all there was to know, but he asked his question anyway.

"How bad is it, Windy?"

"Bad, Matt. As bad as it can get. They were ambushed, and as near as I can tell, nobody lived through it. Several bodies drifted downstream on this side and I went out to check on 'em, but they're all dead." Mandalian watched Kincaid closely and then added, "I didn't find your friend, but there's some bodies on the other side that I didn't get to yet."

Kincaid took the news with a tight-lipped nod. "And the wagon? Is it there?"

"Nope. There's a set of tracks leading out of the river on the far side."

"I see. Then it's safe to approach?"

"Yup, it is. Come on up here to the edge and I'll show you why."

Kincaid allowed his horse to follow the scout's, and they stopped at the lip of the trail while Mandalian pointed to the dark indentations in the bluffs above them. "Those are caves up there, and they've been here since before Noah, I reckon. So have those little fellers," he continued, pointing to the swallows gliding gracefully to their nesting places and alighting with a flutter of wings. "If there was anybody up there, they'd be raisin' hell like a momma with clean wash on the line and two kids throwin' dirt clods. They're the best eyes a man can have in a place like this, but if you ain't smart enough to look at 'em in the first place, I guess they don't do you a helluva lot of good. I think you know what I mean."

"I do. Maybe Ed spent a little too long behind his desk to remember that. Let's go down and get it over with. But, just for safety's sake, I'm going to leave one squad up here to cover us just in case whoever did this happens to come back."

"Good idea. Them birds have a way of lettin' a man know things when it ain't too late for them, but unless he learns to fly damned quick, it might be too late for him. I'll lead the way."

After Kincaid lined out the second squad along the trail, they had just covered, he and the first squad followed Mandalian down toward the river. The sight that met their eyes sickened each man to the aching pit of his stomach. Dead soldiers and their mounts were strewn along the banks, some half in the water and others bobbing in the current where they had been caught upon a boulder or the limbs of a fallen tree. The silence was deafening, and it appeared to be a scene from some macabre play in which a stage director might suddenly step to the front, clap his hands, and everyone would rise and move about normally. But there was no handclap and no one moved, including the soldiers who sat on their mounts at the water's edge and stared at the cold, brutal scene in total awe.

"Jesus Christ!" mumbled one private toward the rear. "Those poor bastards didn't have a chance."

As though suddenly spooked by the reality of death coming so quickly, the other soldiers allowed their gaze to drift upward to the bluff walls, and heads jerked in rapid, searching motions.

Sensing the feeling of the men behind him, Kincaid barked sharply, "Sergeant!"

"Yessir!"

"Take your squad and collect the bodies of the dead. Bring them back here and find a suitable place to leave them for the time being—a cave or washout, something along that order. After you have retrieved them all, cover the bodies with brush or anything that will keep the animals away. We'll send a detail back from Fort McKinney and have them brought in for proper burial. Strip the saddles from their mounts and drag them from the river as well. Check both banks. I want two squads, a teamster, a paymaster, a sergeant, and a lieutenant accounted for. Is that understood?"

"Yes, sir."

"Then get to it. I want to move out of here within the hour."

"I understand, sir."

Kincaid moved his horse into the water without pausing for a salute, and forded the river with Mandalian by his side. Neither man spoke, and when they reached the far shore, Kincaid reined his horse in and stared at a body half submerged in the water, with legs adrift and hands clutching the muddy bank like the roots of a washed-out tree.

"Is that him?" Mandalian asked softly, with a nod toward the dead man.

"Yes it is." Kincaid replied just above a whisper. "The General Mercantile is closed forever."

"I'm sorry, Matt. It's too damned bad and that's all I can say. You likely crave to be alone for a few minutes, so I think I'll take a little ride up the trail and see if I can't find the wagon that made the tracks up yonder. I should be back in an hour or so."

"That's good, Windy," Kincaid replied without taking his eyes off his dead friend. "We should be ready to move out by the time you get back."

Mandalian offered no reply except for a nod and quit the riverbed with a clatter of hooves on rock while Kincaid stepped slowly down and waded through the calf-deep water to where Lieutenant Springer lay. He gently dragged the dead man up on the bank and turned him over on his back. The hole in his chest was filled with mud and the front of his uniform was caked with congealed blood. There were specks of sand in the lieutenant's open, filmed-over eyes.

Kincaid lowered his head to his hand and let it rest there momentarily, with one elbow propped on his bent knee. He could hear the whisper of the river, the soft moaning of the wind, and the gentle sounds of birds tending the needs of their young high above him. It was as though nothing had changed

75

in the world of nature, only that another insignificant creature had ceased to breathe. The careless had ventured into the jaws of death, and the jaws had closed and opened again to await their next victim. Life went on, and somewhere a mother was nurturing a child within her womb while a little girl smoothed the hair of a rag doll by her side. Dreams, the stuff of man's battle against fate, drifted slowly toward the sea and were carried westward on the currents of indifference.

Nearly five minutes passed by before Kincaid rose and took up his reins once more. He turned back to look at the work detail behind him, then led his horse to the nearest bluff and left the animal at its base as he slowly climbed upward to the cave yawning above him. Once inside, he crouched and trailed his hand across the floor, mindless of the irritated swallow that had been searching the rearward portion and now fluttered past his head on the frantic beat of flailing wings.

His hand closed about a hard, cold object and he raised it to the light and trailed a thumb across the cylindrical opening and down the narrowed neck. It was a brass shell casing, and he could tell almost by feel that it was designed for use in an army-issue Spencer. Further gropings turned up more shells, and when Kincaid's curiosity had been satisfied, he sat down and leaned his back against the cave wall.

What kind of men were these, he wondered, who would lie in wait and slaughter other men, innocent men, for money?

The hatred that had been building in him now washed over him in a torrent.

I will find them, he thought. *And when I do, they will know the same mercy they showed the men they killed. They will die like the vermin they are.*

Then the sergeant's voice, calling from below, brought him abruptly back to the present.

"Lieutenant Kincaid? Are you up there, sir? We've done the best we could. It's a grisly mess, but I think we got them all. There's one thing I'd like to talk to you about, sir!"

Kincaid scrambled to his feet and stuffed the cartridge casings in his pocket.

"I'll be right down, Sergeant. Has Windy come back yet?"

"No, sir. At least I haven't seen him. But I've been kind of busy, if you know what I mean."

"I understand," Kincaid replied, lowering himself over the ledge and working his way down the bluff. When he reached the bottom, he dusted off the front of his tunic and turned toward the sergeant. "You mentioned something you wanted to talk about. What is it?"

"Well, sir, we collected all the bodies like you said, but there's one missing."

"Missing?"

"Yes, sir. We got the lieutenant, the paymaster, the sergeant, two squad leaders, and their men, but we couldn't find the teamster."

"Corporal French wasn't among the dead?" Kincaid asked with a raised eyebrow. "That's interesting, isn't it?"

"I don't know, sir," the sergeant replied with a shrug. "You'd think he would have made the best target, sitting on the seat of the wagon like he was."

"Yes, that is strange. Did you look all up and down the river, on both sides?"

"Yes, sir. The only things missing were the four horses we found and the teamster. Everyone else has been accounted for."

"Good. You've done the best you can. Have the detail mounted and prepared to move out the minute Windy gets back."

"I'll do that, sir."

Kincaid returned the sergeant's salute before taking up a twig and turning it pensively in his hands.

The clatter of hooves from up the trail broke Kincaid's reverie, and he looked up to see Mandalian's horse galloping down the trail toward him at reckless speed. The scout reined his mount to a grinding halt, and leaped down to approach Kincaid.

"I found them, Matt," Mandalian said. "They must be a pretty cocky bunch, 'cause they only went about four miles up the river."

"Where?" Kincaid asked anxiously, snapping the stick in two.

"Like I said, about four miles up river. There's a long sandbar along the riverbank, and it's hard enough to drive a wagon on so that any tracks would be washed out. I couldn't see exactly how many of them there are, but there's a cave there, and I'd guess that's where they're holed up. There's a guard posted by the entrance, and I think I could make out four dead mules laying off to one side."

Kincaid thought for several moments before asking, "Could this be a trap? It sounds kind of ridiculous, doesn't it? Killing this many men and then making no better effort than that to hide or escape?"

"Like I said, Matt, they must be a cocky bunch. This crossing is seldom used, and they must think they'll be safe until daylight. They wiped out the wagon tracks with brush several hundred yards from where they turned off, but they forgot to cover up the fresh mule shit. I saw some droppings and followed them down through the trees. Several of the trees were skinned up where the wagon brushed against them going past. They're in there, all right, I'm sure of that. The question is, when do we take 'em?"

"Tonight," Kincaid said firmly. "Just after dark. Did you get the layout of the terrain around that sandbar?"

"Yeah, I did. I couldn't get real close because of that guard, but I'd say we should have one squad approach from the north and one from the south. I'll take care of that guard personally, and he won't kick no more than that horse did back there. After that, it's a matter of surrender or die."

"Is there any way that any of them could escape?"

"Not that I can see."

"Good," Kincaid replied, his teeth gritted. "I want all of them, every damned last one of them dead, killed where he stands."

Mandalian pushed his hat forward on his forehead before speaking again. "Do you mean that, Matt? It doesn't sound like you. Sure, you lost a damned good friend, but you've never gone in for blood vengeance in the past, that I know of. I'm all for killin' the sonsabitches where they are without sayin' a damned word, but that's not your way. Don't you do something against your grain and suffer for it the rest of your life."

Kincaid smiled wearily and reached out to touch the scout's forearm. "You're right, Windy, and I'm wrong. No matter how personal this is, there's a right way and a wrong way. Anything else would put me on the same level with them. Let's get into position now, and move in after dark. I'll give them one chance to surrender, and if they refuse, then what happens is on their heads. Is that fair enough?"

"That sounds more like the Matt Kincaid I know," Mandalian replied with an easy smile. "They ain't gonna surrender, you know that as well as I do, but at least your conscience will be clean after they don't."

"Thanks. I owe you one. Can we be seen from the trail by that guard by the entranceway?"

"No. Besides, he's drinkin' whiskey, just like I imagine the rest of 'em are. He's there, right enough, but he ain't worth a pisspot throwed clean to hell."

"Good. I'll get the troops ready to move out."

"One more thing, Matt," Mandalian said, touching Kincaid's shoulder lightly and stopping his forward progress. "I thought you just might like to know. While I was hidin' in the bushes and watchin' 'em, I saw one man come out of the cave and drop his drawers to piss. He was a yellowleg, wearing cavalry blue."

"Corporal French?"

"One and the same. He's in this thing all the way up to his balls."

The muscles twitched along Kincaid's jaw, and he stared toward the riverbank where he had found Lieutenant Springer.

"I want him, Windy," Kincaid said in a barely audible voice. "I want him myself. He's dead right now and doesn't even know it. But first I want to try and get him to talk. He isn't smart enough to have planned this whole thing himself, and I want to know who's behind it. Then we'll get whoever that is, as well. But no matter what, I want French. He's mine, and the devil can have his soul."

six ━━━━━━━━━━━━━━

    The hush of chilling darkness settled over Farley's
Crossing, and a brilliant silver moon rising steadily into the
cloudless sky gave the appearance of a cold, distant enemy.
The river resembled an iridescent black snake, catching moonlight on its ripples and writhing along with oily smoothness
while wisps of evening fog rose along its banks like a shroud.
There was silent, ominous determination in the faces of the
men standing beside their mounts near the river as they waited
for Lieutenant Kincaid to give them the signal that would send
them into battle. Kincaid stood alone a short distance away,
watching the trail for the return of Windy Mandalian, who had
gone back to the cave to await the cover of darkness while
further assessing the strategy to be employed. Concern nagged
at Kincaid's mind because the hour was growing late and Mandalian had said he would be back shortly after sundown. It was
wellpast that time now. He wondered if some treachery had

befallen the scout as well, but then he heard the sharp click of shod hooves on stone, and saw a buckskin-clad figure emerge from the shadows of the bluffs and break into the moonlit clearing next to the river.

Mandalian stepped down next to Kincaid, and there was a sly grin on his face. "Evenin', Matt. Sorry I'm a little late, but somethin' came up that I wasn't counting on."

"That's all right, Windy. We've still got time. What's the situation?"

"Well, about half an hour before sunset, one of those assholes came out of the cave with a pair of saddlebags over his shoulder. He was too far away for me to recognize his face, but he's a tall, slim feller with hair down to his shoulders. He got on his horse and took off, so I circled around and picked up his trail and followed him until I lost the light. Mostly, I just wanted to make sure which direction he was going. He was headed steady to the south-southeast."

"Then he isn't coming back?"

"Nope, doesn't look that way anyhow."

"And you say he's going straight south-southeast?"

"Yup. He didn't know I was followin' him, and he never tried to throw me off with a false trail. Seems he knows exactly where he's headin', and he's damned determined to get there. I'll pick up his trail in the mornin'. I could have killed him tonight, but I think he's our best way of findin' out who was behind the massacre. If my hunch is right, he'll lead us straight to the man we want, or at least to the place where they were supposed to meet. I'm sure he has his share of the take from the payroll in his saddlebags, and whoever's behind this is gonna want his cut."

"Good. If he continues in the direction he's traveling, what would be the next settlement or town he'd come to?"

Mandalian worked the cut-plug in his cheek and spat before offering a reply. "There ain't a hell of a lot he could hit except Fort Fetterman or Douglas. Since I don't think he'd be too damned welcome at Fetterman with part of an army payroll in his saddlebags and the blood of this many soldiers on his hands, my guess would be Douglas. These fellers are pretty confident of what they're doin', and I don't think they had any idea we'd be on 'em so fast."

"We'll keep it that way until the time is right."

"Speakin' of the time, Matt, I got a little better look at things back up yonder. They're forted up pretty good in that cave, and I think they must've hidden some supplies in there while they were planning this thing. If we take 'em tonight like we talked about, they might be able to hold us off for quite a while. If we try to take 'em from the front, it might cost us some men. If we don't, we'll likely have to starve 'em out, and that could take some time, like maybe three, four days."

"Yes, I wondered about that," Kincaid said thoughtfully. "First of all, I don't want to lose any of my men and second, I don't want them to tie up that much of our time. Any suggestions?"

"Yeah, I think we can get around both of those problems. They think they're safe and secure, and it'd be best to let 'em keep on thinkin' that. If we do, they'll move out in the morning. Meantime, we'll get into position tonight, and when they're all out of the cave and ready to go, we'll have 'em covered with one squad to the front and one to the rear. If they don't lay down their weapons and surrender, the rest will be history."

"What's the ground cover like?"

"Perfect. Thickets, scrub brush, and boulders. We can keep both squads out of sight until they're movin' around and ready to go."

"Good. That's what we'll do, then. Just to make sure we don't wind up firing into our own ranks if it comes to a fight, we'll have one squad along the river to the south, and the other higher up in the trees to the north. We'll still have the same crossfire. You take the first squad and I'll take the second."

"Just as soon as this is over, I'll be lightin' out on that other feller's trail. I suppose you'll be takin' the prisoners, if there are any, on in to McKinney?"

"Yes. Then we'll go back to the post. You find out what you can on the one who escaped tonight and wire me at Number Nine."

"Consider it done," Windy replied, swinging up on his saddle once more while Kincaid turned to his sergeant.

"Have the men mount up, Sergeant. You take the first squad with Windy, and I'll be taking the second with me. Windy will fill you in on the plan before we get there. We will give them a chance to surrender. One chance, and that's it. When the shooting starts, if it does, have your men keep a lookout for Corporal French. I want him alive, if possible."

"I understand, sir. I think you're being more than fair by even giving the miserable bastards that one chance."

"They don't deserve it, but I have no other choice. Leave a handler behind with your mounts and approach with Windy on foot. Maintain absolute silence."

"Fine, sir. They want this just as bad as we do. There won't be any mistakes."

"Good. Let's move out now," Kincaid replied, taking up his reins and swinging into the saddle while listening to the sergeant pass along his instructions to the two squads. "Windy," he said, moving up beside the scout, "I don't think I've ever felt this coldblooded in my life."

"That's the way it should be, Matt." Mandalian replied as he gazed into the darkness. "You're sure as hell not wastin' feelings on the wrong people. Let's go, and I'll show you where to position your troops."

The sounds of soft laughter and the conversation of self-satisfied men died down shortly after midnight to be replaced by the occasional cough or rasping snore. On three occasions, one of the gang staggered from the cave, relieved himself, then wandered back into the cave again with a big yawn. The last guard change came at three o'clock in the morning, and the relief sentry promptly leaned his rifle against a tree, wrapped his blanket more tightly about his shoulders, and dozed on the fallen log where he sat. All activity died until the first rays of the rising sun crept across the riverbank and touched the black hole of the cave entrance.

Realizing he had gone to sleep, the guard jerked upright with an immediate glance toward the cave, then stood, yawned, and relieved his bladder before taking up his rifle and striding toward his sleeping companions.

"All right, you lazy bastards," came his muffled exclamation from within the cave. "Off your asses and on your feet! Time to get the hell out of here! Any whiskey left in that jug over there?"

Curses and groaning protestations drifted from the cave on

the frigid air of morning and there was the scuffling sound of boots being pulled on while the first insults of the day were exchanged.

As he lay on his stomach in a thicket of alder no more than thirty yards from the cave, Matt Kincaid listened to the sounds below him and slightly off to the left, and wondered if those same complaints might never be spoken again.

The thought of waiting in ambush was disconcerting to Kincaid; had it not been for the events at Farley's Crossing, it would have been totally repugnant. But the situation at hand was blessed with two major exceptions: the opportunity to surrender would be given, and the acceptance or refusal of that offer would be the choice of men guilty of coldblooded murder, not soldiers fulfilling their sworn duty, however errantly performed.

The hot flush of anger had long since faded from Kincaid's cheeks, but the black hatred simmering in his heart had not diminished in the slightest. He felt a nearly total lack of compassion for the men now preparing to step forward beneath the sights of army weapons, and as he had mentally composed the telegram he would soon be sending to Springer's widow, any thoughts of cowardly conduct had faded from his mind.

Kincaid's fingers tightened on the grips of the Scoff he held in his right hand as he saw two men, then a third, wander from the cave with bedrolls and saddlebags dangling over their shoulders. Hats had been draped disinterestedly on their heads, and rifles were held loosely in their grasp. The first man stopped in the warming sunlight to yawn and stretch before moving to where the horses had been tethered. He began to saddle his mount with something less than enthusiasm in his motions. The other two duplicated his actions with desultory, stiff-jointed movements while yet another four men exited the cave and angled toward the picket line.

His heart quickened as he saw a man walk downward and to the left with a wad of paper in one hand and the other clutching the waistband of his pants, heading directly toward where Mandalian lay in wait with the first squad. Kincaid knew the scout was watching as well, and he was confident that the outlaw would never complete his bowel movement. And as the outlaw disappeared in the deep brush, Kincaid dismissed him from his mind and vainly searched the bearded faces below in an effort to locate and identify Corporal French.

It was then that he remembered he had never seen the corporal and that he could only identify him by his cavalry uniform. His heart sank when an eighth man stepped into the sunlight and he too was wearing civilian clothes. He had a bundle tucked beneath one arm, and Kincaid thought he saw a flash of blue with a yellow stripe, but before he could make a positive identification, the man had moved in among the horses and begun to saddle his own mount. Several of the other men were already seated on their saddles, and as the last man pulled his cinch strap tight and swung up, there was only one riderless horse waiting. Another man turned with hands cupped to his mouth and yelled toward the brush.

"Come on, Kushing, damn you! Pinch it off and get your ass up here! I saddled your horse on that bet we made last night, but I'm damned sure not gonna ride the son of a bitch for you, too!"

No sound came from the brush, and the speaker glanced at his companions before hollering again. "Come on, dammit! We're waitin' for you!"

After another long, silent pause, a man off to the speaker's left said, "What do you think, Kingsley? Want me to go over and look for him?"

"Yeah, you'd better do that. He sure as hell should have been able to hear me."

Kincaid had heard and seen enough. It was obvious there was no one else left in the cave, and he wanted to make his move while he had the outlaws all in one tight group. Inching his head up slightly to raise his mouth above the fallen tree in front of him, he took in a deep breath and brought the Scoff up to the level of his eyes.

"Stay where you are! Nobody moves! We're the United States Army, and you're all under arrest! Throw your weapons down and put your hands on your heads! I have you under a crossfire, and this will be your one and only chance to surrender! You have thirty seconds to think it over!"

Startled looks were exchanged, and bleary eyes turned sharp in bearded faces while searching the surrounding timber to locate the source of the voice. No attempt was made to hide the open shock they were experiencing, and as horses were turned in tight circles, it was obvious that a decision was rapidly being formulated.

"What are we gonna do, Frank?" one man hissed as his horse breasted Kingsley's.

"We'll all hang for damned sure if we surrender," Kingsley replied through gritted teeth, as his eyes continued to search the shadows. "The only thing we can do is to make a break or it."

The strain and tension was building on their faces, and the absolute silence surrounding them only added to their panic. Kingsley's head jerked in a glance toward the river and stopped at the sound of Mandalian's voice coming from a concealed position in the brush.

"I wouldn't try it over here, fellers," the scout said laconically. "A bowie knife just split your friend from his asshole to his eyeballs, and I'd be more'n happy to do the same for you."

Kingsley's mouth dropped open and he twisted frantically in the saddle to look back in Kincaid's direction.

"Your thirty seconds are up, mister! Drop those weapons and do it now!"

A look of wild desperation flashed across Kingsley's face and he instantly raised his revolver and fired three quick shots toward where he thought the voice was coming from, before slouching low across his horse's withers and spurring the animal toward the sandbar along the river. His companions fired as well in the blur of rearing, spinning horses, their shots crashing into the brush on one side and the timber across the way, while they jerked their mounts toward the narrow neck of sand.

Chips of bark exploded from the log in front of Kincaid's face, and then he was on one knee and raising his Scoff. The first shot caught Kingsley squarely between the shoulderblades and he pitched forward to dangle with one leg caught in the stirrup while his terrified mount kicked and bucked in headlong flight. As arranged the night before, Kincaid's first shot was the signal to open fire, and now weapons blazed on either side of the clearing. Riders and mounts were spinning to their deaths while wounded men struggled to remain upright in the saddle.

Kincaid swung his weapon and brought it to bear on the

man whom he had seen earlier with the bundle beneath his arm, then lowered the sight and shot the man's horse out from beneath him. Its rider hit the ground in a tumbling roll, his saddlebags burst open, and thick sheaves of money scattered across the ground. The rider staggered to his feet and stared momentarily in disbelief at the bills floating about him before he grabbed the reins of a riderless horse and tried to drag himself into the saddle. Hoping to keep Corporal French alive, if he was indeed the man under his sights, Kincaid swung the barrel once more to kill the second horse and in the same instant that he fired he saw the man's hands fly up, and then he sprawled across the horse that had dropped in front of him. Kincaid knew he had not hit the corporal, but he was equally aware that the man's identity was as unknown to the others as it was to him, with the exception of Mandalian.

Two outlaws had managed to get to the sandbar, but were cut down there. One was killed instantly and the other rolled twice before attempting to crawl away and then slumping forward with a pained scream that echoed off the river. That was the last sound of the battle, and then a deadly calm settled over the clearing.

After waiting several seconds to make certain the men sprawled before them were dead, Kincaid rose slowly and glanced off to his right.

"Any casualties, Sergeant?"

"None that I know of, sir. But let me check just to make sure."

"Do that," Kincaid replied, stepping over the log and advancing toward the clearing. "Have the men keep their weapons trained on these people, just in case."

"Yes, sir."

"Windy?"

"I hear ya, Matt."

"Let's have a look here. Help me identify Corporal French."

"Headin' your way now," the scout said, stepping out from behind his cover and shoving fresh shells into the Sharps as he walked. "I think that was him tryin' to get on that second horse. Must've taken his uniform off, and that's just what got him killed, if he is dead."

"Somehow that seems kind of fitting after what he did yesterday, Windy," Kincaid said softly as the two of them met and the scout knelt down to turn the man over, then lowered an ear close to the chest to listen for breathing.

"It's him, Matt. He's still alive, but not for long," Mandalian said, indicating the pinkish blood spread across French's chest. "He took one through the lungs."

Kincaid knelt beside the corporal and reached out to turn the man's face toward him. "Yes, I see that. Let's see if we can't get something out of him while there's still time." As he hovered over the dying trooper, a sense of almost uncontrollable revulsion swept through Kincaid's mind and he felt a strong desire to strangle the man rather than interrogate him, but he managed to contain the impulse.

"Corporal French? Can you hear me?" he asked softly while holding the man's head partially upright. "I'm Lieutenant Kincaid, and I would like to ask you some questions."

French's mouth sagged strangely to one side, and there was great pain in his eyes when they fluttered open. "Ain't got nothing to say."

"Don't you have any regrets for what you've done?"

"I . . . I . . . needed the . . . money. No regrets."

"I see," Kincaid replied stiffly, while staring down at the traitor. "You have betrayed your own kind in the worst way imaginable, Corporal. And you are now dying for it. Your only hope for salvation is to confess who was involved in this with you, so they can be brought to trial. The money will do you no good now, but a confession might save your soul."

His eyes glazed over and French blinked twice as he stared upward into the bright sunlight, as if attempting to recognize the man speaking to him. "You . . . you a preacher or somethin'?"

"No I'm not. But I do know my way around a Bible. I can take your confession."

French smiled weakly and licked his dry lips with the tip of his tongue. "Ain't that a dandy thought now? Old French confessin' his sins. 'Fraid we ain't got that long, Lieutenant."

"I'm not interested in chapter and verse, Corporal. I want to know the name or names of the men behind the ambush of that paywagon yesterday. As it is now, the deaths of those cavalry troopers are directly on your head. I'll see that your involvement in this is kept off the record and it will be assumed that you were killed in the ambush." Kincaid watched the corporal closely. "Is that fair enough?"

"You makin' a deal with me . . . sir?" French asked, gritting his teeth against another surge of pain.

"I'm trying to. Even though you are guilty of the crime, this is your one chance to avoid soiling your family name forever. Do you have any living relatives?"

French closed his eyes as if beset by a new, deeper pain. "Yeah. Two brothers, a . . . sister, an' my ma."

"Think of what this will do to them. You might have done a lot of wrong in your life, but this is your one chance to do something right, something for your family, because news of what happened yesterday will be in every damned newspaper clear across the United States. Think of them, branded as the relatives of a coward and traitor."

Kincaid knew he was playing his only ace, and he leaned forward, speaking intently in the hope of igniting one last spark of decency and humaneness in the dying man before him. He saw French swallow with some difficulty, and he knew he was getting through to the corporal's subconscious mind.

"Someone left here last night, and that man who escaped left you here to die alone. Tell me his name."

French coughed, and pinkish phlegm flecked the corners of his mouth. "And nobody'll know I had a hand in it?" he asked, opening his eyes to tiny slits and attempting to focus on Kincaid.

"Nobody. But I want a name and I want it now."

"Jay . . . Jarvis. He was a lieutenant till he got cashiered out . . . out of the cavalry . . . 'bout two years ago . . . ," French replied with a heavy sigh that brought a rattle from deep within his chest.

Kincaid's heartbeat quickened and he knew instinctively by the sound of the corporal's words that he would be dead within minutes, possibly even seconds. "Where was he going last night?"

"Doug . . . Douglas. Said somethin' 'bout . . . Douglas."

"Who else was in on it with him?" Kincaid asked quickly, noticing the eyelids flutter as they closed and feeling the neck sag in his hand. "Was there anyone else in on it with him?"

He felt the head nod weakly one time, noticed the mouth open to speak, then French's head lolled to one side and the rasping sound of tortured breathing died in his chest.

"The name," Kincaid said, leaning close to French's ear. "Give me the name of the other man."

There was no response, and Mandalian reached over to touch Kincaid's shoulder. "He ain't got any more to say, Matt. He's dead."

Kincaid looked up sharply, "Damn it, Windy! He nodded when I asked if there was anyone else involved, and he was about to give the name. Did you catch the first one? It was Jay Jarvis, wasn't it?"

"Yeah, that's what he said. Also something about him bein' in the cavalry up until a couple of years ago."

"That's what I heard too. Looks like you were right about that Douglas hunch, eh?"

"Looks like I was. I'll still pick up his trail, just in case." Mandalian paused to study Kincaid's face. "You gonna do what you told him you'd do? About coverin' up his part in this thing?"

"Yes I am. First of all, it'd give the army a black mark that we don't need, and it won't be necessary if we catch the brains behind the ambush. Corporal French is insignificant in the overall scheme of things. And second, I made a promise to a dying man in exchange for information. There's no way I could go back on that, no matter what kind of scum he might have been when he was alive," Kincaid replied, rising and turning toward the river. "Sergeant? I'd like to speak with you for a moment."

The sergeant crossed the clearing quickly and stood before his lieutenant. "You called me, sir?"

"Yes. First of all, do we have any dead or wounded?"

"None, sir. A couple of near misses and a scratch here and there, but nothing serious."

"Fine. Now here's what I want you to do. Corporal French here"—Kincaid indicated the dead man with the toe of his boot—"was taken hostage by the others. He had no involvement in the ambush, and was only trying to get away with them under the threat of death. They made him change from his uniform to civilian clothes, and I think you'll find his uniform in that bundle lying over beside that dead horse. I want him changed back into his uniform and taken back to be left with the others from the paywagon escort detail. I will sign the report stating that all of the payroll detachment are accounted for and were killed in the line of duty. Is that understood?"

"Yes, sir."

"Fine. Pick a detail to do that, and give them my instructions. I want you to collect all the money here that was taken from the paywagon. I would imagine it's been divided into equal amounts and will be found in each of their saddlebags. Count it, and I want to know the exact amount, including the bills scattered on the ground here. When that's done, have the remaining bodies carried into the cave and left there for the burial detachment out of McKinney. Drag the dead horses off to one side and leave them there, but stack their riding gear in the wagon. I'll be sending a team back for it as well after we get to McKinney."

"We'll get right on it, sir. Do you want me to send someone to have the mounts brought down?"

"Yes, do that. Windy and I have some things to talk over, and we'll be over by the cave when you get through."

"I'll be back with a money count for you in ten minutes, sir," the sergeant said, turning away and immediately beginning to relay Kincaid's orders to the troops.

Mindless of the flurry of activity going on around them, Kincaid and Mandalian wandered toward the cave and talked as they moved.

"Once I find out how much money is here, Windy," Kincaid began, "I'll know how much Jarvis took with him. Then, if you do pick up his trail and it does in fact lead to Douglas, kind of lie low and snoop around a little bit. Get to know who is new in town, where they came from, what kind of bankroll they have, that sort of thing. Once I get back and report in to the captain, I'll head on up that way and we'll see if we can't pick up some leads from that point. Unless it becomes necessary, don't do anything until I get there, which should be in less than a week. Even if you can locate Jarvis, we've got to leave him alone until he leads us to whoever else was in on the planning of this."

Mandalian nodded and worked a fresh chew of cut-plug in his cheek. "French didn't say for sure that this Jarvis was stoppin' in Douglas, just that he was headed that way. But if he does decide to hang his hat there, he sure as hell won't be using his own name."

"No, I don't imagine he will, and since neither one of us knows what he looks like, we'll just have to wait and smoke him out if he's there. Maybe we can get something about him over the wire from Laramie after I get back to the post. If you do come up with anything on him before I get to Douglas, wire it back to the captain and I'll check in with him. The main thing is to stay with him if you find him, but don't spook him. If he, or they, leave, follow them and then let me know where you're heading from the first telegraph station you come to."

"I'll do that, Matt, and I'll be leavin' just as soon as we find out how much money is missing."

The two of them talked for nearly ten more minutes before the sergeant returned with several saddlebags draped over his arm. "It's all here, sir. Every damned nickle of it that I could find. Twenty-four thousand dollars."

Kincaid took a moment to make some mental calculations. "That would be about right, considering the stops they had to make yet. Thank you, Sergeant. Make sure what's left of that payroll is secured for the ride to McKinney."

"Yes, sir."

After the sergeant had left again, Kincaid turned to look at Mandalian. "Damned near exactly half of what that payroll should have amounted to is missing, Windy. We're looking for a man with twenty-four thousand dollars to spend, invest, bank, or buy with. There aren't too many men with that kind of cash in their pockets who could keep a low profile."

"Especially one who thinks he got away clean, Matt," the scout replied with a wink as he took up his reins. "But he ain't got away yet, not by a long shot. Be seein' you in Douglas, or wherever in hell I wind up," he concluded, swinging onto his saddle and touching his hat brim with the tips of two fingers.

"Take care of yourself, Windy, and don't forget we've got some coldblooded killers on our hands."

Mandalian turned in the saddle just before his horse moved into the trees. "No we don't, Matt," he said with a grin. "We've got some coldblooded killers on the run. They just don't know it, that's all."

93

seven   _____

They had been riding north since just before daybreak, and now, with the sun reaching its zenith, Sergeant Gus Olsen halted the detachment and looked across at Hat Creek, which had been constantly on their right throughout the morning. "Now ain't this a son of a bitch? We ride all the way up here, find the creek we're supposed to find, get jumped by a bunch of Sioux last night, and now we're damn near halfway to Canada and still no sign of that cavalry outfit."

"They mighta heard the shootin' last night and cleared out, Sarge," Jones offered, only half in jest. "The miserable bastards have a way of doin' that in a fight."

"This whole thing is bullshit, if you ask me," Winkleman threw in. "I figure the captain had an IG inspection comin' up back at the post and just wanted to get us the hell out of the way so he might have some chance of passin' it."

Olsen glanced at the big private and smiled. "That's not a

bad idea at all, Winkleman, and the captain would be smart to keep that in mind. But I hope he'll put another NCO in charge next time. I think we'll turn back here and head southwest and see if we can't cut their trail somewhere closer to the border. Might even run into somebody who knows where the hell we are, where they are, or, if we get real lucky, where in hell this stage station is supposedly being built. Come on, I'd like to find the damned thing before nightfall if we can. Those Sioux likely ain't too happy about the whippin' they took last night."

It was well past midafternoon when they saw a strange caravan approaching. As they neared, Olsen could make out five horses—two being ridden and three pack animals on lead ropes. A tall, emaciated man wearing tattered buckskins sat on his horse with a Henry rifle held in the crook of his arm. The woman beside him was an Indian squaw riding a scrawny, diminutive pony. She watched them with ebony eyes narrowed in contempt. She too wore buckskins, with Arapaho markings, and with her corpulent figure, the two of them waited while the army patrol approached.

"Good afternoon, sir, ma'am," Gus offered, tipping his hat slightly while pulling his horse to a stop. "My name is Sergeant Gus Olsen, and we're with the U.S. Mounted Infantry down south a ways." He nodded toward the trappings affixed to the pack animals and added, "From the look of things, you folks must be buffalo hunters."

"Used to be, son," the old man replied with lips bulging around toothless gums, "but we ain't anymore. Lotta difference 'tween huntin' fer 'em and findin' 'em. Decent buff is scarce as hens' teeth anymore, and I'm givin' 'er up. Headed back up north to try my hand at trappin' again. I answer to the name of Josh Blackburn, and this purty little woman over here is my wife, Totum." Blackburn squinted, and deep wrinkles creased his leathery face. "You fellers lost?"

"Well, yes and no. We were sent up here to locate a stream called Hat Creek, but don't seem to be having much luck finding it."

The old man cackled and inclined the barrel of his rifle in the direction from which the five had come. "If you came from that way, as it 'pears to me you have, you'd have to wade it to get across."

Olsen glanced over his shoulder in indication of slight surprise. "Was that Hat Creek? I thought it was, but things aren't the same as we'd been led to believe."

"And what things would that be?"

"We're supposed to locate a stagecoach station being built there by the U.S. Cavalry. We've been the length of Hat Creek now, clear up into what must be Dakota Territory, but haven't seen hide nor hair of any cavalry unit."

The old hunter turned toward his wife with an edentate grin. "Hear that, Maw? Some more of them army folks plumb lost in grass no deeper'n their knees. Sometimes I wonder how them boys beat your folks so durned bad, when they couldn't find the shithouse in broad daylight."

The woman named Totum matched the grin, but it was obvious she hadn't understood a word that had been said, and Blackburn looked back at Olsen once more with a conspiratorial wink. "She cain't understand a danged word of English, so I can say whatever comes to mind around her. To my way of thinkin', that's the kind of wife a man should have."

"Yes, I suppose you're right," Olsen replied, edging forward slightly in his saddle. "You mentioned some more army folks. Did you have any outfit in particular in mind?"

"Sure did, or I wouldn't of said it. Only they're worse off'n you all are. They've got a whole damned stagecoach station on their hands to tote around when they finally get a proper smell of the wind."

"Then you've seen the construction site?"

"Yup, I have. Me and Totum here left there not more'n three hours ago."

"Three hours?" Olsen asked in surprise. "Traveling the direction you were when I first saw you, that'd put them in Wyoming Territory."

"It not only would, son, it does," Blackburn said with obvious delight.

"But you just told me that Hat Creek was back there?"

"I told them that too, but it didn't make no never-mind. I guess if they want to call Sage Creek by the name of Hat Creek, it don't bother me none. Ain't no buff on neither one, no way."

97

Now Olsen was clearly puzzled, and he pulled the map from his pocket and studied it closely. "According to this map, Sage Creek is in Wyoming Territory, not far to the west of the line, and Hat Creek is back behind us about the same distance into Nebraska."

Blackburn eyed the map suspiciously. "Don't know much about them things there, son. Maps is just for people who's already lost and tryin' to find out where the hell they are. The sun, the stars, the direction of the wind, and which side of the stalk the grass seed heads grow on are what tells a man if he's shittin' too close to the house or not and whether his camp's upwind or down."

"Let me get this straight, Mr. Blackburn. You've seen the stage station and you're sure it's being built on Sage Creek, in Wyoming Territory?"

"Son, I've got more miles passed under this old ass, ridin' the prairie 'round these here parts, then you've got threads in them pants you're wearin'. If Sage Creek is where I told you it was, that's where it'll be when you get there, and the same goes for Hat Creek." A chagrined, almost hurt expression crossed the old hunter's face. "Tried to tell that to some smart-mouthed army lieutenant who's supposed to be buildin' the damned station, but he told me to move my ass along afore I had to carry it away in two hands. The young whelp can rot in the wrong place the rest of his damn life, far as I'm concerned," Blackburn concluded with a sniff and a toss of his head.

"Well, I'll be go-to-hell! They're building the son of a bitch in the wrong place!" Jones exulted with a grin. "Sounds about right for a bunch of damned yellowlegs. I can't wait to see the look on their ugly faces when we tell 'em that little bit of good news."

"We won't be telling them anything, Jones," Olsen replied firmly. "At least not at first. When and if we do, it'll come from me and be directed at Captain Gann, not from you and directed at some poor private who had nothing to do with the mistake in the first place."

"Word'll get around, Sarge. You know that as well as I do. Five'll get ya ten the officers know it already and are just too damned stubborn or ignorant to admit their mistake."

"We'll find that out when we get there," Olsen said, dismissing Jones and turning back to the hunter. "Thank you for this information, Mr. Blackburn. If we leave now, we should be able to make it to the station by nightfall, then?"

"Sure. If'n they don't move the damned thing clear over to White River afore ya do. But that's your problem, not mine. Me and Totum are headed for Canada, and if'n you've got nothin' more to say to us, we'll take our leave."

"Of course, Mr. Blackburn. Have good luck with your trapping and thank you for the information."

"Luck ain't got nothin' to do with it, son," Blackburn huffed as he encouraged his horse in a forward direction again. "Luck's fer soldiers like you who run into buff hunters like me, and best it be that way. Seems like you're needin' a lot of it to pick out the bulls from the cows."

With those words, Blackburn was gone, leading his motley menagerie toward the northeast at a plodding pace. The five soldiers watched them go, then Winkleman turned to look at Olsen.

"Know what I'm thinkin', Sarge?"

"What's that, Winkleman?" Olsen asked distantly, again preoccupied with the map.

"Seems to me that if old Blackburn back there rode his wife and fucked that pitiful horse she's sittin' on, he'd make a hell of a lot better time."

"And have a better-lookin' bunkmate to boot," Malone added.

The four privates laughed raucously while Olsen shook his head, folded the map, and resumed a steady gallop in the direction of Sage Creek.

There was possibly an hour and a half of daylight left when the detachment intercepted Sage Creek, and they followed it south until, just before sunset, they saw the stage station, which appeared to be nearly completed. The walls were up, and several troopers were putting the final touches on a cut-lumber-and-sod roof. Others worked on pole corrals off to one side, and yet another crew was busily sinking the stanchions for hitch rails in front of the building. Just beyond the main station building to the south, a low-silhouette barn had been constructed, and the glow of a setting sun turned the raw yellow of freshly cut lumber an orangeish color when viewed from a distance.

Olsen was truly impressed, and as he slowed his mount to a walk, he said to the others, "Say what you will about 'em, boys, but I'd say the cavalry did one hell of a fine job in building that station down there. I've seen a few stations in my time, but none as big and finely constructed as that one appears to be."

"Who's payin' for that damned thing, anyway?" Winkleman asked without totally concealing the hint of awe in his voice.

"The government, I suppose," was Olsen's reply. "The army's building it, so I suppose the army's paying for it as well."

"That sound about right," Garfield said in disgust. "We make thirteen lousy goddamned dollars a month, and they piss away money on somethin' like that. A stage station's one thing, but the goddamned White House is supposed to be somewhere back East, the way I hear tell."

Jones sneered and wiped his mouth with the back of a hand. "And they built 'er in the wrong goddamned place besides. Ain't seen a yellowleg yet who knew his ass from a teakettle."

"All right! That's enough," Olsen said sternly. "Keep that kind of remark to yourselves. We all know why we're here, and that's the extent of it. I'm sure if anyone wanted your opinion, it would have been asked for through the bars of the stockade door. Now keep your mouths shut," the sergeant concluded as they saw the cavalry troopers slow their work and glance up at the approaching detachment. "This ain't gonna be a piece of cake no matter how you slice it, and I don't need any extra grief from any of you."

"Look at 'em grin, Jonesy," Winkleman growled just above a whisper. "Don't think we're gonna have to worry 'bout givin' out a lot of shit."

The cavalrymen laid down hammers, saws, picks, shovels, and other tools almost in unison as they saw the light blue stripe on the mounted infantrymen's trouser legs. A low round of whistles and jeers greeted the detachment from Outpost Number Nine when they entered the construction site.

"Well, lookie there! Five bluelegs done got lost and come to the good old U.S. Cavalry for help."

"Kinda makes a man wanta toss his gut just at the sight of 'em."

"Might be able to find work for 'em diggin' a latrine or two. 'Bout the only thing they could do, and then they'd dig it sideways."

"Know what I heard about the mounted infantry, boys? Ain't man enough to ride and ain't soldier enough to walk. Kinda like a mule with an asshole at both ends."

And so it went as the detachment passed through the ranks of cavalry. Olsen held his breath in the fervent hope that his men would be able to tolerate the abuse while he guided the detail toward the headquarters tent. Then he heard Jones speak up behind him, with no regard for the volume of his words:

"Know why these cavalry shitheads have yellow stripes on their pant legs?"

"No, Jonesy? Tell me, why?"

"'Cause it's a perfect match for that big yellow stripe down the middle of their back."

"No kiddin'? I thought it was supposed to be the color of the baby-shit yeller that runs down their legs ever' time somebody mentions the Little Bighorn."

"No, boys, it's for a different purpose altogether, that bright yellow," Malone contributed. "It's so the poor fellas can find each other after they've run from a fight."

Laughing, Garfield threw his head back and broke into song:

> Yellowlegs have dirty ears
> The miserable sonsabitches.
> They wear their socks for years and years
> And fuck their girls in ditches.

The party atmosphere recently enjoyed by the cavalrymen had subsided to a low growl, and nasty remarks were suddenly transformed to hurled insults. Olsen turned in the saddle to glare at the four grinning privates.

"Knock that shit off, and knock it off now! You'll have me to answer to for this when we get the hell out of here!" Then he turned back to see an officer stepping from the tent, and the look on the lieutenant's face was one of mild interest.

Olsen halted the detachment and offered a smart salute when

they were five yards away from the officer, and he wondered briefly if the privates behind him were following his example. Then, after a long pause, the cavalry officer returned the salute and all hands dropped.

"Sergeant Olsen reporting as ordered, sir. Easy Company, mounted infantry, out of Outpost Number Nine, Wyoming Territory."

"At ease, Sergeant. I'm Second Lieutenant Charles Ecklehart." He leaned to one side to take in the four privates, and while a quizzical, almost unbelieving look passed across his face, he looked up at Olsen. "May I ask what you are reporting *for*, Sergeant? And further, who it was who told you to report in the first place?"

"Thank you, sir. At ease, men," Olsen said over his shoulder, knowing there would be little discernible difference between attention and at-ease among the men of his detachment. "Captain Warner Conway, our commanding officer, directed me to lead this detail here at the request of regimental HQ."

"*Whose* regimental HQ?"

"Yours, sir."

Ecklehart's right eyebrow rose slightly and he touched his neatly trimmed, light brown mustache with one finger in contemplation. He was a narrow-shouldered individual, slight of build, possibly six feet tall, somewhere in his late twenties, and graced with the commanding presence of a man well schooled in proper manners and social graces.

"Mine?"

"Yes, sir, yours. The orders originated at Fort Laramie."

"I see. Would you be so kind, Sergeant, as to tell me the exact nature of these orders?"

"I would prefer to discuss that in private with you, sir. At Captain Conway's request."

"Yes, of course," Ecklehart said with a moderate wave of his hand and a pleasant smile. "It's nearly time for the evening meal—or 'grub,' as the troops call it. What a ghastly name for food, don't you agree? At any rate, have your men dismount and partake of this repast, such as it is, with mine. Meanwhile, you and I will have a little chat and you can dine later."

Olsen glanced toward the cavalrymen lining up in the grub-line with tin cups and spoons in hand before looking down at the officer again. "Begging the lieutenant's pardon, I'm afraid that wouldn't be such a good idea, sir. We've brought field rations along, and my men are quite accustomed to them."

"Nonsense, Sergeant. They've had a long ride, and certainly a hot meal would do them no harm."

"Begging the lieutenant's pardon, I do think it would be in the best interest of all of us if my men and yours weren't mixed together too much."

Again the raised eyebrow. "This is most unusual indeed. I do believe we are all in the same army, and I can see no reason why, considering our mutual purpose, a prepared government meal can't be shared by all. As a matter of fact, I insist upon it. Consider it an extension of hospitality from one military organization to another."

Olsen swallowed hard and shifted uneasily in his saddle. "When you say you insist, sir, is that the same as saying you're giving an order?"

"If that's what's required," Ecklehart replied with his easy smile. "Consider it an order, since nothing seems to be accomplished in this army without relying on that damnable imperative term. Dismiss your men, then join me in the tent. I suppose it's improper for officers to drink with enlisted men along with all the other restrictions, but if you will allow me, I'd like a brandy and shall offer you the same." Ecklehart turned toward the tent and then stopped just inside the flap and looked back. "I assure you it's an entirely civilized custom, and one practiced quite frequently in my home state of New Hampshire when two gentlemen sit down to discuss a simple business matter. Don't be long, Sergeant."

Olsen had been trying to place the lieutenant's strange accent throughout the entire conversation, and now identified it as belonging to an Eastern gentleman of high breeding. An uneasy feeling settled over him and he looked back at his detachment. "You heard the lieutenant. You're going to have grub with the cavalry, and since it's obvious he doesn't understand what he's done, I'm goint to remind you of what I expect. We're here to observe and report, nothing more. If they give you any shit, laugh it off. If they push you, back away. Is that understood by all four of you?"

"Sure, Sarge. We understand," Winkleman replied dryly.

"It's as plain as the nose on your face that they were just kiddin' when we rode in here."

"That's exactly what I mean. You assholes didn't exactly go out of your way to make yourselves popular, either. Now shut up, eat, and go make camp somewhere away from this damned cavalry outfit."

Jones grinned and raised up on one stirrup in preparation to dismount. "Like maybe to Hat Creek, Sarge? That's where we're supposed to be, ain't it?"

"Damn it, Jones! I'm warning you!" Olsen said with a threatening stab of one finger toward the private. "Give me any shit on this patrol, and you won't see town for six months!"

"Easy, Sergeant, easy," Jones replied, stepping down and grinning again. "We don't aim to start nothin'. You've got my word on that."

"And that's about as much good as a fart in a windstorm," Olsen snapped, dismounting and thrusting his reins at Garfield. "Take care of my damned horse."

"Sure, Sarge. Be glad to," the private said with a broad smile. "Don't let that yellowleg lieutenant feed ya no bullshit now, hear?"

"This is the dumbest damned thing I ever heard of," Olsen growled, pulling off his gloves and ducking beneath the tent flap.

Ecklehart stood beside a drafting table, with a glass of brandy in either hand, while admiring the drawing spread out across the wide, flat board. "I'm quite pleased with what we've done here, Sergeant," he said, turning and handing one cup across while raising the other in toast. "To your health and to the successful completion of this facility."

Olsen raised his glass, then drank without replying to the toast.

Ecklehart went on, "This is the first major project I've been involved with, and I'm finding it both challenging and enjoyable. I'm a graduate of the Massachusetts Institute of Technology, and other than enduring a brief stint in officer's training, I'm fairly new to military life."

"You mean, sir, that this is your first time in the field?" Olsen asked incredulously.

"Yes it is," Ecklehart replied with a tight smile. "I'm quite pleased that Captain Gann had enough confidence in me to select my qualifications over other candidates for this assignment. There were others with a great deal more experience than mine in this type of structure, not to mention general knowledge of the area."

Olsen wondered momentarily if he should mention the fact that even though the lieutenant had performed excellently, his magnificent work was misplaced by some twenty or thirty miles, but he decided not to.

"Speaking of Captain Gann, sir, you don't mind my asking where he is, do you? I'm supposed to talk with him as well while I'm here."

"Ah, Captain Gann," Ecklehart said with a wistful smile. "What a magnificent soldier he is. He commands with an iron hand, while I occupy myself with mere lines and figures. But in response to your question, the captain is in Douglas, a small town in the area, and his responsibilities seem to require a great deal of his presence there. I believe he intends to return this evening, perhaps within the hour."

"Good. I'd like to conclude my affairs here and return to my post as soon as possible. Tell me, sir," Olsen asked, swirling the remaining drops of brandy in the bottom of his cup, "who chose the construction site for this station?"

"The captain himself, Sergeant. And he couldn't have done better had he ridden on the back of an eagle and surveyed the entire landscape from the air. Perfect soil conditions, a more than ample water supply—year 'round, I might add—and a plenitude of materials with which to build."

Something was troubling Olsen that he couldn't quite put his finger on, so he downed the last of the brandy while stealing a moment to think, and when he lowered the glass, he looked at the officer again. "How'd he do that, sir? Choose this site, I mean." Olsen allowed himself a smile. "That part about the eagle sounds good, Lieutenant, but I reckon Captain Gann's a mite bigger than that."

"Indeed he is," Ecklehart replied, his face brightening with discussion of the project. "First, he is extremely familiar with the area, having patrolled every inch of it, by his account. So he had a natural feel for the land—drainage, accessibility, and all that. Then, through the use of maps supplied by the government, we pinpointed the location and came up here for a look, and I knew it was the place to build the minute we arrived here."

Olsen squinted one eye without consciously knowing he had done so. "Did you say maps, sir? The captain chose this site from official government maps?" Catching the puzzled look in Ecklehart's eyes, Olsen corrected himself immediately. "What I mean is, I had one hell of a time finding you. All I had to go on was dead reckoning and what some drunk old Indian scout told me. I wish I had known there were detailed maps of this area available."

"Of course there are, Sergeant," Ecklehart replied. "Step over to the table here and I'll show you."

Olsen followed the lieutenant to the drafting table and waited while several large square sheets were flipped over, then stepped forward at Ecklehart's beckoning to bend over the displayed map.

"See here," Ecklehart began, shifting his glass to the other hand while trailing the index finger of his right vertically and then horizontally along the map. "Here is the Wyoming border, and there is the border between Dakota Territory and the state of Nebraska. Note the drainage; to the south we have the Niobrara River in Nebraska and Wyoming, the White River draining to the north and fading to the east while Sage Creek, here, feeds into the Cheyenne. Over here to the west we have Hat Creek, Old Woman Creek, and Lightning Creek, all draining eventually to the Cheyenne as well. As you can see, we have a perfect drainage situation with all major streams, creeks, or rivers flowing away from the location. It's my understanding that that's quite an important consideration when the winter storms come."

"Yes, it certainly is," Olsen observed while continuing to study the map and attempting to memorize the location of the various waterways. Finally he glanced up. "That's a mighty fine map, sir. I'll have to say that. Did you mention that it was drawn up by government surveyors?"

"Yes it was. To be frank, I'm quite surprised that outfits like yours don't have maps of this quality as well. After all, if they're going to send you wandering all over the damned place, they certainly should feel some responsibility as to where you're going."

Olsen smiled disarmingly. "We're kind of a small, mostly forgotten outpost, sir, and what we get usually has been pretty well worn out by somebody else."

"I see. It's a pity, but I guess that's the way things go sometimes." Ecklehart folded the pages over once again and then looked up at Olsen. "Now that the formalities are over, as I assume they are, might I inquire what government business brings you this far north? You did say your post was to the south, didn't you?"

"Yes it is, sir. But I'm supposed to answer that question when Captain Gann asks it and nobody else."

"I see," Ecklehart responded somewhat stiffly while reaching for the bottle. "More brandy?"

"No, thank you, Lieutenant. I'm afraid I still have some work to do tonight."

Ecklehart nodded and tucked one hand behind his back while picking up his refilled glass with the other. "You are aware, Sergeant, that when the commanding officer is not available, the executive officer is in complete charge?"

"I'm aware of that, sir."

"And as previously stated, Captain Gamm is not available at this time. Therefore I am the commanding officer. I'd like to know your purpose here."

Olsen studied the hard look in Ecklehart's previously friendly eyes and shook his head. "I'm afraid I can't tell you that, sir."

"I see. Well then, since orders seem to work so damned well in this army, I guess I'll have to issue one of my own. I order you to tell me the purpose of your mission."

Olsen's face tightened and the muscle along his jaw twitched once. "Sorry, sir. Your orders aren't worth a bucket of water in a wildfire." He reached for his pocket and started to draw out the orders given him by Captain Kincaid as he said, "The orders from my commanding officer supersede—"

But that was as far as Olsen managed to get before the clatter of pans banging together and the angry shouts of dozens of men shattered the calm outside the tent.

"What the hell is that?" Ecklehart demanded, staring slack jawed at Olsen.

"What that is, is the reason why your men and mine shouldn't have had supper together, Lieutenant. If you'll excuse me, I'm afraid that work I mentioned earlier is just starting."

"Hold on a second," Ecklehart yelled at the sergeant, who was already ducking beneath the tentflap. "I'm going with you!"

Ignoring the lieutenant's words, Olsen sprang through the opening and paused momentarily to shake his head before running toward the brawl erupting in the grub line.

Private Malone had one man on his back and another by the throat, whom he decked with a mighty punch, while Garfield had two men by the backs of their necks and was slamming their heads together. Winkleman had knocked a trooper into the pan rack and kicked him beneath the jaw as he staggered to his feet, then turned and knocked a cavalryman flat who was in the process of swinging a broken table leg at the mounted infantryman's head. Farther down the line, Jones had just thrown one man, butt first, into a cauldron of soup and slammed a backhand across another's jaw, while swinging a boot upward to catch a third full in the groin. More cavalrymen charged into the fray, and the four privates somehow managed to maneuver themselves into a ragged circle with their backs toward each other, and were taking on all comers while suffering severe punishment themselves.

A big man grabbed Olsen's arm as he ran by, and Olsen, seeing the sergeants's chevrons on the other man's sleeve, unleashed a mighty punch to the solar plexus and a right to the jaw. The opposing sergeant staggered backward, grinned through split lips, then landed a powerful blow on Olsen's right eye. Olsen stumbled, caught himself, and threw a combination of left to the belly, left to the jaw, and right to the temple, and the cavalry NCO dropped to his knees while Olsen felt two men men jump on his back.

"Welcome to the party, Sarge!" Wilkleman yelled, knocking one man off Olsen's back with a hard left to the kidneys and turning to take on a fourth while the sergeant threw the remaining trooper off his back and vaulted a fourth over his shoulder.

Once Ecklehart had recovered from his shock, he ran toward the brawl, pushing cavalrymen aside with either hand and shouting, "Stop this nonsense now! Stop it, I say! That's an order! What are you, a bunch of animals?"

Private Jones caught sight of the gold second lieutenant's bars on Eckleman's shoulders and a vicious, vengeful glint came into his eyes. While working his way toward the lieutenant through the stumbling, flailing mob, he caught one man on the chin with an elbow and another one in the throat while taking a punch alongside the ear and a second one on the corner of the mouth. But Jones seemed not to notice the effect of the blow, and when his hand finally closed over Ecklehart's shoulder, he spun him around and slammed a mighty blow against the officer's chin, sending him crashing backward over two fallen cavalrymen. Another crashed into Jones's knees and he went down just as a single revolver blast split the night air.

All fighting stopped instantly as a tall, fierce-looking officer rode his mount into the middle of the throng with his Scoff raised and cocked, leaving no doubt as to his intention to use it.

"What in the goddamned hell is going on here?" Captain Gann raged, staring down at Ecklehart, who lay on one side while gingerly testing his jaw before scrambling woozily to his feet.

"I'm at a loss to explain it, sir," Ecklehart replied, continuing to work his jaw in a testing motion.

"You'd better find a way damned quick, mister!"

Jones had regained his footing and he glanced up at the captain with a broken grin. "Beggin' the cap'n's pardon, sir, I think I can help the lieutenant out."

Gann stared down at him as though transmitting the wrath of God. "Who the hell are you?"

"Private Jones, Cap'n. Mounted infantry, U.S. Army."

"All right. I don't know what in hell you are doing here, but you'd damned well better come up with an answer. Speak your peace."

Jones grinned again and pointed to Ecklehart. "It appears the lieutenant there called a short-arm inspection, sir. Seems cavalry lieutenants don't like fuckin' women who ain't been spoke for already, and that's the only way they can tell if they stand a chance or not." Jones's grin widened. "We was all just tryin' to get in line, sir."

eight _____

"The captain wants to talk to you, Sergeant."

Olsen glanced up from the cup of lukewarm coffee he had been nursing and looked at the cavalry trooper who stood above him with his rifle held crosswise across his chest in portarms position. Two of his comrades stood similarly off to one side, as they had throughout the night, and now, with early-morning sunlight flooding the construction site, there was a guard relief approaching from the opposite direction. Olsen's four privates were seated beside him on the ground near a small fire, and each of them showed the effects of last night's battle—a mouse under the eye here, a pair of split lips there, a cheekbone skinned raw, and various other lumps and bruises.

Olsen shrugged, tossed the remainder of the coffee away, and rose to follow the guard toward the command tent. Inside, Captain Gann sat at the drafting table and Ecklehart stood off to one side, slightly behind him, explaining a set of drawings with the aid of a ruler. Both men looked up as Olsen entered the tent, came to attention, and saluted.

"Sergeant Olsen reporting as ordered, sir."

Gann stared coldly at the NCO before saying, "At ease, Sergeant. I'll deal with you in a moment." Then he looked down at the plans once again.

Ecklehart attempted an equally severe glare, but his enormously swollen left cheek rendered his facial expression more comical than threatening, and he abandoned the effort to continue his explanation of the drawings. Nearly five minutes passed before Gann nodded, shoved the papers to one side, rose, and advanced on Olsen to circle with his hands folded behind his back. He looked the sergeant up and down, as if examining some strange animal, until he had made a thorough inspection. Then he came to the front again.

"You're in the shit up to your neck, you know that, Sergeant?"

"I don't believe I am, sir," Olsen replied in a tone that indicated military propriety but no hint of reluctance.

"I'm afraid I'll have to be the judge of that, soldier," Gann snapped. "But first, I would like to know just what in hell you think you're doing."

"Following orders, Captain."

"Whose orders?"

"Those of my commanding officer, Captain Conway."

"I see. And this Captain Conway of yours sent you here to engage in fisticuffs with my men, including my executive officer?"

"No, sir. Whatever happened last night was started by your men, not by mine or myself. As far as your executive officer being struck goes, I doubt that he could identify the man who did it, and it could well have been one of your own. I was hit myself, but I couldn't pick out the man responsible this morning."

Gann's eyebrows arched sharply. "You've got a bit of sass about you, Sergeant, that I don't like and won't tolerate. I don't care if you're artillery, mounted infantry, cavalry, or a goddamned low-life cook, you're still in the presence of an officer and you'd damned well better keep that fact in mind when asked a question."

"I haven't violated any code of conduct, sir. I'm only answering the captain's questions in the same way they're asked."

Gann spun on his heel and his eyes blazed with anger. "You mentioned some orders from your commanding officer. What the hell are they?"

"Merely that I proceed to this location, make a visual observation, and report back to him, Captain. And that's what I've been trying to do." Olsen stared straight into Gann's eyes. "But being held under armed guard all night and this morning, sir, has made the carrying out of my orders slightly more difficult."

"You were placed under armed guard for your own protection, soldier!"

"Thank you, sir," Olsen replied dryly.

"Just what in hell's name does your captain think he's doing, sending you here to inspect anything that's being done on this site?"

"Following orders, sir, just like I am."

"Orders, Sergeant? Orders from whom?"

"Fort Laramie, sir. They were sent by a major."

"What was his name?"

"I have no idea, sir."

"What did his orders specifically say?"

"I can't tell you that either. I can only tell you what Captain Conway told me regarding my orders, and I've already done that, Captain."

Even though he was being honest in his answers, Olsen was being purposely vague and he felt that the less the captain knew about his findings or suspicions, the better that information would serve Captain Conway. He was certain that the stage station was being built in the wrong location—the conversation with the buffalo hunter, the futile search along Hat Creek, Mandalian's observations, and the map in his pocket had convinced him of that—but he had no idea why. However, the fact that Gann had chosen the location himself struck Olsen as very odd indeed, and he intended to convey the entire curious set of circumstances to Captain Conway the minute he got back to Outpost Number Nine.

Deeply in thought, Gann had walked toward his desk and

now rested a hip on the desk corner and folded his arms across his chest while looking again at Olsen.

"Let me get this straight, Sergeant. You were ordered to come here simply to take a look and report back to your CO?"

"Yes, sir."

Now Gann smiled coldly. "And what have you seen? What would be the basis of your report?"

"That a stagecoach station is being built, that it is nearly completed, and that it is located at the headwaters of Hat Creek, in the state of Nebraska. Nothing more, sir."

"And would you consider that to be a set of findings worthy of your time and effort, Sergeant?"

"Yes, sir. I've done as ordered by my CO."

"I see," Gann replied speculatively while tracing the tip of one finger across his mustache. "I don't believe you, Sergeant. Not for one damned minute. I'd like to see the orders this Captain Conway gave you. You must have been given a written copy just in case a situation like this came up."

"Yes I have, sir," Olsen said, reaching into his pocket and pulling out the folded orders, but making certain the map was not seen. "Here they are."

Gann nodded to Ecklehart, and the lieutenant crossed to Olsen, took the orders, then passed them to the captain, who quickly snapped them open and read them. Although expressed in greater detail, the orders said exactly what the sergeant had stated, with the exception that they superseded any other orders that might be given by another officer.

Gann flipped the orders toward Ecklehart and focused his attention on Olsen. "I don't know what the hell you and your CO are up to, but I don't like it one damned bit, and if I give you an order, you'll damned sure obey it or be shot on the spot. Is that understood, soldier?"

"I understand, sir. And that's exactly what you'd have to do."

"We'll see about that when the time comes. I don't like smartasses, and especially not smartassed NCOs. Furthermore, I don't like anybody snooping around in my affairs and I god-damned well am not going to put up with any mounted infantry captain taking liberties of that nature. I'll be sending an inquiry to Fort Laramie, and I intend to get to the bottom of this heap of bullshit. And when I do, Captain Conway, whoever the hell he thinks he is, will have his ass on the line so damned fast it'll make his head swim. You tell your CO that for me, and that I intend to have a full inquiry into this matter just as soon as my work is completed, which will be in ten days, maybe less. We're damned near done here now, and the station will be turned over to a civilian contractor as was originally planned."

"I'll pass that word along, sir."

Gann's eyes narrowed to tiny slits and he gritted his teeth before speaking again. "Now I'm going to give you a bit of advice, Sergeant, that you'd better consider an order. I don't ever want to see you around any project I might be involved with, no matter when or where. If I do, I'll personally see to it that you are stripped and flogged, or worse. Men have a way of getting killed on construction sites, and no one ever knows when or how an accident might happen. Just consider yourself lucky that one hasn't happened to you."

"I've always been fond of a bit of luck, sir," Olsen replied with a slight smile.

"You're dismissed, Sergeant! You and your detachment have five minutes to be off this site or I'll arrest you without a second thought and have you taken to Laramie under armed guard. Now get your ass out of here! I've got work to do!"

Olsen offered a salute that wasn't returned, ducked through the tentflap and paused beside the guard standing outside.

"My men and I have been given permission to leave. Check with the captain on that if you want to."

"I heard, Sergeant."

"Good," Olsen replied, striding toward his four privates. "All right, shitheads, we're moving out on the double. Saddle up and prepare to leave."

The privates scrambled to their feet and expertly slipped blankets and saddles onto their waiting mounts. In less than five minutes they were swinging up. As Olsen reined his horse around, he stopped by Private Jones and said just loudly enough to be heard, "You're an asshole, Jones, but nice work anyway. That lieutenant looks like he tried to kiss a mule's ass and got kicked for his efforts. Too bad I can't say the same about the captain."

Jones grinned his satisfaction. "Thanks, Sarge. I said I never hit a woman, but that's as damned close as I've ever come and it didn't feel all that bad. Maybe I've been missin' out on somethin'."

"Yeah. You'll make up for it. Let's go. I've got a real powerful urge to talk to Captain Conway about now."

The main street of Douglas was tinted red by the sunset behind him as Jay Jarvis dismounted, looped his reins over the hitch rail, and stepped onto the boardwalk in front of the babershop. An elderly man with an apron around his middle was backing out the door with a broom in his hands, and Jarvis moved to one side and waited until the barber had finished his sweeping.

"You still open, Pop? I'd like a shave and a haircut."

The barber eyed Jarvis's long, stringy hair, soiled clothing, stubbled face, and worn-out boots before offering a reply. "Usually close at six o'clock, which it is right now, young fella. But if I ever seen anybody who needed some barber work done, it's you. Come on in. Gonna cost ya two bits extra, though."

"Fine. Be glad to pay it," Jarvis replied, hanging his hat on a rack and turning toward the chair.

The barber watched him and inclined the end of his broom toward the gunbelt as Jarvis settled onto the seat. "You gonna take that thing off?"

Jarvis grinned easily, and there was a disarming boyishness about his smile. "If it's all the same to you, I don't think I will. Once a man gets used to one of these things, he feels kind of naked without it."

"Never shot one myself, and don't aim to," the barber sniffed, leaning the broom in a corner before beginning to strop his razor. "You new 'round these parts?"

"Yup, sure am. Come up from down Texas way. Been workin' cattle for an outfit over toward the west. My daddy's got a big spread down home, and he sent me up here to take a look around and see if there was anything worth investing in. Haven't seen an outfit that I'd spend fifty cents on yet, let alone fifty thousand dollars." Jarvis glanced up at the mirror and smiled at the barber's visible look of shock. He was pleased with the reaction, and he knew that the first part of his job had

116

already been accomplished, but he continued on in easy conversation while an apron was being draped around his neck.

"That's a lot of money, fifty thousand, and my daddy'd get plumb mean if I threw it away on something that wasn't damned good. He's kind of sour on me anyway, and this is kinda his way of tellin' me to grow up or get the hell out. But to tell you the truth, I'm having a damned hard time finding something I can sink my teeth into. I'm tired of the cattle business and I'd sure like to get into something else, if I knew what that was."

The barber had been listening intently as he worked his brush in a cup of soap and spoke as he began to lather Jarvis's face. "You ain't tryin' to tell me your pa sent you up here with fifty thousand dollars, just like that."

"Hell, yes I am. A thousand dollars to him is like one lonely dollar to you and me."

"And you're carryin' that kind of money around with you?"

"Hell, I wouldn't be that stupid," Jarvis said with a chuckle. "I've got it put away in a safe place till I can get to the bank tomorrow morning."

"Damned smart on your part," the barber replied in a distant voice as he concentrated on the strokes of his razor down the left side of Jarvis's face. "Damned smart indeed. Ever hear of a feller named Canfield? Senator Rankin Canfield?"

Jarvis paused as if searching his memory. "No, can't say as I have. Why?"

"No reason, maybe, but he might be able to help you find that investment you've been talkin' about."

"That a fact? How?"

"Well, I shave the senator every mornin', leastwise I have been every day since he's been here, and that's more'n a week now. He kinda gets to talkin' while he's gettin' his shave, and he was tellin' me about some kind of investment he's interested in. Nothin' real particular, you understand, just that he's got the inside information on somethin' real big."

"Sounds interesting. Any idea at all what it is?"

"Nope. Just that he's got somethin' big and that he's kinda lookin' around for a partner or two to take in. Hell, it ain't every day that you get the chance to shave a senator's face, so I just listen and let him do the talkin'." The barber wiped the blade clean on a towel hanging from his shoulder and grinned slyly. "Got himself a beauty for a daughter, too. I've seen her around town a time or two, and she's a real looker. I make her to be 'bout your age, maybe a little younger. If I was lookin' for somebody to invest with and had the kind of money you do, the senator's the man I'd damned sure start my talkin' with."

Jarvis grinned. "For the business or the girl?"

"Both. Marla's her name, and it fits her perfect as all get-out."

"Sounds interesting. How would I get in contact with this Senator Canfield? Will you be shaving him in the morning?"

"'Spect I will."

"Then do me a favor. Tell him I'm in town and that I'll be having breakfast at the restaurant over there across the street. My name is Phil Bradley and I'd be mighty pleased to make his acquaintance."

"I'll do that for you, right enough. Our town banker sometimes comes in with him. He's Otto Bruner—tight-fisted son of a bitch he is, but honest as the day is long. He'd be somebody for you to talk to as well."

"Fine. Tell them breakfast is on me. How late is the mercantile open?" Jarvis asked as the barber finished the shave and began on the haircut.

"Another hour."

"Good. I'll be wanting some new clothes and then a room. I noticed the Grayson Hotel when I was coming down the street. Is it any good?"

"Best in town. Matter of fact, that's where the senator and Miss Canfield are stayin'."

"Well now. How's that for luck?"

The old barber chuckled and carved off another lock of long, stringy hair. "Son, when you've got fifty thousand dollars to play with, I'd say you've had all the luck any one man deserves."

They talked amicably until the haircut was completed, and in the process of the conversation the barber came to like the young man, who had an air of trustworthiness and believability about him. He seemed like an entirely different sort of person after his shave and haircut than he had appeared to be upon arrival. There was a handsomeness about him, even the look of a gentleman, perhaps.

Jarvis stood, retrieved his hat and saddlebags, and paid the barber with the addition of a handsome tip before offering a handshake and moving toward the door. "Thank you once again for your help in passing my message on to the senator. I'll be looking forward to seeing him in the morning over breakfast."

"You're welcome, son. I'll pass it along. Good luck, and I'm sure I'll see you around town if you find something suitable. Oh, one more thing," the barber said innocently. "Do you enjoy a friendly hand of poker from time to time?"

Jarvis grinned as his hand went to the door latch. "You're damned right I do. Is there a good game in town?"

"Well, probably nothing on the order that you're used to, but me and a few of the boys get together in Radly's Saloon on Friday nights. If you care to join us, feel free to sit in for a few hands. I'll be there tomorrow night at eight o'clock sharp, myself."

"Thank you. I'll do that. See you then."

Jarvis stepped onto the boardwalk again, tipped his hat to two ladies, found his way to the mercantile store, and went inside. He selected trousers, boots, three shirts, and a charcoal-gray coat of Western cut, along with a new Stetson, then paid for his goods, collected his packages, and crossed to the run-down boardinghouse across the street. There he paid for a hot-water bath, with soap, and an hour later he was back on the street, a new man. He paused to light one of the slim, long cigars he had bought in the mercantile, and then ambled toward the Grayson Hotel, entered, and approached the desk.

The clerk looked up from his work, gave Jarvis an approving glance, and asked, "May I help you, sir?"

"Yes, I believe you can. I'd like the best room you have available. I'll be in Douglas for quite an extended stay, and I'd like something comfortable."

"I see. Our finest accommodations are rooms sixteen and fourteen on the second floor, but they are presently occupied by the senator and his daughter. Let's see now—"

"Is there a senator staying here at the hotel?" Jarvis asked with great surprise. "How interesting."

"There certainly is, and he's a marvelous man as well. His

daughter defies description," the clerk said, clearing his throat and adjusting his glasses with a sly smile, before turning to the ledger once again. "I can't let you have number twelve, since the army captain has reserved it indefinitely. So—"

"An army captain as well? I must say, you have some interesting guests. I hope my humble presence won't be too easily noticed."

The clerk's face turned sour at the mention of Gann, and his tone became cold. "We certainly have, and they are all guests, but that doesn't mean that they are gentlemen, with regard to certain of the males. Ah, here we are. I think room number thirteen will quite suit your needs and be comfortable as well. Now if you will just sign the register," he continued, turning the book toward Jarvis, "I'll help you with your baggage and you can settle your account with us on a weekly basis."

"Thank you," Jarvis replied, signing the register with the name he had given the barber and turning the document back toward the clerk. "I once served some time in the military myself. Cavalry, as a matter of fact. Wouldn't it be a coincidence if that captain you mention and I had served together at some point or other?"

"Quite so. His name is Captain Raymond J. Gann," the clerk offered, studying Jarvis's face for the slightest reaction. "He's a cavalry officer, as I understand it."

A look of total shock filled Jarvis's eyes. "Are you serious? Captain Gann is staying here?"

"In a manner of speaking. He does stay here on his frequent visits to town." The clerk's eyebrows arched perceptibly, and there was a slight curl to his upper lip. "I presume that you do know the gentle—ah, the captain?"

"I most certainly do. He was my commanding officer some years ago."

"Then I can understand why you are no longer in the military, sir," the clerk said in a sepulchral tone, barely above a whisper.

"What was that?"

"Nothing, sir."

"When do you expect the captain to return?"

"He mentioned something about tomorrow night, but one cannot be certain. Shall I tell him you are registered when he arrives?" the clerk concluded with a long hard stare at Jarvis.

"By all means. Now I think I'll go up to my room and rest briefly. As far as luggage goes, I have nothing of consequence with me at present, since I arrived on horseback, other than these saddlebags. My animal is the sorrel just down the street in front of the barbershop. Please have someone take it to the livery stable."

"I shall, sir," the clerk responded in a tone lacking any of its previous cordiality.

"You're a good man," Jarvis offered, taking up the package containing the two shirts he'd purchased and moving toward the stairway. He didn't notice the stare given his back by the clerk, nor was he aware of the careful study his signature was given once he had gone up the stairs.

Just as Jarvis turned the corner landing at the top of the stairs, the door to room sixteen opened and he saw the senator and his daughter step into the hallway. He tipped his hat grandly and stood to one side with a pleasant smile to allow passage. The senator nodded his appreciation and responded to Jarvis's greeting with a pleasant "Good evening." The senator's daughter studied his face intently for a fleeting second as they passed before Jarvis continued down the hallway. He stopped at the door to room thirteen and glanced in the direction of the stairwell at the couple who were just turning on the landing and preparing to descend the steps. The senator had taken the first step in preparation to escort his daughter down, and Marla looked quickly down the hallway while Canfield was preoccupied with proper balance. Jarvis nodded toward the door to his room, and Marla responded with a warm, almost wistful smile and then disappeared down the stairwell under the guidance of her father's hand.

Feeling a thrill run through his body, Jarvis stepped into the room, deposited his packages and saddlebags on the bed, then stepped before the mirror to examine himself after removing his hat. He smoothed his hair back carefully, removed his coat, and knelt down beside the bed to shove the saddlebags out of sight after removing a bottle of whiskey from one of them. He straightened and realigned the creases in his trouser legs, poured a glass of whiskey, and leaned back against the pillows on the bed to sip his drink and stare at the ceiling. *I pulled it off*, he

121

thought, occasionally nursing the whiskey and puffing on his cigar just frequently enough to keep it lit. *I'm here with all the money we'll ever need, and Marla is coming to me. The first half of the plan is in motion,* he thought before a troubled look crossed his face. *And the second half will be done without mercy or feeling.*

Downstairs, the senator and his daughter paused to bid the clerk a good evening.

"And good evening to you, Senator Canfield. And you as well, Miss Canfield. Are you going out to dine?"

"Yes we are. But we'll return early. My daughter just mentioned a headache as we were coming down the stairs. Strange how women get those damned things at just about every opportunity, but I guess that's a curse we men have to live with."

The clerk smiled thinly. "Yes, I am quite familiar with that problem, being a married man myself. Good night, and I hope you have an enjoyable dinner."

"Good night," the senator replied while Marla smiled demurely and the two of them went out onto the boardwalk.

After a safe period of time had elapsed, the clerk closed his ledger, twisted the combination lock on the safe in one corner of the office, then slipped on his jacket and stepped outside. Walking quickly, he went to the barbershop and took up the reins of the sorrel and led the animal toward the livery stable and into a stall at the back of the building. Working quietly to keep from awakening the old hostler, whom he knew would be drunk and passed out in the back room, he stripped saddle and bridle from the horse, forked some hay into a trough, and then lit a lantern and bent down closely, lantern in hand, to examine the riding tack. After a search of nearly five minutes had yielded nothing, he puzzled for a moment before noticing the stock of a rifle protruding from the saddle scabbard. He pulled the rifle out and held it beside the light, turning the weapon and carefully examining the stock and chamber for markings, which revealed only the brand name "Spencer" and caliber identification. Just as he was about to give up on the weapon as well, he noticed a loose screw in the buttplate, and he removed it and a second screw with a thumb nail.

Setting the rifle aside, he held the plate up to the light and studied its interior face. There, barely discernible in the weak light, he could make out a name that had been inscribed in the brass with a knifepoint. The clerk strained his eyes and held the plate even closer to the yellow light and read a name softly to himself.

"Second Lieutenant Jay Jarvis, U.S. Cavalry."

The clerk smiled to himself in the semidarkness and replaced the plate while remembering a slip of the tongue Marla Canfield had made the previous day. She had been inquiring about a guest who might be registered at the hotel, and he recalled her words exactly:

"Yes, I'd like to know if a Mr. Jay Jarvis—ah, I mean Phillip Bradley, is registered in the hotel?"

The clerk remembered how he had checked the register and failed to find the name, and then his surprise at having Mr. Bradley check in the following day and mention a previous acquaintance with Captain Gann. The clerk had long since come to assume that snooping was an integral part of his job, and that preoccupation had sharpened an already inquisitive mind that had even been more finely tuned by a loathing of the army captain. He had not the vaguest idea what his findings would lead to, but it was a game to be played and thoroughly enjoyed, and one that he would pursue until all possibilities had been exhausted.

After the buttplate had been secured and the lamp extinguished, the clerk left the livery and returned to the hotel, where he took up a notepad and pencil and cautiously ascended the stairs. After a careful look in all directions, he went to the end of the hall and opened the broom closet and slipped into his observation post. He wondered briefly if he was about to waste an entire night for nothing, but quickly dismissed the thought from his mind. Listening to the events in Miss Canfield's room that had transpired with Captain Gann had been more than sufficient to whet his appetite for more, and he settled back to wait, with the door slightly ajar. No more than an hour had passed before he heard voices in the hall and peeked through the crack to see the senator and his daughter enter the hallway and pause before the lady's door long enough for her to give him a peck on the cheek and a hasty good night. Then Miss Canfield went into her room. The senator turned and left again and the clerk, hearing the heavy steps on the

123

stairway, knew Canfield had had several drinks with dinner and was returning to the saloon for a nightcap.

Fifteen minutes later, the door to Miss Canfield's room opened and she crossed the hall in a flimsy nightdress, knocked on the door to room thirteen, and, after a brief pause, entered the room. The clerk made a notation on his paper; then, fearing the senator might return and catch him listening in the hallway, he gave a reluctant sigh, closed his book, and quit his hiding place. He was pleased on the one hand, but extremely disappointed on the other. He had gotten the information he was after, but he desperately wanted to hear what was going on inside — something he had heard only once before and probably would never hear again, at least not from the matronly wife waiting for him at home with five children, a determined scowl, and not one single loving word in her entire vocabulary.

nine _____

At the sound of the door opening, Jarvis slid off the bed and stood on the small oval rug, wearing nothing but his trousers. His lithe body tensed as he slid the revolver from its holster and thumbed the hammer back in one motion. Marla stepped into the room and a slight gasp escaped her lips at the sight of the heavy pistol, which Jarvis instantly lowered.

"I'm sorry, Marla. I didn't expect you this early." Jarvis lowered the hammer cautiously and replaced the revolver in its holster before straightening to look at Marla again. "God, but you're beautiful, honey. Come here and let me touch you."

Marla quickly crossed the room and her lips hungrily went to his while her hands closed on the back of his head and she forced her body against his. Jarvis's palms slid down the filmy fabric of the nightdress and he slowly massaged her firm buttocks while they rocked back and forth in a clinging embrace. When Marla finally pulled her mouth away, she leaned her head against his chest and rubbed his back with circling strokes of her hands.

"I love you, Jay. I love you so much," she said softly, almost in a whimper.

"And I love you too, honey," Jarvis replied with eyes closed, pressing his cheek against her soft blonde hair. "It won't be much longer now."

"How much longer, Jay?" Marla asked, looking up at him. "I don't know if I can stand it anymore."

"We have to, honey. I've gone too far to back out now. I have the money and I'll soon be a partner with your father in a major business venture, then we can get married and live our lives on our terms." A hard tone came into Jarvis's voice and a distant look filled his eyes. "I won't be looked down on anymore, and I won't be just a kid from an orphanage who had to fight his way to the top and educate himself without any help from schoolteachers."

"But why couldn't we have done it without all this?" Marla's pleading eyes searched his face. "I would have run away with you when we met in Washington."

"No, that wouldn't have been any good. We would have been broke and struggling all our lives, and I couldn't stand the thought of your living like that. Besides, you were Ray's woman when I met you at that party. He would have hunted us for the rest of our lives. He's that way, and you know it as well as I do."

"I know," Marla replied, lowering her head to his chest once again. "I don't think I can stand to go to bed with him again. I have to get half drunk just to do it now, and then it's all an act. I try to make it seem like he drives me crazy, just like you told me to, but he's so rough and not gentle and loving like you are at all. He—he hurts me sometimes."

"I know, and I hate it as much as you do, but we need him and it couldn't work without him. We have to make him think you love him, or at least are willing to marry him, until this thing's over. Has he asked you to marry him yet?"

"Yes he did. The last time he came to my room."

"And you said?"

"That I didn't know, only that I wanted to make love to him that night and not talk about anything else." A tear leaked from Marla's eye and Jarvis could feel its warm moistness on his chest. He pressed his head against her hair more tightly as she said in a whisper, "God, but he was brutal that night. It was the worst it's ever been."

"It'll only be a few more times, honey. Once he's concluded this deal with your father, we won't need him anymore. Stall him if he asks you again to marry him, and just pretend you love him. But if he even thinks you're not going to marry him, he'll pull out of this whole deal and we'll be left with nothing, possibly not even our lives. I know too much and he couldn't let me live if things go bad."

"I'll do anything you say, Jay. You know that. I get so lonely for you I can't help myself sometimes. I—I even went to the desk clerk yesterday and asked if you had checked in yet."

Jarvis pulled away quickly and took her by the shoulders. "Don't do that," he said sternly. "Don't ever do that, because no one can know we're even acquainted until this is over. What name did you ask for?"

"The one you told me to use. Phil Bradley." She looked down at his white-knuckled hands on her shoulder and her lips formed a pained expression. "Please, Jay, you're hurting me."

"I'm sorry, honey," Jarvis said, releasing his grip and pulling her to him once more. "It's just that we can't afford any mistakes now. Not when we're so close. I'm meeting with your father tomorrow morning to invest a sizable amount of money in his venture, and I think the banker will be there as well. They will have no reason not to think I'm legitimate, since I'll be dealing in cash."

"You keep mentioning a venture, Jay. What kind of venture? You've never told me any of it."

Jarvis looked down at her tenderly. "I can't tell you that even now. Just believe me when I tell you that we need Ray for a few more days, that I love you and we'll be both rich and married in no time at all. I will no longer be Jay Jarvis, and you'll be Mrs. Phil Bradley. It's all in the works and will just require the proper timing. When it's over, I'll be your father's partner, a respectable businessman, and married to the most beautiful woman in the territory."

"But what about Ray? He must have something to gain from all this."

Jarvis's face tightened and his gaze drifted to the far wall.

127

"He thinks he does, and to be honest with you, the whole thing was his idea in the first place. But he doesn't deserve you. I'll take care of him in my own way."

Marla turned her lips up to him once more, and her eyes were misted with tears. "Kiss me, Jay. I don't want to talk about it anymore. I just want you, and I want you to make love to me. I want to feel your body against mine and have you hold me tight. I'm frightened about this whole thing and I need reassurance that everything is going to be all right. Make love to me, Jay," she whispered as his lips closed on hers. "Make love to me right now."

"Oh, Christ, Marla. Yes. I want you so badly," Jarvis whispered as he slid the nightdress from her shoulders. "I dream about you and your body every night."

Later, after they had fallen to the pillows in exhaustion, Marla fell asleep in his arms with her head on his shoulder. As he began to doze, he stroked her hair. And as he fell into a deep sleep, he was no longer touching her hair in a comfortable bed, but was instead stroking the feathers of a dead swallow in a distant cave. His hand slowly went to her neck, where it rested the remainder of the night, encircling her soft throat, and he slept fitfully with nightmares racing through his brain.

The sun was well up the following day when Jarvis crossed the street to the restaurant across the way. He glanced once toward the barbershop and saw two thick-bodied men rise to glance out the window at the barber's instruction, and then sink back down again to await their morning shave. Jarvis smiled to himself, stepped inside, and found a seat in a rear corner of the room.

No more than twenty minutes passed before the two portly men entered the cafe and approached Jarvis's table. He glanced up nonchalantly over his steaming cup of coffee.

"May I help you gentlemen?"

"Only if you happen to be a man named Phil Bradley," Senator Canfield said with an appraising glance that openly revealed that he liked what he saw.

"I'm Phillip Bradley," Jarvis replied, affecting a slight Southern drawl that he'd perfected as a ruse to employ in poker games to lull his opponents into a false sense of confidence regarding his intelligence. "I'm at your service," he continued, rising and offering his hand.

"I'm Otto Bruner," the banker began, accepting the handshake and then referring to the senator, "and this is Senator Rankin Canfield. We'd like a moment of your time, if you don't mind."

"Certainly. Please join me. Would you care for coffee?"

Both men nodded and took seats while Jarvis signaled for more coffee and additional cups. Once the coffee was poured and they were alone again, Jarvis leaned back and lit one of his cigars. "Now tell me how I may be of service."

The banker's bushy dark eyebrows nodded over his coffee cup and he took a sip before looking up. "Old John over at the barbershop said the two of you had had a conversation yesterday. Something about your desire to invest a considerable sum in a business venture of one kind or another. Is that correct, Mr. Bradley?"

"Yes, as a matter of fact it is. He mentioned to me that he knew some influential people in town and that he might consider putting me in contact with them. I suppose you are the two men he had in mind?"

"Yes we are," Canfield replied, ignoring the coffee and surreptitiously casting about the room for something more substantial. "I happen to be the individual in question, and Mr. Bruner is my good friend and advisor, the first man to get to know when you come to town with the prospect of making money on your mind."

"Yes, I am quite aware of that. Certainly you wouldn't care to discuss this matter in public, so may I suggest breakfast first and then perhaps a visit to your offices? I seem to think better on a full stomach." Jarvis risked one of his boyish grins. "Must be a holdover from my days of working on my daddy's ranch."

Both men chuckled appreciatively and their heads bobbed in agreement with Jarvis's suggestion. They chatted amiably throughout the course of the meal about generally meaningless topics, even though the two guests continued to probe Jarvis regarding his background and financial standing at every opportunity.

When they had finished eating, Jarvis insisted on paying the bill and peeled the price of the meal from a generous stack he withdrew from his pocket to the approving stares of the other two. Then they walked down the boardwalk in the direction of the bank. Walking between the two big men, and maintaining constant concentration on which words would best maintain his image, Jarvis didn't notice a lone rider slowly walking his horse down the street.

The rider sat on a tall roan horse and wore fringed buckskins. A huge Sharps rifle was held casually in the crook of one arm. A wad of cut-plug bulged against one cheek, and his dark eyes seemed unblinking as he watched the street scene before him. A bowie knife and revolver hung from his narrow hips, and there was a look of deadly seriousness about him that was in complete contrast with the three men now turning into the bank's front door. Windy Mandalian watched them disappear, then spat and reined his horse in before the ramshackle boardinghouse. He had never felt any love for banks, or the people who frequented them.

Throughout the long ride back from Fort McKinney, the memory of a particular message Kincaid had sent while there continued to haunt his mind. Not the one to Captain Conway, nor the one to Fort Laramie, but the one to the newly widowed Mrs. Edward Springer. He wondered if he had said the right things in the proper way. No matter how he had tried to phrase it through several handwritten drafts, he could not properly express his sorrow or sense of loss.

Even now, with the main gates of Outpost Number Nine in view, he felt that he had somehow failed, and a great weariness swept over him as he saluted the guard standing by the gate and led his two squads into the compound. It was as though he were returning empty-handed, and the battle that had taken place at the cave were as senseless as the ambush that had caused the deaths of so many soldiers. The sense of futility and loss were overwhelming, and after the searing fire of vengeance had died in his heart, it had been replaced by a gnawing emptiness.

Kincaid stepped down, gave instructions for the dismissal of the squad to the sergeant, handed his reins to a waiting private, and walked wearily toward the orderly room.

Captain Conway met him at the door and offered his hand,

which Kincaid accepted with as much enthusiasm as he could muster.

"I'm damned sorry about your friend, Matt," Conway said with deep sincerity, "not to mention the loss of the escort detail. It's been tough on you, I know. Come on into the office and let's have a glass of brandy."

"Thank you, sir," Kincaid replied with a tight smile. "I think I could use one."

After the drinks were poured, Conway took a seat behind his desk and Kincaid sank down into one of the facing chairs. Matt related all the details of the patrol, which had been too numerous to relay by telegram, and when he finished, the captain leaned forward to take up a message lying before him.

"I guess it's a little too late for this to mean anything, Matt, but you and Windy asked me to send a telegram inquiring about the reasons for Sergeant Benjamin Harrison's not having been the teamster on that trip, and here's the reply."

"I remember, sir. I thought at the time that it might be a hunch that could help sort things out. Unfortunately, I learned the answer firsthand. But it still could do some good. What was the reason for Harrison's absence? Did he fall down while drunk and break his arm, like French said he did?"

Conway smiled with a shake of his head. "No, not at all. It's true that he had a broken arm, but he's never had a drink in his life and still hasn't. He was attacked in the stables late one night and beaten. They say they haven't found out who did it yet, but they'll let me know when they do."

"They won't ever find out through any investigation, sir. I'm positive that I killed the man who did it."

"After what you told me a few minutes ago, I'm afraid I have to agree with you. And now this whole thing's got me wondering," Conway continued, folding his fingers together across his chest and leaning back in his chair. "Let's put a few of these coincidences together and see if we come up with anything. First of all, you told me this was Lieutenant Springer's first escort patrol, isn't that correct?"

"Yes, sir. At least that's what he told me. I find it strange myself, since he's been pretty much confined to desk duty. He said the officer who was normally in charge of that responsibility had been reassigned."

Conway nodded. "All right, that's coincidence number one.

Then we have Sergeant Harrison being replaced by Corporal French, and the reasons given for that by French have been proven entirely false. Then Springer decides to alter his course to Farley's Crossing, where an ambush has been set up, instead of staying with the assigned route via Baker Flats. Now what does all that tell you, Matt?"

"It tells me that someone put this whole thing together, someone in a position of responsibility who could manipulate the duty roster to fit his needs and control both the route and the destiny of that escort detachment."

"But we don't have any idea who that might be, do we?"

"No, sir. But I would suggest another message to Fort Laramie requesting any information on who made up the detachment, where and why the regular officer was transferred, who authorized the transfer, and what officer, if any, is disgruntled enough with the army to take his revenge out on innocent men or desperate enough financially to do something of this nature."

"Exactly what I had in mind, and I'll draft that message just as soon as we've finished talking," Conway said, leaning forward to take a sip of brandy. "Unfortunately, as late as it is in the day, we probably won't be able to get the answer we want until sometime tomorrow."

"Yes, I'm aware of that. Has anything come in from Windy yet? He should have been in Douglas by this morning."

"No, haven't received a thing. There's no doubt that he's there if he said he would be, but he might not have had time to do much snooping around yet. The only thing we can hope for is that this Jay Jarvis intended to stay there and hasn't got any knowledge of what French told you."

"He couldn't have any knowledge of that, sir. There was no one left who could have told him. I firmly believe he thinks he got away scot-free, and let's hope that confidence will make him a little less cautious than he might be otherwise." Kincaid paused and allowed a determined smile to cross his lips. "If he does leave Douglas, I wouldn't give him much chance of getting away. With Windy on his trail, he'll be tracked clear to the gates of hell if necessary."

"Yes, he's got the wrong man after him, no matter how confident he feels," Conway agreed. "When you were telling me about what went on up there, you mentioned wanting to go to Douglas yourself. Would you mind explaining that a little further?"

"Not at all, sir. It's my opinion that Jarvis and whoever else is in on this can be taken only if they're not spooked. A large patrol would attract attention and might prevent them from doing whatever it is they stole that payroll to do. If I join Windy there, in civilian clothes, we can work as a team and maybe get to the bottom of this." Kincaid's eyes hardened and he stared into his brandy glass. "Aside from army business, I've got a personal interest in this and I would like permission to pursue any possibility that might help me avenge the death of a friend. Perhaps I would feel differently if it had happened in open combat, but for him to die in such a coldblooded manner, being killed from ambush, is something I take personally."

"I understand, Matt, and your request is granted. We can get along around here without you for however long it takes. When do you want to leave?"

"Tomorrow morning, sir. I think I'd better get some rest tonight."

"That's what I would suggest. You're going to need a civilian mount and weapons too, Matt. I'm sure you can get some weapons on loan from the sutler's store, and those stray horses we picked up are still in the paddock. As for a saddle and bridle, Pop Evans has got a set of those over at his store as well. Remember that trapper he took them from because he didn't pay his bill?" Conway asked with a grin.

"Yes I do. He can be a miserable old bastard when he wants to be," Kincaid replied with a smile. "It's going to feel kind of strange playing civilian again after all these years."

"Don't get to used to it, Matt. We need you here. Now—"

Conway hesitated at the knock on the door and turned to see Sergeant Cohen stick his head inside the door.

"Sorry to disturb you, Captain, but Sergeant Olsen just returned with his detachment, and from the sight of 'em, it looks like they got into a brick fight and didn't have a brick. He's pretty anxious to talk to you, sir. Shall I send him in?"

"By all means, Ben. I'm anxious to talk to him as well."

Sergeant Olsen stepped inside, and grinned somewhat

sheepishly as the two officers studied his bruised cheek and swollen eye. He started to salute, but Conway said, "Never mind that, Gus. Come on in and have a glass of brandy. From the looks of things, you kind of wound up with your hands full down there."

"Yes, I guess we did, sir." Olsen accepted the brandy poured by Kincaid and took a deep swallow. "Thanks, Lieutenant. But those yellowlegs knew they'd been out behind the barn themselves. They started it, sir, and the four men I had with me were more than happy to oblige."

"I imagine they were. How were they otherwise?"

"Dumber than a board, crazier than hell, and downright infuriating sometimes, but deep down inside they're damned good, tough soldiers. We got jumped by a band of Indians the second night out, and killed four."

"What tribe?"

"Sioux, sir. I'll make out a full report on it for you."

"Fine. How's that stage station coming along at Hat Creek?"

"Excellent, sir. Except for one thing."

"What's that, Gus?"

"The station's not being built at Hat Creek. It's being built at Sage Creek."

"What?" Conway exclaimed while Kincaid looked up in surprise. "Sage Creek? Isn't that in Wyoming Territory?"

"Yes it is, sir. According to what I understood, the station was supposed to be built in Nebraska, wasn't it?"

"It was. You'd better tell us the whole story, Gus. Have a seat and start at the beginning."

Olsen eased down onto a chair and detailed the search along Hat Creek, the encounter with the buffalo hunter, and their eventual arrival at the construction site. He mentioned the initial greeting they had gotten from the cavalrymen, and outlined his discussions with Ecklehart.

"The lieutenant showed me the maps they had used to select the site, sir, and those maps show the two creeks located in exactly the opposite positions from where they are on your map over there on the wall. It was an official government map, I made sure of that."

Conway pondered for long moments before looking up at Olsen again. "Then you believe it's just an honest mistake,

Gus? That somehow they were given a faulty map?"

"That's what I wanted to believe at first, sir. Until I met Captain Gann. He's probably one of the meanest, most ornery officers I've ever met in my time in the army, and that includes a whole pisspot full of officers."

"Sounds like a real dandy. Did you tell him he was building in the wrong location?"

"I was going to, but then I changed my mind. It was something the lieutenant mentioned. He said that the captain had chosen him specifically to do the engineering job, even though he was a green lieutenant to both the area and military procedure. He said that Gann had supplied him with the maps. On top of that, he said that the captain had personally chosen the site and that the choice was the result of his complete knowledge of the area. Now I ask you, sir, if he knows the area that well, how could he get two creeks mixed up that are almost forty miles apart?"

"That does sound a little strange," Conway mused. "And Captain Gann personally chose the location for the stage station?"

"Yes he did, sir. At least that's what the lieutenant said. And I'd say he chose Wyoming Territory over Nebraska for some reason."

Conway looked at Kincaid and asked, "What do you make of it, Matt?"

"It's pretty hard to tell. There is still the possibility that Gann was using incorrect maps, and had been for some time, so he wouldn't actually know which was Hat Creek and which was Sage Creek. On the other hand, he might have had a reason of his own, as Gus suggested. I think the first question to look into is who owns the land the station is being built on? Doesn't the government build those stations on private property mainly because they don't have any desire to be in the stagecoach business?"

"That's correct. There are usually influential people with political pull involved, and the government, wanting to expand service but not wanting a hand in running it, will build the station for those people at government expense and turn over operations to them."

"How would we go about finding out who the particular

135

civilian is who owns the land at the Sage Creek construction site?"

"They would have a record of land ownership for that whole military district at Fort Laramie. After we locate the exact area that Gus is talking about, I'll get a wire off requesting that information. But no matter who owns it, it seems kind of unlikely that an army officer could benefit from building a station in the wrong place. After all, he's just getting paid his monthly wages to oversee the construction, wherever it's built."

"You mentioned, Captain," Kincaid said with a questioning look in his eye, "that those stations are usually built for influential people with political pull. Those same people are generally quite wealthy, and I would imagine some of them wouldn't be above a payoff of some sort. It would be a hell of a risk for the officer involved—Captain Gann in this case—but once the station is built, there wouldn't be much the government could do except leave it there and cashier the man who made the mistake. But if the payoff was large enough, that could well be of interest to some unscrupulous officer, and we both know there are a number of those in the military."

Olsen drained his brandy and placed the glass on Conway's table. "If you'll pardon my saying so about one of your fellow officers, sir, that Captain Gann seems to me like he'd fit the bill just right. There's something about him that'd leave a bad taste in a preacher's mouth."

"Your experience with him doesn't sound like one of the best, Gus," Conway allowed.

"I didn't finish telling you all of it, Captain. He held us under armed guard all night and told me that if he ever saw me on one of his construction jobs again, he'd have me shot on sight. Later he changed his mind and threatened to have me killed in some freak accident. I think he meant it, Captain. He's a mean customer and I wouldn't be surprised if he isn't as crooked as a dog's hind leg."

Conway's eyes flashed in anger for the first time since Olsen had arrived. "He told you that?"

"Yes, sir. In so many words."

"Then that's that. Turning his troopers loose on four of my men is bad enough, but threatening to shoot one of my NCOs is something I will not tolerate. We were ordered to look into

136

this matter, and by God we will! I'll be sending a full platoon back down there tomorrow morning to get this mess straightened out." Conway glanced at Kincaid. "Since you'll be on your way to Douglas to settle that other matter, I think I'll send Lieutenant Fowler along. Think he can handle it?"

"I'm sure he can, sir. Second Platoon is due for patrol anyway."

"Good. And I'll send along a correct copy of the map of that region to show both Gann and Ecklehart. Then, when we get some answers, we'll file our report to Laramie as requested."

Sergeant Olsen folded his big hands and cracked his knuckles with several loud pops. "Captain? I'd like to make a request for myself and that asshole group that went up there with me last time."

"Sure, Gus. The only thing I can promise is that I'll listen to your request, but fire away."

"We'd like to go along with the Second, sir. I know that's not our regular platoon and all that, but we took an awful lot of shit off those boys the last time, and I'd kind of like to have 'em try it again when the odds are a little less in their favor."

Conway smiled and rocked back in his chair. "You sure you want to do that, Gus? You've had a long and mighty rough patrol."

"Positive, sir. Never been more positive about anything."

"And the other four?"

"They'd swim through a mile of shit to get back there if they thought they had a chance to even the score."

"Matt?"

"We sent them down there virtually alone last time, sir. Seems only fair to me that they should have the right to be there when the numbers are close to even, if it comes down to something like the situation they were in last time."

"Then it's settled. On your way out, Gus, find Lieutenant Fowler and send him in here for me, will you? Then you're off duty until tomorrow. Get some sleep and be prepared to move out in the morning."

"I'll find the lieutenant, sir, but I'd like to hold off on that sleep for a bit."

"Oh? What have you got in mind?"

137

"To find me four of the dumbest, ugliest, toughest, and fightingest damned privates on this post and take them over to the sutlers and buy 'em a beer." Olsen grinned and rose from his chair. "I was damned proud of those fellows for the way they tied into that cavalry outfit against that kind of odds. They don't follow orders very damned well, but when it's too late for orders anyway, I'll have those four bastards backing me up anytime."

Kincaid laughed, dug in his pocket, and handed a silver dollar over to Olsen. "Here, Gus. The first few rounds are on me, but don't tell them where it came from. Knowing them, I'll still have to restrict them to post next payday."

"I'm sure you will, sir, and I'll have to kick their butts from here to East Jesus again in the near future. But for right now, we're kind of in on a little something together."

ten

After securing a room in the boardinghouse and taking a hot bath, Windy Mandalian stopped by the restaurant for a meal, then wandered down the street at a leisurely pace, taking in the layout of the town. He paid particular attention to the Grayson Hotel as he passed by, as well as the seedy Smith House and the three saloons breasting Main Street while he walked toward his first objective, the livery stable.

As he stepped into the dimly lit building, rich with the pungency of horseflesh, he paused to allow his eyes to adjust to the dimness and finally located an old hostler forking straw and dung from a vacant stall. Walking slowly down the passage between the stalls, Mandalian examined each of the six horses he passed before stopping behind the old man and leaning his elbows on the top rail.

"Not tryin' to make a joke, pardner, but that's a pretty shitty job you've got there," Windy said in a cordial voice.

The hostler straightened with some difficulty while turning to see who was behind him, and his eyes took in the length of the tall scout. "Betcher boots it is, mister. And the pay ain't much better. Somethin' I can do fer ya?"

Judging from the broken veins in the man's face, his pock-marked, bulbous nose and yellow eyes, Mandalian could tell he was looking at the town drunk. "Not a hell of a lot," Windy replied. "Just admirin' the horseflesh and killing a little time."

"Last damned place I'd be killin' time if I had money to kill it somewhere else," the old man snorted.

"Well, I'll tell you what—maybe I can help you out. A man could work up a powerful thirst doin' a job like that, and I'll bet a little drink of whiskey would taste mighty good when you get through."

The hostler squinted his eyes and licked his lips uncon-sciously at the same time. "Whatcha got in mind?"

"First off, my name's Windy. What's yours?"

"Folks 'round here call me Oly."

"Proud to know you, Oly. Now you've got a problem and so do I—you'd like to have a drink when you get through there, and I'd be real pleased to get some information."

Now the eyes became suspicious. "What kind of informa-tion?"

"Nothin' that could cause you any harm, and enough to be worth about two dollars in your pocket."

"Did ya say two dollars, fella?"

"I didn't stutter."

"What'd ya be wantin' to know?" Oly asked, laying his pitchfork aside and edging forward while wiping his grimy hands on his pants in anticipation.

"Mostly, which of these horses are boarded here regular-like, and which ones come from somewheres else."

"That all?"

"For now."

"Well, this'll be the easiest two damned dollars I ever made." Oly said with a toothless grin. "Only one what ain't from 'round hereabouts is that sorrel down in the end stall. Rest of 'em belongs to townsfolk."

"Is that a fact?" Mandalian asked as his eyes went to the horse mentioned. "When did that one come in?"

140

"Sometime last night."

"When last night?"

"Damned if I know," the hostler replied, scratching the shaggy hair behind one ear. "I usually go to sleep not long after sundown, so I couldn't say for sure. Know it was afore nine o'clock, though, 'cause I got up to take a piss 'bout then and the horse was there, and it wasn't when I went to sleep."

"Any idea at all who brought it in?"

"Nope. Most likely a guest over to the Grayson Hotel. They got a standin' deal with the owner to board saddlehorses, teams, and the like anytime, day or night."

"Anybody else have that same kind of arrangement?"

"Nope. Not that I know of, leastwise."

"I see," Windy said musingly as he wandered toward the far stall and looked at the riding gear stacked in one corner. "I reckon this belongs to the feller who owns the horse?" he asked, glancing over his shoulder at the hostler, who had hobbled down the walkway behind him.

"Yup. And it ain't much of a horseman who threw it down there like that. There's saddletrees and pegs to hang bridles and blankets on over by the wall."

"That was kind of what I was thinkin'. Mind if I have a look?" Windy asked, opening the latch on the stall gate.

"It's your two dollars. Look all ya want."

"Thanks." Mandalian stepped inside and ran his hands over the horse, before checking each hoof. "Needs to be shod pretty bad, besides," he observed, letting the last hoof drop and kneeling beside the tack thrown in one corner. "I picked up the trail of a horse on the way in here with shoes worn down 'bout like those."

After searching the tack thoroughly and finding nothing of interest, Mandalian pulled the Spencer from the saddle scabbard and turned it in his hands. "Looks like army issue. Kinda strange for a civilian, but unfortunately not for an Indian these days," he said as he returned the weapon to the scabbard. "The feller who owns it could've picked it up most anywhere for the right price."

Mandalian turned away and dug in his pocket for the promised two dollars and held the coins out to the hostler's eagerly outstretched hand, but did not release them. "Like I said before, there's one more thing I want from you for this whiskey money."

Oly watched the scout with watery eyes. "I heard ya."

"I want you to let me know if anybody comes for this horse, anytime. I want to know what he looks like and which direction he went. I'll be down at the boardinghouse or in one of the saloons. Have we got a deal on that?"

"Sure have, mister. I'll find ya."

"Thanks, old-timer," Windy said, dropping the coins into the hostler's hand and clapping him lightly on the shoulder as he walked by. On the street once again, Mandalian angled toward the Grayson Hotel, entered the foyer, and approached the desk.

The clerk watched the man in buckskin with obvious distaste, and adjusted his glasses with an irritated twitch of his fingers. "I'm sorry, sir, but you must have the wrong establishment. The boardinghouse is just across the street and down to the left."

"I'm not interested in a room," Mandalian said flatly. "I'm interested in a man whose already got a room."

The clerk, startled by the cold, deadly tone in Windy's voice, cleared his throat nervously. "I'm quite sorry, sir, but it's not our policy to give out the names of our guests."

"This one you will. His name is Jay Jarvis." Mandalian noticed the startled look flit through the clerk's eyes but gave no indication that he had seen it. "But he's probably usin' another name. I'll have a look at that register there, if you don't mind."

"I—I just said that—"

Windy's hand shot out and pulled the register from beneath the clerk's protective palm. "Save it for somebody who's listenin', friend," he said, flipping the register open to the most recent entry, which was the first on a new page and marked by a ribbon. He ran his finger under the name and noted the time and date before looking up at the clerk once more.

"This Mr. Phil Bradley checked in yesterday at seven in the evening. What'd he look like?"

"Well, he's kind of hard to describe."

"Try."

"Tall, slender, a handsome sort of fellow, neatly dressed,

well-groomed, and possibly in his late twenties."

"Well-groomed—does that mean he had a shave and a haircut?"

"That, of course, and the clothes."

"I noticed he's in room thirteen. Is he up there now?"

The clerk turned and pointed to the key rack behind him. "No, of course not. His key is right there, as you can plainly see."

Mandalian leaned on the counter, and the hard expression on his face made the clerk swallow sharply. "This little conversation we had is just between you and me," he said. With that, he turned and walked out of the hotel without waiting for the clerk's affirming reply.

After Mandalian left the hotel, he went to the nearest saloon and drank a few beers. He engaged the bartender in idle chatter and when it was obvious he would learn nothing of importance, he thanked the man and left. Things were much the same in the next place, and finally, when he went across the street to Radly's, the afternoon had passed and the sun was sinking.

The saloon was fairly crowded, and Mandalian could tell upon entering that it was the classiest drinking establishment in town with its mirrored backbar, brass spittoons and foot railing, and highly poslished mahogany bar. Off in one corner he saw a large round poker table with seven chairs but no players. Even though there were a few men present of a rougher cut, several well-dressed businessmen stood in a cluster at one end of the bar, and Mandalian thought he recognized three of them as the men who had been walking down the street when he rode into town. Windy worked his way to an opening beside the group, leaned nonchalantly on the bar, and ordered a beer when the bartender arrived. Then he nursed the brew as though concentrating on something else while listening to the unusually happy men beside him.

The only names exchanged that he could make out were "Otto" and "Senator." Shortly, something about a dinner celebration was mentioned and the three men he thought he had recognized left the saloon.

While ordering another beer, Windy casually drew the bartender into conversation. "I hope I'm not out of place in your saloon with these buckskins on, pardner. From the look of the three that just left, I was standin' next to money that I don't have and never will see."

. The bartender laughed. "You're fine just the way you are. To tell you the truth, I'd rather be in the company of men like you any day, as long as you stay in line, than a tightwad banker and a puffed-up senator."

"A banker and a senator, huh?" Windy remarked, raising his eyebrows in exaggerated surprise. "They from around here?"

"Old Otto Bruner is, but the senator isn't. He just came to town a few days ago, him and his daughter, and what a beauty she is."

"I see. I couldn't help but overhear 'em when they said they were gonna have a victory dinner. What the hell happened? Did the senator get reelected or something?"

Again the barkeep chuckled. "No, nothing like that. Did you notice that young feller with 'em?"

"Yup, by damn I did."

"Well, him and the senator just made some kind of big business deal and old Otto handled the cash through his bank. So all three of them are pleased as all get-out, but you can bet your ass some poor bastard's gonna take a fuckin' somewhere along the line. Otto don't make deals that don't line his pockets, and the senator looks like he'd steal his grandma's corset if he thought she had a nickle hidden in it somewhere."

Windy chuckled appreciatively and waited a proper length of time before asking, "How 'bout the young fella? Looks like he's tryin' to ford a pretty damned fast stream, dealin' with them other two."

"Don't know him," the bartender replied. "Just came to town yesterday, the way I hear tell. Word gets around pretty fast here in Douglas, though, and word has it that he's got big money to burn. Old John, the barber down the street, says he looked like a saddle tramp when he came in here, but left lookin' like a new man. Long hair and beard was gone and he said he was goin' down to the store to buy some new clothes."

Windy shoved his glass across for another beer and observed, "Sounds like he's doin' better'n most saddle tramps I know."

"That's the funny part. He ain't a saddle tramp at all. His

daddy's a rich cattleman down Texas way, and the boy was sent up here to invest in some kind of business. He told old John he had fifty thousand dollars to put to work, and John sent Otto and the senator over to see him this mornin'. Looks like he must've been telling the truth, 'cause those two wouldn't hang around with anybody who had less."

Knowing he had better not make his questions obvious, Windy turned to rest one elbow on the bar and point at the poker table with his glass. "What time's the game start?"

"Usually about eight, but it doesn't get going real good till about nine. It's an open game, and you're welcome to sit in if you feel up to it."

"What kind of stakes do they play?"

"Depends on who's in the game. If it's players like the men who just left here, the senator and Otto and like that, it could be no limit." The bartender thought a moment. "Usually, though, fellers like John the barber are in the game and the pot limit is three raises until they're gone, then the big boys play for whatever they want. It's a clean game, and no under-the-table bullshit."

Windy drained the last of his beer and shoved the mug across the bar. "It's been nice talkin' to you. Think I'll get myself a nice big steak now and I'll probably be back when the game starts."

"Good luck to ya," the bartender replied.

Windy crossed the street to where his horse was tied, led the animal to the livery stables, and had started to call out the hostler's name when he heard a gentle snoring sound coming from somewhere in the back. Realizing the two dollars had been spent for their intended purpose, he put his horse in a stall next to the sorrel, stripped his tack and hung it, then forked in some hay and ran a curry brush over the animal's back for several minutes. From there he went back to the restaurant, found himself a table off in a corner where he could be alone but still watch the door, and ordered his evening meal from the portly woman with a stained apron who finally appeared from the kitchen.

He had no trouble finding things to think about while he chewed his steak and washed it down with coffee. And his meal took nearly two hours as he mentally evaluated the events of the day. He was certain he had found his man, but he was at a loss to do anything, just in case there was another individual involved. Besides, the only evidence he had was the money taken from the paywagon, and even though he was sure it had been deposited in Bruner's bank, there was no way he could verify that it was the stolen army payroll. What had happened in the livery stable had fairly well convinced him that the horse he had looked at belonged to Jarvis, and he was certain the outlaw hadn't unsaddled the horse himself, judging by the way the tack was strewn around. In addition to that, if Jarvis was trying to pass himself off as a rich young man from Texas, he certainly wouldn't unsaddle his own mount. But there was one thing more than anything else that convinced him he had found the man he was looking for, and that was the stunned look in the clerk's eyes when he had mentioned Jarvis's name. He had known at the time that he was taking the risk of revealing his presence to Jarvis by mentioning his name to the clerk, but he also felt that it was a chance worth taking in light of the fact that time was working against him. If he had not actually found Jarvis, then the longer he waited in Douglas for a man who was no longer there, the less chance he had of catching him where ever he had gone.

Windy's mind went to the hotel clerk again. Since Jarvis, if that was actually him, had registered under the name of Phil Bradley, how could the clerk possibly have known his real identity? Windy decided to keep an eye on the clerk at all times when things started to break. He seemed like a small man in a fairly high place, and Mandalian knew well that those type of people were easily bought, and not usually for an extremely high price. Maybe he was the man who had unsaddled Jarvis's horse the night before. Possibly he had come up with some information that Windy had missed, or had had the chance to overhear something that had transpired before Mandalian arrived.

Windy couldn't be certain, and while he wiped up the last drops of beef drippings with a chunk of bread, he decided that with the hostler on his side, at least Jarvis's escape without notice was sealed off and that his next clues, if any, would probably be obtained at the poker game that night. With that

146

thought in mind, he checked the clock, which said eight-thirty, paid his bill, and wandered again toward Radly's saloon.

Windy had noticed the town gradually filling up throughout the course of his meal, and now there were numerous horses tied at the hitch rails along the street. The sounds of men drinking and laughing spilled from the doorways of the saloons. Radly's was nearly full when he pushed his way through the batwing doors. The bar was lined with an assortment of men— range hands, tradesmen, businessmen, and drifters lined up shoulder-to-shoulder—while the groups at the tables were more segregated according to social standing.

As he worked his way through the milling crowd, Mandalian glanced toward the poker table and saw a game in progress with five players, none of whom he recognized. Two drinkers stepped away from the bar midway down as Windy approached, and he stepped into their slot and raised a signal to the bartender. There were two men working the evening shift, and the barkeep Windy had talked with earlier in the day approached while hurriedly wiping up spilled beer.

"Evenin'," the bartender said cordially. "Same thing?"

"Howdy. No, I'd like a whiskey this time. I think I'm gonna have to burn that steak I just had out of my stomach."

"Sure thing." The bartender snatched a glass from the back-bar, picked up a nearby bottle, and poured expertly while looking up at Mandalian. "Know that young feller you were askin' about this afternoon? The one from down Texas way?"

Windy nodded. "Yeah, I remember. What about him?"

"His name is Phil Bradley. He's gonna be in here about nine o'clock to play a little poker with Otto, the senator, John, and a few of the other boys. Thought you might like to know that and maybe lighten up that young feller's pockets a little bit." The bartender winked as he collected money for the drink and moved toward another customer. "Told ya word gets around fast in Douglas."

"Seems like it does," Mandalian allowed. "Thanks. I might just do that little trick."

It was roughly nine-fifteen and Mandalian was on his second whiskey when the doors swung open again and the three men the bartender had mentioned stepped inside. The two older men

147

were obviously quite intoxicated, judging from the senator's flushed face and the banker's hearty attitude. But it was the younger man that attracted the scout's attention, and he noticed an air of self-composure about him, even though he too must have overindulged in the course of their celebration. Windy was well aware that nothing infuriates a drinking man more than to be in the company of a conservative tippler when he feels like tying a good one on, and he assumed that the man called Bradley must know that as well. That premise led Windy to the logical conclusion that the man either could hold his liquor well or knew how to drink at his own pace without drawing attention to his limited consumption. *Which of them is the lamb, and which is the wolf?* Mandalian asked himself as the man who he was certain had to be Jarvis steered his drunken companions toward the poker table.

Three of the lesser players gave way to the big money, and when the trio were seated and had chips arranged in front of them, the cards were passed to Jarvis. With the first shuffle it was obvious that he was no stranger to a poker table. While not ostentatious in his dealing and handling of cards, there was an artfulness about his manner that bespoke a skill not often seen in small towns like Douglas.

Windy was watching, waiting for a pattern to develop that he knew wouldn't be long in coming, before entering the game himself. If Jarvis played as Windy thought he would, he would win the first few hands merely to gain the attention of the other players and show them he was at least a mediocre player while not showing them any of his greater skills. If he lost several of the first hands, they would immediately assume he was baiting them and keep their wagers small. It was a case of doing exactly the opposite of what was expected of him. Then he would begin to lose steadily, winning only occasionally, and the hounds would go for the scent and chase the fox to ground.

After Jarvis had won the first four hands, lost the next, and then won the following three, Windy knew the time to get in the game had arrived. With his limited funds, he would have to win his playing money while Jarvis was on his planned losing streak. Windy was certain that would begin the next time the deal came Jarvis's way, which would be on the up-coming hand.

He signaled for a refill and watched as one disgruntled player began to scoop up what few chips he had remaining, and then he crossed to the table and stood behind the man's chair as he rose and left.

"Mind if I try my luck at a hand or two, gents?" he said, glancing around the table and allowing his eyes to glide past Jarvis without special notice.

There was a silent evaluation of the tall man in weathered buckskins, and finally the senator nodded. "It's an open game. Twenty dollars buys in."

"Sounds right to me," Windy replied, easing his long frame into the chair directly across from Jarvis and shoving a double eagle to the center of the table. "Twenty dollars' worth."

Once the chips were stacked in front of him, Windy was pretty much forgotten as the cards went around, and while Jarvis steadily lost, the scout rapidly accumulated enough money to stay in the game, while making certain not to win every hand.

"Your luck's kind of gone to hell on you, hasn't it, Phil?" Canfield said, while scooping in the pot with one hand and signaling for another round of drinks with the other.

Jarvis smiled tightly, as if pained by his losses. "Yes, Senator, this just doesn't seem to be my night. Fortunately I'm a better businessman that a card player." His hard eyes went to the growing pile in front of Windy Mandalian. "The mountain man there seems to have stolen my luck."

Windy tilted his glass and watched Jarvis over the rim. "Can't steal luck, son. Either you're born with it or you ain't."

A low round of chuckles circled the table while the cards were dealt again by the man next to Jarvis. Windy knew the trap had been baited; the ante would now be raised and the fox would be chasing the hounds.

Just as he had predicted, when the cards were passed to Jarvis for the shuffle, he glanced at each of the other players while his fingers fanned the deck.

"What do you say, gentlemen? Shall we make this a little more interesting? I've lost a lot of money here tonight, and I'd like a chance to win some of it back. Shall we double the ante and make it an unlimited raise?"

Bruner swallowed the last of his whiskey, signaled for another round, and wiped his fleshy lips with the back of his hand. "Sure you can afford that, son?" he asked in jest. "You aren't doing so damned good the way things are now, to my way of thinking."

Mandalian noticed a hard glint in Jarvis's eyes, which went unnoticed by the others.

"If things get real bad, sir, I'll just wire down to Texas and have Daddy send up more money," Jarvis said dryly.

"Don't think you need to worry about that, Phil," the banker rejoined. "With the money you've got in my bank, your credit's good in our game anytime."

The other players laughed, and all agreed to the suggested change except Windy, who made no indication either way. Jarvis's eyes held on Mandalian's face, and there was a tightness to his lips.

"How about you, mountain man? Most of that money sitting in front of you is mine. You gonna stay in and give me a chance to get it back, or are you gonna fold and run?"

"Money has a way of changin' hands mighty quick, young fella," Windy replied laconically. "One day it's yours and the next day it's somebody else's. But when it's in front of me, it's mine. Deal the cards."

Jarvis's luck changed immediately with the raise in ante, and he began to win steadily. The conversation loosened up, and what Windy had entered the game for in the first place finally happened. Both Canfield and Bruner were thoroughly drunk by now, and talking about subjects that would normally have been reserved for the seclusion of a private office. With the raise in stakes, Mandalian was the unknown player left in the game and it was obvious the three business associates had accepted him as nothing other than a grizzled mountain man.

"Well, fellas," Canfield said, studying his cards with one narrowed eye, "I said it before, but I'll say it again. The deal we made today could be the biggest one we'll ever make in a lifetime."

"My daddy's gonna be right proud of me," Jarvis said in agreement.

"The success of your mutual venture could mean a lot to my bank," Bruner added. "I'm behind you boys one hundred percent, and don't you ever forget it."

"We won't, Otto, you can bet your boots on that. Open for thirty," Canfield said, pawing the required number of chips from the scattered pile in front of him.

"Call."

"I fold," Bruner grunted, slapping his cards down and reaching for his drink.

"I'm in," Mandalian said softly while matching the bet.

As cards were being discarded and replacements dealt, Canfield spoke again. "With Phil over there comin' in as a forty-percent cash partner, and my owning the four sections we're building on, along with a sixty-percent investment, we should be in pretty damned good shape financially at the start. We'll probably need that help you mentioned, Otto, when it comes time to expand."

"When do you figure you'll be open for business, Senator?" Bruner asked. "That's the only thing that's a little vague about the whole proposition."

"Construction should be completed within a week, and then the army pulls out. The captain said he'd be here early tomorrow morning, and we'll know the exact date then. After that, all we need is equipment, stock, and some paying freight, and we're set to go."

Jarvis looked up sharply. "Did you say the captain wouldn't be here until tomorrow morning?"

"Yup, that's what I said. He's a pretty busy man out there, and as we all know, any job takes more work to finish than it does to start. I think he's going to take me out to see my property pretty soon. Could be tomorrow, or maybe the next day." Canfield squinted over his cards. "Would you like to go along, Phil? We're partners now and you've got damned near as much in this as I have. We're going to have all of Wyoming Territory in our pocket once we get going."

A startled look crossed Jarvis's face, which only Mandalian caught because the senator was studying his cards and Bruner had turned to signal for more drinks.

"No, I don't think I can make it, Senator. Not just now. I've got a lot of business to take care of in the next few days.

Things my daddy asked me to do, you understand." Jarvis offered one of his boyish grins. "Gotta keep him happy at all costs."

"You bet. Always take care of the man with the biggest donation, son. Just a little political advice from an old politician to a young one. Now are we going to finish this hand or not?"

"I kinda had that same question in mind, Senator," Mandalian said quietly. "You boys are dealin' more business than cards. I ain't here to talk bank talk, I'm here to win enough for a grubstake and outfit my trapline up in Canada again next spring."

"Sorry, stranger," the senator replied, almost as if he meant it. "I guess we got a little carried away."

"No problem. You opened, you raise, Senator."

"Thirty again."

"I'll see your thirty and go you thirty more," Jarvis said.

"And I'll double that," Mandalian replied, shoving his chips toward the center and glancing across at Canfield. "Cost you a hundred and twenty to play, Senator."

Canfield studied his cards with a pained expression before folding and tossing them on top of the banker's. "Too rich for my blood with that hand."

Jarvis studied Mandalian closely, calculating the number of cards he had drawn and remembering it had only been one. He had drawn one himself and filled a queen-high straight. Finally he nodded and reached for his chips. "Call, and raise fifty."

"I'll see that," Windy said without consulting his hand again while matching the bet. He smiled at the man across from him. "I call, you show."

Jarvis hesitated, then fanned his cards out. "Straight. Queen through ten."

"That's pretty damned good," Windy allowed. "But not quite good enough. Full house, kings over tens."

"You're pretty damned lucky for a mountain man," Jarvis said heatedly as he watched Mandalian scoop in the chips.

"Whatcha think us mountain men do all winter, son? Sit around and scratch our asses?"

Jarvis kicked his chair back and stood. "I don't know, and couldn't give a goddamn. I think I've had enough for the evening, gentlemen. Time to turn in."

Windy pretended to stifle a yawn and nodded his agreement. "Think I'll crawl under the old bearskin myself. Thank ya all for the help in gettin' back in business again." Then he grinned and looked at the other three men. "Looks like we're *all* goin' into business now, don't it?"

eleven ━━━━━━━━━━━━━

Even though they certainly didn't need one, Canfield
and Bruner said they were going to the bar for a nightcap, so
Jarvis bade them good evening and left the saloon without
saying a word to Mandalian. Windy waited a moment before
leaving the saloon himself, and as he stepped into the night he
glanced down the boardwalk in the direction of the hotel.
Jarvis's sharp reaction to the senator's remark about the captain's arrival early tomorrow morning had aroused his curiosity,
and he went across the street and looked up at the hotel win-
dows. Shortly, a lamp lit the panes of a window on the second
floor with a yellow glow, and he could see the shadow of a
man moving around inside.

Mandalian had almost dismissed his hunch as being overly
suspicious, and he'd started to turn away toward the boardinghouse, when a second shadow appeared and merged with the
first. He had no doubt that the couple up above were sharing

a long embrace. The remark the bartender had made about the senator's daughter came to mind, and he combined that with Jarvis's sudden departure. His conclusions made no sense to the overall picture, but he was certain they represented pieces of the puzzle, and when the lamp went out he entered the boardinghouse and slipped into his cot. Long into the night he lay there thinking, calculating, and attempting to come up with some positive conclusions before finally giving up and rolling over on his side and allowing himself to slip into a light sleep.

Up in room thirteen, Marla lay in her lover's bed with her arms wrapped tightly about him and her head resting on his shoulder.

"I haven't seen you all day, Jay. I get so lonely up here all by myself."

"I'm sorry, honey. I was with your father and Bruner all day, and everything is set. I'm an investor with your father, and they accept me for what they think I am."

"Investor in what, Jay? Can you tell me now?" Marla asked, twisting her head to look up at his face in the darkness.

"Yes, I guess I can," Jarvis replied, hugging her tightly. "Remember when I first met you, when I was on temporary assignment in Washington with Ray?"

"How could I forget, silly? That's when I fell in love with you."

"And me with you. Anyway, Ray had known your father for quite a while—and you as well, unfortunately. They struck up a friendship and Ray could see that your father was his only way out of the army life and into the big money where he thinks he belongs. Later, after I resigned my commission, Ray learned that a stage station was going to be built on the Nebraska border just east of the Nebraska-Wyoming line. He contacted your father and had him buy four sections of land on the Wyoming side, knowing that whoever controlled the first station in the territory would control the entire territory. Your father bought the land and Ray built the station, and he's finishing it right now, on your father's land instead of on the Nebraska side where it was supposed to be.

"Ray contacted me because he knew I'd won a lot of money in several big poker games, twenty-four thousand dollars to be exact, and offered to take me in on the deal as an equal partner with him. Together we would buy in with your father, which I've just done. When the station is complete, the army will turn it over to the civilian who's on the contract, namely your father, and Ray resigns his commission in the army and comes into the business."

Now Marla sat bolt upright. "But what happens to us? I mean, if Ray is a partner with my father and you're a partner with my father, how could we possibly ever get married? You know how mean and insanely jealous Ray is."

"I know, honey, I know. The only way we can get rid of Ray is for me to kill him." Jarvis felt Marla's body tense, and he patted her thigh gently. "Don't worry about it, he'd do the same to me. It's us that count, not Ray, your father, or anyone else. What has to be done, has to be done."

"This is all so terrible, Jay. What if you get hurt or . . . or killed?"

"I won't. I've got it all planned and I just have to wait for the right time, and that won't be until the station is officially and legally turned over to the senator."

Marla slowly sank back down to rest her head against his shoulder again. "I'm scared, Jay. Really scared. What happens to my father?"

Jarvis hesitated, knowing the truth but looking for the perfect answer. He had nearly stolen the entire plan from Gann now, and he wanted to be sure he said the right thing to the person who would share the senator's fortunes with him.

"He'll be just fine, honey. He likes me, he really does. Once Ray is out of the way, we can have an open and proper courtship. I'll be his partner, and I'm sure he would be delighted to have me for a son-in-law as well."

"I want that. I want it so badly, Jay. To be treated like a lady, to be seen in public on a gentleman's arm and to have people know that I'm in love and that I am loved. Daddy has been so bad about trying to pick my husband for me, and every one of his prospects has been a pinch-faced congressman in Washington. That's how I got involved with Ray; he was wild, exciting, and unpredictable."

Jarvis kissed her lightly on the lips and his hand moved up to her breast. "And me?" he whispered as his mouth moved to her ear.

Marla shivered at the feeling of his warm, searching kiss, and she squirmed more tightly against his body. "You're gentle and kind and good and honest. I can't imagine you ever being mean and cruel to anything or anyone."

Jarvis groaned and rolled on top of her as her thighs opened willingly to him.

Captain Raymond J. Gann had been pushing his horse hard in the pale moonlight, but he had made the trip to Douglas so many times before that he knew the trail well and had no fear of riding into unseen obstacles. Even though he had had a full two days to cool off, he was still seething inside about the visit from that mounted infantry detachment. Not from a professional point of view, but because he couldn't figure out exactly why they had been there and what they had learned during their patrol. Nearly six months had gone into setting up the arrangements that were now only three days from fruition, and the last thing he needed was to have the actual location of the station brought to the attention of his superior officers. Surely the station would remain where it had been built, but he would be transferred or cashiered, the blind faith the senator had placed in him would be gone, and Marla, the key to wealth and power, would be lost to him forever.

Further, he had learned in a dispatch from Fort Laramie that the army payroll destined for Fort McKinney had been lost and all escort personnel killed from ambush. That would mean that Jarvis was safely in Douglas, but if the error regarding the location of Hat Creek station was discovered too quickly and the senator pulled out of their arrangement for fear of political embarrassment, then the money would be lost as well, because it had been deposited by Jarvis under an assumed name.

Gann pushed his horse mercilessly while his mind continued to mull over the next steps of the plan. Jarvis would have no reason to suspect him of any treachery because he knew that Gann intended to marry Marla, and once the senator was out of the way, there would be plenty of room for two men in the stage business. With the late senator's wealth and holdings behind them, it would be too big a plum for a nobody like Jarvis to turn down.

Gann smiled to himself as he slowed the horse at the entrance to town. *Old Jay,* he thought, *won't know what his ultimate role in the plan is until he feels that slug go deep into his chest. Then, no one can implicate Captain Gann in anything, except having built a stage station in the wrong place.*

It was nearly midnight when the captain walked his horse into the livery, led it to a stall, pulled off the McClellan saddle, and left the stable to head toward the hotel. A substitute night clerk was dozing in the chair behind the desk, and Gann slammed his hand down on the counter.

"Wake up, you lazy son of a bitch! I want the key to my room!"

The clerk spluttered to wakefulness and scrambled to his feet. "Yes, sir. What room is it, sir?"

"Number twelve. And I want to have a look at the register."

The clerk, a frail, elderly man, was not inclined to argue. "Yes, sir. Here's your key," he said, reaching below the counter, "and here's the register."

Gann flipped the pages open to the ribbon marker, noted the name *Mr. Phillip Bradley,* and the room number, then slammed the book closed again. He glanced at the key and noticed that the keys to room thirteen, fourteen, and sixteen were also missing, and turned toward the stairway without another word.

He mounted the stairs cautiously, taking care to make no undue noise lest the senator not be asleep yet. Memories of Marla's body swam through is mind. Just as he raised his knuckles to rap on the door of room fourteen, he heard what he thought was a moan coming from Jarvis's room, and he stepped across the hall and lowered his ear to the keyhole. Words, faint but discernible, came from within, and the voice was unmistakably Marla's, in the throes of passion.

Gann straightened and turned as rigid as stone. He stood there motionless for nearly a minute as the hands hanging by his sides slowly turned into white-knuckled fists and trembled with nearly uncontrollable rage. Finally he turned and tiptoed down the hallway while watching the slight crack in the broom closet door at the end of the hall. Gann unlocked his door, stepped inside, and pulled his boots off in two swift motions. Then he was through the door again like a cat and down the hall on noiseless feet to swing the broom closet door open.

The clerk's eyes were wide in terror as he sat there, hunched in a corner, with his notepad on one knee. He stared at the enraged Gann and his lips moved in a futile search for words, but the captain's hand closed about his throat before he could say anything. Gann slowly raised the clerk to a standing position and stared at him with cold detachment.

"You've been here every night, haven't you, you slimy bastard?" Gann growled through gritted teeth.

Nearly in shock, the clerk attempted to nod.

"And you've written everything down on that little pad of yours, haven't you?"

Again the clerk attempted to nod.

"Who's in there with her now?" Gann asked, loosening his grip just enough to allow croaked words to escape the clerk's mouth.

"Mr. Bradley...sir."

Gann stared at the clerk a moment longer, then his hand began to close. He increased the pressure slowly, feeling the clerk's throat constrict within his grasp and watching the pleading eyes bulge behind thick glasses. Ignoring the frantic wrestling at his wrist, he tightened his grip even more, feeling the rage pour through his extended arm and into the other man's throat, and he saw the eyes finally roll upward in the clerk's head. Gann held him there for nearly another minute, then shook him like a cat might shake a mouse, and finally lowered him soundlessly to the floor.

Gann stopped, picked up the notepad and pencil, backed out of the closet, and softly closed the door before turning and going back to his room. He lit a lamp, stripped, washed his upper body while admiring his torso, then turned to look around the room. The brandy bottle was where it was supposed to be, and Gann poured a glassful before slipping into bed and adjusting the lamp so he could read the clerk's hurried scrawls on the notepad. When he had finished going over each page twice, he stood, held the pad to the chimney of the lamp, and waited until it burst into flame before stepping over to the washbasin. Just before the flame touched his fingertips, he dropped the pad into the porcelain bowl and watched it burn until there was nothing left but ashes. He poured a liberal amount of water on the smoldering remains, then blew out the lamp and climbed into bed. Gann laughed softly to himself in the darkness, and within minutes he had fallen into a deep, dreamless sleep.

Windy Mandalian was up well before dawn, and by the time the first rays of sunlight crept down Main Street, he was seated on a wooden bench in front of the boardinghouse and absently whittling on a stick of wood while watching for the man who was due to arrive early that morning. An hour passed, then an hour and a half, and the town slowly came to life with shop doors opening, mop water being thrown out in the street, and early risers beginning their day.

Mandalian heard the clomping of clumsy footsteps on the boardwalk off to his left, and his head jerked in that direction to see the old hostler making his way as fast as he could toward him. When he stopped and sucked in a deep breath of air, Windy lowered both stick and knife and turned toward the hostler.

"Helluva way to treat a hangover, Oly," Mandalian observed. "Bet you haven't run that fast since you got caught in your pa's smokin' tobbacco."

The hostler held his words until his panting had finally subsided. "I ain't here fer a social call, mister. I made a deal with you, and ol' Oly always sticks by his word."

"I'm proud of ya, Oly. What's on your mind?"

"Remember I said I'd tell ya if anything went on down at the livery with that sorrel?"

Mandalian's face sobered. "Yes, I remember. Is it gone?"

"Nope. But another horse come in last night whilst I was sleepin'. It was a cavalry horse, judgin' from the saddle pad. Had to come in after nine o'clock 'cause that's when I always get up to take a piss."

"I remember your nine o'clock piss, Oly," Mandalian said with a smile.

"And it had to be afore midnight, 'cause I woke up and finished my bottle then, and the damned thing was there when I did."

"Why do you think I'd be interested in a cavalry mount?"

"'Cause you was so danged interested in that Spencer rifle. Said somethin' 'bout it's bein' military issue. Cavalry's military issue too, ain't it?"

Mandalian rose and took another dollar out of his pocket. "Sure is, old-timer. And that horse is of interest to me, and it's the reason why I'm sittin' out here like a damned fool whittlin' on a stick. Thanks, and you deserve this," Windy said, handing the money across. "Keep an eye on things down there for me, will you? I want to know every horse and every damned rider who uses that stable for any purpose."

The hostler squinted through perennially watery eyes. "Dollar fer ever' time I tell ya somethin'?"

"That depends on how bad I want to hear what you've got to say. Get on back to the stable now, and when you buy your jug tonight, don't tell anybody where you got the money. Keep an eye on things and let me know what's goin' on."

After a leisurely breakfast, Mandalian went down to the stable, checked on the horse that Oly had mentioned, curried his own animal and checked its shoes, then slowly meandered toward Radly's saloon. He noticed a crowd of people milling around in front of the Grayson Hotel, and there seemed to be an unusual buzz of excitement up and down the street. There was a different man behind the bar at Radly's, and when he approached, Mandalian ordered a beer while turning to look at the tables behind him. The senator and Jarvis were seated in one corner of the saloon, their heads bowed close together in deep conversation. Windy turned back to the bar and paid for his drink, and since the bartender wasn't busy at that time of day, he struck up a conversation.

"What's all the excitement about, pardner? The way people are carryin' on down at the Grayson, a man'd think somebody got killed or something."

"Somebody did," the bartender replied flatly.

Mandalian blinked in surprise. "They did? Who?"

"The hotel clerk. Fella by the name of Everett. Nosy bastard, and I'm surprised it didn't happen before."

"How'd he die?"

"Strangled. Some army captain checked in early this morning and found him dead in the broom closet at the end of the hall."

162

"I'll be damned," Windy said casually, turning his beer mug in thought. "The army captain found him this morning, you say?"

"Yeah. 'Bout six o'clock this morning, I guess. The sheriff won't be back for a couple of days yet, so I guess whoever did it got away clean as a whistle. The only bad thing about it, to my way of thinkin', is that he had a whole passel of kids, and however bad he was, Everett was a better daddy than none at all."

"Damned shame. I suppose they robbed the place, huh?"

"Nope. That's the funny part. Mr. Grayson, the owner, said nothing was missing. Good thing too, 'cause as I understand it, the senator over there and his daughter have quite a bit of money and jewelry in the safe. Wouldn't make the town look too good if a senator got robbed while he was here."

"No it wouldn't," Windy agreed as the bartender moved away to serve a new customer. His mind went back to his conversation with the hostler, and he was sure that Oly had said the army horse came in after nine but before midnight. If the soldier found the body at six o'clock this morning, why didn't he find it at midnight?

"Say, bartender?"

"Be right with ya," the bartender replied, making change for the other customer and moving Windy's way. "Another?"

Still deep in thought, Windy nodded, and when the beer was served he looked up at the bartender. "How did that soldier happen to find the clerk? What I mean is, why would he be looking in the broom closet in the first place?"

The bartender shrugged. "The way I hear it, the door was wide open and Everett was lying half in and half out of the closet. Don't see how he could've missed him."

"I understand," Windy replied. "Sure, there's no way you could miss a dead man lying in the hall."

The bartender moved away again and Windy rested one elbow on the bar while turning toward the doorway to think about what he'd said.

"I'd like a beer, please, bartender."

Mandalian heard the familiar voice from probably ten feet off to his right. As surprised as he was, he kept himself from reacting immediately, concentrating instead on the mug in his

163

hand. After the beer had been served and paid for, there was a long pause and then he heard the same voice again.

"Pardon me, mister."

Mandalian glanced toward the speaker. "You talkin' to me?"

"Yes I am," Matt Kincaid replied. "I just got into town and I'm wondering what's the best hotel. Could you help me out?"

Mandalian shrugged as he looked at what appeared to be a well-dressed rancher. "I'm stayin' at the boardinghouse, but you look like you could do a little bit better'n that. Try the Grayson, just down the street."

"Sounds good. Buy you a beer?"

"Sure, why not?"

They made small talk until the bartender had set up another round and moved to the other end of the bar to talk to a regular customer, and when they were certain that no one was within earshot, the scout tapped Kincaid's elbow with his own.

"Good to see you, Matt. Don't look now, but when the time's right, have a glance at the two men talking at that table in the corner."

After a prudent lapse of time, Kincaid casually looked toward the table then turned back to the bar again.

"What about them?"

"The young one's our man. He's passing himself off as Phil Bradley, son of a rich cattleman in Texas. The other one is Senator Canfield, and they're both staying at the Grayson, along with some army captain that might be of interest to us."

"What's the senator got to do with this?"

"I don't know yet. When you finish that beer, go on down and register at the Grayson. We'll talk in your room. I'll be along in about five minutes."

"All right. I saw the hotel when I dropped my horse off at the livery. What the hell are all those people doing standing around out front?"

"Same damned thing everybody does when a man gets killed."

"Killed?" Kincaid asked in surprise.

"Yup. The clerk at the Grayson got killed last night. Strangled, and I think our army captain had a lot to do with it. I'll explain when we get to your room. There should be a lot of confusion in the lobby right now, so when you register, take

164

a look at the names on the previous page if you can."

"I will, but first I want to check the telegraph office and see if there's a message from Captain Conway. He said he'd wire me here when he got the information I asked for."

"I'll give you ten minutes. There's an old hostler that should be lookin' for me about now," Mandalian said with a wink, "and I'd hate to have him rupture a gut over a lousy damned dollar."

"What the hell are you talking about, Windy?"

Mandalian grinned. "That's another thing I'll tell ya when we get to your room. The army owes me three dollars now, and damned soon it's gonna owe me four. I'll bring along a jug since you've had a long ride. Ten minutes."

Kincaid finished his drink, shook Mandalian's hand, and left. Five minutes later, Windy walked toward the door with a final glance toward the table. Both the Senator and Jarvis were watching him, and Mandalian smiled easily while touching the brim of his hat with the tip of a finger. Oly slammed into him just as he stepped onto the boardwalk.

"There ya are, by damn," the hostler wheezed as he sagged against the hitch rail. "Drinkin' yerself to death while I'm doin' all yer damned work for ya."

Windy took the hostler by the elbow and guided him onto the street while pressing a dollar into his palm. "This one's on me, Oly. The horse is a buckskin, its owner is a rancher, and he's probably staying at the Grayson Hotel."

The hostler squinted up at the tall scout. "Now how in hell did you know all that?"

"Just a lucky guess, Oly," Mandalian replied, slapping the hostler lightly on the back. "Keep all this under your hat."

Oly watched Windy curiously as he walked away, and hollered after him, "Keep *what* under my hat?"

"Everything you know," the scout replied over his shoulder.

"Now that'd take a damned small hat," the hostler growled as he shuffled toward the livery once again.

Fifteen minutes later, Windy Mandalian walked up the steps of the Grayson Hotel and turned down the hallway toward room number ten. At the same time, Captain Gann and Marla Canfield stepped out of number fourteen and Mandalian stepped to one side to allow them passage. Windy tipped his hat but received no response from the grim-faced captain, and he noticed a look of fear, almost pleading, in the woman's eyes. From the descriptions he had heard, he knew he was looking at Senator Canfield's daughter and he wondered if the army captain was the man who owned the horse boarded in the stable across the way. Once they had passed, Windy tapped lightly on Kincaid's door and stepped inside.

The lieutenant was holding a telegram in his hands and staring blankly at the wall, deep in thought. His head jerked toward Mandalian as he stepped inside and closed the door.

"I see the cap'n had somethin' for us, huh, Matt?" Windy observed as he pulled the cork from the bottle, splashed whiskey into two glasses, and handed one to Kincaid.

"Yes he did. Thanks, Windy," Kincaid said, taking a drink. "Good to see you, you old bastard."

Windy appraised his old friend for several minutes. "You might've made a mighty handsome civilian, Matt, but you look damned funny to me."

"I feel a little strange myself."

"Then you'll fit into the situation around here just fine," Windy said flatly as he sank into one of the two chairs. "Have a sit-down, Matt, and let's get to it. What'd the cap'n have to say?"

Kincaid took a seat and crossed his legs while glancing at the telegram a second time. "What did you say that senator's name was? The one back in the saloon?"

"Canfield. Rankin Canfield. Why?"

Kincaid shook his head in puzzlement. "This is really strange, but we'll get to the telegram later. You said the other man was Jarvis. Fill me in on whatever I should know."

Mandalian detailed everything that had happened since he arrived in Douglas, including his suspicions that the captain registered at the hotel was very likely responsible for the clerk's death. He told how and why he believed that the senator and Jarvis were somehow involved, and that he was certain Jarvis's investment money was the same as that stolen from the pay-wagon. When he had finished, he sipped his drink and looked across at Kincaid.

"But what I can't figure out, Matt, is what the hell they're up to. That night at the poker game, when Bruner asked when

166

they'd be open for business, Canfield said, 'After that, all we need is equipment, stock, and some paying freight, and we're set to go.' Those were his exact words, but I'm damned if I can come up with what they're plannin' to haul. At first I thought of the stage station, but that's over in Nebraska, and Canfield said Wyoming Territory plain as day."

Kincaid smiled tightly. "Well, friend, you can quit wondering. That station isn't being built in Nebraska, it's being built here in Wyoming Territory."

"What?" Mandalian asked, stopping his glass halfway to his mouth. "It was supposed to be built on Hat Creek, and Hat Creek is in Nebraska."

"Where it was *supposed* to be built and where it's *being* built are two different kettles of fish, Windy. It's being built on Sage Creek in Wyoming, not Hat Creek in Nebraska. Now this is starting to make some sense," Kincaid concluded, tapping the telegram with his thumb.

"Might be to you, old son, but it ain't to me. I've been doin' more figurin' and thinkin' in the last coupla days than in all the rest of my damned life put together, and I still come up with empty pockets."

"Would you care to know who owns the ground the station is being built on?"

"I ain't here to pick ducks, Matthew," Windy said in his most ironic tone.

"Senator Canfield. He bought four sections along Sage Creek six months ago."

Mandalian's eyebrows arched in surprise. "You mean it's bein' built in the wrong damned place on purpose?"

"It has to be. It didn't make any sense to me, either, until I talked to you and put what you had to say together with the captain's telegram. The man who hand-picked that site at Sage Creek was Captain Gann. There is no way he could have made a mistake. He even had false maps drawn up, supposedly to convince the senator and his engineer, one Lieutenant Ecklehart, that everything was legitimate. Now if you're sure the man you pointed out to me is Jarvis, and he's talking to the senator and has invested money in the stage station—and eventually a stage line, I would presume—then we have a situation that's pretty much open-and-shut. You mentioned an army officer who you thought had killed the hotel clerk? Guess what the name is of the only army officer registered in this hotel?"

"Matt, dammit! I ain't long on guessin' in the first place, and my old head's plumb wore out with all the thinkin' I've been doing. If you've got something to say, just say whatever in hell it is."

"Sorry, old friend. Captain Raymond J. Gann is registered in this hotel, room number twelve."

"Then that—that was him I just met in the hall?" Windy exclaimed, waving his glass toward the door. "But he was coming out of room fourteen."

"That room is occupied by Miss Marla Canfield, the senator's daughter. A Mr. Phillip Bradley is in room number thirteen."

Mandalian held his hand up. "Just a minute, Matt. Just a minute here now. Last night I followed Jarvis out of the saloon after the poker game. From out on the street I watched him light his lamp inside his room, and some woman came into the room and they were huggin' and kissin' like two youngsters out behind the barn. Now if this is ten, then that would be eleven across the hall, and thirteen would be next to it." Windy slapped his hand against his thigh and grinned in triumph. "Damned if I wasn't right, Matt. That had to be Canfield's daughter in there with him."

"I have no idea."

"It was, I'm sure of that now. But the lady in question just walked down the hall arm-in-arm with Gann. She didn't look like she was likin' it a whole lot, but they were as close together as a saddle and a horse's back."

Now it was Kincaid's turn to think. Suddenly he looked up sharply at Windy. "Gann is the one who set up that ambush," he said grimly.

"Now how in hell do you know that?"

"Because of this," Kincaid replied, raising the telegram. "The last thing Gann did at Fort Laramie before coming up here was to draw up the duty roster for the paywagon. I asked Captain Conway to find that out for me. He's the one who assigned Ed as escort officer, a man who had never been through that area before. He has to be the one who made sure

168

Sergeant Harrison wasn't the teamster, and he's the one who made damned sure Corporal French had the detachment cross the Powder at Farley's Crossing instead of Baker Flats. He is the one responsible for all of this," Kincaid said in a hard, deadly tone. "He is the man we're after."

"Then we'll get him, Matt," Mandalian replied firmly. "But we still ain't got all the buff skinned here yet, to my way of thinkin'. Let's say Gann and Jarvis are in on this thing together. Where does the senator fit in? And his daughter? She just walked down the hall with a coldblooded killer, if we've got this thing put together right. Is she in on it too?"

Kincaid pursed his lips. "I can't answer that, Windy. As far as Canfield goes, I believe he's in this strictly for a profit. He's in it for what he stands to gain personally, and he probably doesn't know how deeply he's been drawn in. Now, like I said, that's only a guess, and we have to assume that the senator and his daughter are just as much a part of this as Gann and Jarvis. Time will prove them innocent or guilty."

Mandalian swirled the remaining whiskey in his glass before glancing across at Kincaid. "If they're innocent, time might just be the one thing they haven't got, Matt. We're dealing with men here who would kill a whole detachment of soldiers for a coupla sacks full of money. What would they do to a beautiful woman and a fat-assed senator for the same thing?"

169

twelve ────────────────

"Ray, you're hurting my arm," Marla complained without looking at Gann as they descended the stairs. "And you hurt me this morning when we made love, too. You were . . . brutal, in fact."

Gann continued to stare straight ahead with a tight smile on his lips. "You weren't quite as interested as I thought you would be, dear. Your sexual appetite seems to have lessened since I've been gone."

"I've . . . not been feeling well, Ray. I'm just tired, that's all, and that clerk's getting killed has me a little upset as well." Marla looked up at the tall officer and searched his stern face. "I don't want to do this, Ray. Not like this. Not this fast."

"Nonsense, love. The last time I was here, I told you we were going to get married in secret, and now is the time to do it. I already talked to the Reverend earlier this morning, and he's going to marry us at his house in a legal and proper manner. In ten minutes it'll be over, and you will be Mrs. Raymond J. Gann."

Marla started to say something, but fell silent in response to the increased pressure of Gann's fingers on her elbow as they passed through the lobby. Once outside, the captain quickly turned to the left, ducked into an alley, and walked toward a collection of houses arranged behind Main Street.

Marla looked up at him again. "I'm serious, Ray. Maybe this isn't the right thing. I'd like some more time to think about it before I make a final decision."

"I'm surprised at your attitude, darling. You were deeply in love with me a few days ago, and when I suggested a secret marriage, you didn't object at all. Now the arrangements are all made and we're going through with it." Gann smiled down at her with something less than warmth as they turned onto another street. "Do you remember a junior officer I had assisting me while I was in Washington, by the name of Jarvis? Jay Jarvis?"

Marla studied the rutted street and massaged her forehead as if deep in thought. "The name does sound familiar."

"I thought the two of you had met at one of those endless parties your father was always throwing. Anyway, after he left the army, he changed his name to Mr. Phillip Bradley. The funny thing is, there's a man by that same name registered at the hotel. Have you seen anything of him?"

"No . . . no I haven't," Marla stammered. "But then, I spend most of my time in my room."

Gann nodded. "I'll bet you do," he replied in a tone that left little doubt as to his meaning.

They were silent for the remainder of the walk, and a hundred yards farther on, Gann opened the gate in a white picket fence and ushered Marla down the walkway. After he knocked on the door, there was a momentary wait before a thickly built woman opened the door and beamed out at them.

"Ah, Captain Gann! My, but you are punctual. And is this the lucky bride? My, my, what a lovely couple you make," she gushed, clasping her hands before her and scrutinizing the bride and groom.

"Thank you, Mrs. Peterson," Gann replied, removing his hat and encircling Marla's waist with his other arm. "Miss

172

Marla Canfield, I'd like for you to meet Mrs. Peterson. She's the Reverend's wife, and has been kind enough to agree to witness the ceremony for us."

Marla smiled weakly, offered a half-curtsy, and said, "I'm pleased to meet you, Mrs. Peterson."

"The sight of young love is something I never tire of," Mrs. Peterson said with eyes aglow, while stepping aside for them to enter. "I was a bride once myself, Miss Canfield, so I can understand any nervousness you might feel. Just trust the Reverend, and you shall be delivered into marital bliss by the guiding hands of God's humble servant. Please come in now. The Reverend is waiting."

The ashen look on Marla's face didn't go unnoticed by Gann, and he took her elbow firmly once more as they entered the house. The tight, unrelenting fingers pressing into her arm told Marla that she had no choice but to comply with Gann's wishes, and she was suddenly terribly frightened of the man. Her body shook and her knees felt weak, but Gann supported her as they moved into the living room. Reverend Peterson, a short, thin man, looked up from his Bible with a funereal smile. After the necessary introductions were made, he explained to them their part in the ceremony and where to stand, then cleared his throat and began to recite the standard marriage ceremony. When he asked Marla if she took Gann for her lawfully wedded husband, she didn't reply and the Reverend had to ask a second time.

"Do you take Captain Raymond J. Gann to be your lawfully wedded husband?"

"I—I—do," Marla replied in a tortured whisper, without looking into the eyes of her husband-to-be.

Gann gave his vows with military crispness, and when the Reverend pronounced them man and wife, the captain leaned down, turned her face toward his, and kissed cold, unresponsive lips.

"Your five-dollar fee includes a marriage certificate, I presume, Reverend?" Gann asked as he looked at Peterson again.

"It certainly does, my son. I have it all filled out, with the exception of your bride's maiden name, of course. It won't take but a minute to complete."

"And that makes this thing completely legal?" Gann asked

173

with a hint of impatience. "No one can deny the fact that we are man and wife, with all legal privileges and obligations taken care of?"

Peterson looked at the big captain as though he had been struck a terrible blow. "This is a house of God, Captain Gann, or at least the house where a man dedicated to God's work happens to reside. Your marriage is as binding as any performed in the name of the Lord, our Heavenly Father, on any day in any year."

"That's what I wanted to hear. Just fill out that certificate and we'll be on our way. My wife hasn't been feeling too well, and I think it would be best if she got some much needed rest."

"I'll attend to that matter instantly," the Reverend said, laying his Bible aside and turning to his ledger. "If you would be so kind as to give your donation for my services to Mrs. Peterson, it will be greatly appreciated. She seems to feel that she has the Lord's confidence in financial matters more than I," he concluded in a tone that was nothing less than acrimonious.

"Thank you, Captain," Mrs. Peterson gushed as Gann handed the half eagle across. "I was hoping you and your lovely wife could stay for tea and cookies, but what with the poor dear's illness and all, I can understand."

"We both thank you, ma'am, don't we, honey?" Gann asked, leaning down toward Marla and hating her for having her eyes closed. The fingers tightened around the elbow again. "Don't we, honey?"

Marla's eyes fluttered open and her lashes were filmed with tears. "Yes, ma'am."

Minutes later, the gate had closed behind them and they were walking back toward town. Mrs. Peterson turned toward her husband, who had joined her in the doorway.

"Rather a strange couple, wouldn't you say, dear? I swear I've seen more joy in the eyes of the condemned that I saw in that girl's face."

"Marriage has a strange effect on some people, Irma," the Reverend replied as he turned away. "You should know that as well as anyone else."

Marla was crying freely when Gann opened the door to her room and shoved her inside, and she refused to even look at

174

him when he touched her shoulders to remove her shawl.

"I'm not sure if you're acting the way wives are supposed to act or not, Marla," Gann said coldly as he laid the shawl across the foot of the bed, "but we'll find that out soon enough. Take your clothes off."

Marla looked at him and nibbled her trembling lower lip. "Please, Ray. Not now. Please?"

Gann had already removed his boots and was unfastening his belt buckle to lower his pants. "Now! Take them off. I'm going to make love to you now, as my wife, and maybe even get started on a son in the process."

"Oh, God!" Marla cried. "Oh, God, no!"

Gann stared at her evenly. "Either you take them off or I tear them off. It's your choice, as simple as that. We are going to consummate our marriage and I'm going to show you once and for all what kind of man your husband is in bed. That way you won't have any thoughts about other men who might be interested in you."

He stood there before her, completely naked, and she glanced once at his rising erection, shuddered violently, then began to slowly unbutton the bodice of her blouse.

It was roughly half past one when Captain Gann stepped into Radly's saloon and went immediately toward the table where Senator Canfield, Otto Bruner, and Jay Jarvis sat. At another table on the opposite side of the room, Windy Mandalian and Matt Kincaid were sipping beer and playing a game of gin rummy, apparently oblivious to the events at the senator's table.

"Ah, Captain Gann!" Canfield said, standing and offering his hand in greeting. "First let me say how distressed I am about the unfortunate circumstance that greeted you this morning. I assumed that you would have some legal matters to clear up in that regard, and might want to catch up on a little sleep as well, so I didn't come around to call."

"That's perfectly all right, Senator, and correct as well. I didn't get out of bed until half an hour ago."

"Good. Then you're refreshed and ready to discuss business. But first, the introductions. Gentlemen, I would like for you to meet Captain Raymond J. Gann, United States Cavalry. Captain, please meet Otto Bruner, a local banker, and Phillip

Bradley, my new business associate."

"It's my pleasure, gentlemen," Gann said, returning their handshakes while allowing his hard gaze to remain on Jarvis for several seconds before taking a seat.

Canfield splashed whiskey into a fourth glass and handed it to Gann while raising his own in salute. "A toast to our mutual success, gentlemen." After a drink had been taken by each of the other three, the senator lowered his glass and looked at Gann.

"Now, Raymond, on to the business matters at hand. When do you expect the construction at Hat Creek to be completed? Before you answer, let me point out that both Otto and Phil are well aware of everything that's gone on up to this point. So, without further delay, when can I expect to begin operations?"

"Sooner than we had expected, Senator. I'm pleased to report that we've made remarkable progress and should evacuate the area within two days. At that time, you can set up shop." Gann paused to reach inside his tunic and draw out a set of legal documents. "To prevent undue delay, I've brought the proper forms along with me for you to sign here today. Once your signature is written on these, along with mine and that of a responsible witness, such as Mr. Bruner here, you will be proprietor and operator of the Hat Creek stage station. That means, from this point on, you or your heirs have legal rights to that facility, even though we have some finishing touches to carry out yet."

Canfield's eyes lit up with delight. "Splendid! I had thought we were more than a week away from this moment. Phil, would you be so kind as to get a pen, ink, and a blotter for me from the bartender? Certainly they have them around here somewhere."

"Sure," Jarvis replied, rising with a cautious glance at Gann, whose eyes were riveted on his face. "Be back in a minute."

When he was gone, Gann looked again at the senator. "Your operations will link up with the Deadwood stage line out of Dakota Territory. The iron bridge across the North Platte is nearly completed, and I would assume you will want to initiate service south to Cheyenne just as soon as possible. That should prove quite lucrative, considering the mining going on around

Lead and Deadwood in Dakota, and the number of passengers wishing to travel between there and Cheyenne. If handed properly, you should have a controlling interest in all stage service from this point on, as far as the Wyoming Territory is concerned."

"And handled properly it shall be, Captain," Canfield exulted as his eyes skipped over the documents. "Everything seems to be in order here, so let's affix the proper signatures in the proper places and drink to a golden future. You don't know how much I appreciate this, Raymond, and how much in your debt I am," he said, passing the papers to Bruner for inspection.

"No, I suppose not, Senator. Neither one of us can tell that at this point. Time will determine any gratitude I deserve."

Jarvis returned with the writing implements just as Bruner handed the papers back with an approving nod, and Canfield dipped pen in ink while Gann pointed out the proper places to sign. Each man in turn signed in the designated places, and then Gann folded the papers again and returned them to his breast pocket.

"I'll have these recorded at Fort Laramie when I get back there, but bear in mind that you are now the legal owner," Gann said, before his gaze drifted to Jarvis. "That is, you and your partner here, Mr. Bradley. I assume you have your investment protected by papers drawn up to cover any eventuality that might arise, don't you, Mr. Bradley?"

"Yes, of course I do," Jarvis replied somewhat nervously. "The senator and I have a binding agreement written into the original proposal, which states that if something should happen to either one of us, the other has full control of our mutual enterprise. We both thought it would be better that way," he concluded weakly.

"Sounds like a wise decision. Now, Senator, I think this would be the proper time for us to ride out and take a look at what you've just received. I'm quite proud of the work my men have done, and I'm anxious for you to have a look at it."

Canfield looked up in surprise. "Now? You mean today?"

"I can't see why not," Gann said innocently. "As I said earlier, we're well ahead of schedule, and everything else has to be pushed up as well."

177

"But . . . but you said you wanted to have a detachment of your cavalrymen along to ensure my protection. Are they here with you?"

"No they aren't. But I've made that ride several times by myself, and there's no greater risk to you than there is to me. Perhaps I was being a bit overprotective when I said that, and besides, I thought we'd have more time at our disposal."

"How long does it take to get there?"

"It shouldn't be too much after dark when we arrive." Suddenly Gann smiled in a self-deprecating way while holding his hands up, palms outward. "No, wait a minute. I'm wrong. We wanted to look at your land as well, and we'd be better off to leave at first light in the morning. I guess I was just so pleased with what we've done that I got a little overanxious. We'll leave in the morning."

A relieved look swept over Canfield's face, and he sagged in his chair as though all the strength had drained from his body. "Thank God," he said, taking up his glass again. "I need to brace myself for a journey of those proportions."

"Yes, I suppose you do," Gann replied while directing his attention toward Jarvis. "Mr. Bradley, do you own that sorrel over at the livery stable?"

"Yes, as a matter of fact I do. Why?"

"I was there to check on my mount just before I came here, and the hostler was saying something about its having gotten some bad feed. He's a little concerned and asked me to tell you to stop by if I saw you. I'm quite familiar with horses and their ailments, so, if you'd like, I'll go back over there with you and we'll see what can be done."

An apprehensive look flashed across Jarvis's face, but he concealed it quickly with one of his patented smiles. "Of course, Captain. I would very much appreciate that. If the senator and Mr. Bruner will excuse us?"

"Of course, my boy," Canfield boomed jovially. "I would like for the two of you, along with Otto, of course, to join my daughter and me for dinner tonight. Say, seven o'clock?"

"Well . . . I, ah, don't know, Senator," Jarvis stammered. "I'm really kind of tired and—"

"Of course we'll be there, Senator," Gann said, cutting Jarvis off. "It might be the last time the five of us will have a chance to be together. May I ask the privilege of escorting your daughter to dinner, sir? I haven't seen Miss Canfield in some time now."

"Certainly, Captain. She would be delighted, I'm sure. Call for her promptly at six-forty-five, and we'll be waiting for you in the dining room."

"I won't be a minute late, Senator," Gann replied while turning Jarvis toward the batwing doors. "Shall we have a look at that horse, Mr. Bradley?"

Jarvis nodded and trudged toward the door with anything but enthusiasm in his step.

After the two had left the saloon, Kincaid looked up from his hand of cards with a casual glance toward the senator and Bruner, who had immediately fallen into conversation.

"What do you think, Windy? Did you hear it all?"

"Yup. I think the chick's startin' to peck at the shell. Shouldn't be too long before something happens."

"That's the way it sounded to me too," Kincaid replied. "The problem is, we still don't have anything that will prove those two were responsible for that massacre at Farley's Crossing. Sure, we know who did it, and most likely who planned it, but we don't have any absolute proof. Jarvis could lie about where he got that money, even if we could prove he's lying about being from a rich Texas family."

Windy worked the cut-plug in his cheek, expertly sailed a stream of tobacco juice into the spittoon by his chair with a loud clang, then played another card. "We'll just have to wait 'em out, Matt. They're gonna have to make a mistake sooner or later. Don't worry about those two goin' over to the livery by themselves. If they say anything we need to hear, old Oly'll get it to me. Gonna cost the army another dollar, but when they stand to get twenty-four thousand back, that ain't nothin' more than dribble on a baby's chin."

Kincaid studied his cards in thought. "Gann's going to have to make a move shortly, since he's already signed the station over. I wonder what it'll be?"

"Beats me, but I do know one thing."

"What's that?"

"It's your play."

179

Neither Gann nor Jarvis spoke as they crossed the street, but when they were in the sheltered coolness of the livery, Gann glanced around once and then drew Jarvis off to one side.

"How did it go at Farley's?" Gann asked.

"Like clockwork," Jarvis replied with a relieved grin. "Our split was twenty-four thousand, and I put twenty of that into the stage line, like you told me to. The other four thousand we can split for operating money."

"Good. Once the old man is out of the way, we'll be free and clear. I'll take care of him tomorrow." Gann paused to allow his steely gaze to sink into Jarvis's mind before speaking again. "You seemed to be a little nervous in that saloon over there, Jay. That's not like a cool poker player like you. You aren't planning on doing me a little shit on this deal, are you?"

Jarvis laughed with as much gusto as he could muster. "What are you talking about? We're partners in this, and you're the last man I'd try to double-cross."

"I hope you mean that, Jay. For your sake. Once the old man is dead, you'll have complete control of the station, according to that agreement I had you sign with Canfield. That might be a little bit tempting to a person with an extra ace up his sleeve."

"I gave that up a long time ago, you know that, Ray."

"Yes I do. But I also know a man like you only plays with four aces until he needs a fifth. Have you seen Marla since you've been in Douglas?"

Jarvis shrugged to show total lack of interest. "A couple of times, maybe. She's always with the senator, though."

"She's a beautiful woman, isn't she?" Gann asked.

"The best, Ray. You're a lucky man."

"I am indeed. You missed the big event this morning. I would have invited you, but there wasn't any time for that sort of thing."

"Oh? What did I miss, Ray?" Jarvis asked, trying to control the sinking feeling in the pit of his stomach. "You mean that business with the hotel clerk?"

"No, that wasn't an invitation affair," Gann replied acidly. "I mean the wedding. Marla and I got married this morning.

She is now Mrs. Gann," he continued with a wink. "It's all legal and proper. After the senator's gone, you and I will be partners. One more day, and it'll all be ours."

A sickly expression crossed Jarvis's face, which he made a failing attempt to conceal, and he tried to speak but no words came forth.

"What's the matter, partner?" Gann asked with a hearty slap on Jarvis's shoulder. "Aren't you going to congratulate me? Hell, man! It's my wedding day!"

Jarvis swallowed hard several times and finally managed to look up at Gann. "Congratulations, Ray," he mumbled.

"That's more like it. Now we'd better get out of here before we're noticed," Gann said, turning away. "I'll go first." He stopped in the entranceway and looked back. "Oh, one more thing. The senator doesn't know about my being his son-in-law yet, so keep it under your hat. And another thing—don't trouble yourself with going up to congratulate Marla. I'll be with my new bride from now until we meet the senator for dinner, and you know what newlyweds do when they're alone for the first time, so I'd appreciate no interruptions." The captain grinned at Jarvis's pained expression and said cheerfully, "See you at dinner, partner."

Jay Jarvis sank onto a stool and stared at the floor between his boots until long shadows stretching across the street marked the sun's progress toward the horizon. Finally he left the stable and went back to the hotel to prepare for the dinner party that evening, but he felt sick deep inside and wanted to face no one. What he had known all along was proving to be true once again—he was no match for Gann. The man was so intimidating, arrogant, confident, and ruthless that Jarvis could not deal with him face-to-face.

He knew there was only one way he could conquer Gann, and it was the same ploy he'd used at Farley's crossing—a shot in the back from ambush. As his key went toward the lock, Jarvis vowed to do it that night, after the dinner party. Everyone would think it was the same murderer who had killed the clerk, and no one would be the wiser. Then he would find the marriage certificate, destroy the document, and Marla would be his again, with the senator knowing nothing of what had transpired. The station had been turned over to Canfield already, so there was no reason to wait any longer.

That decision having been made, Jarvis felt stronger and more sure of himself as he turned the key, noted with mild surprise that the door wasn't locked, and stepped into his room. The first thing he noticed was that his bed had been torn apart, and then he froze at the sight of something dangling from a rafter. It was a bedsheet with a noose fashioned at one end, hanging directly above a chair placed in the center of the room. Almost afraid to turn his head, he slowly looked toward the far corner where another chair was situated, and was greeted by the cold, cruel smile of Captain Gann.

Seated with his legs crossed, his revolver in one hand and a drink in the other, Gann waved the pistol toward the door. "Come on in, Jay, and close the door. If I have to, I'll kill you right there, so don't give a second thought to running or going for your gun."

Stunned, Jarvis closed the door and moved to the center of the room in response to a second waggling of Gann's revolver.

"That's good, Jay. Very good. Now take that gun out of your holster with the tips of two fingers and toss it on the bed."

Again, Jarvis did as instructed and Gann nodded toward the bottle sitting on the nightstand. "Pour yourself a drink. I don't have long to chat because I've got a dinner engagement, but we do have a few minutes to waste."

As Jarvis poured, the bottle shook in his hand and its neck clinked against the side of the glass with a loud chatter. "Why are you doing this, Ray? I haven't double-crossed you, and I wouldn't, you know that. Otherwise, why would I have come back here with that twenty-four thousand?"

"You didn't come back here from any loyalty to me. I would never have trusted you with that kind of money on your word alone. I know why you came back, and you do as well, so don't bullshit me."

Jarvis tried to control the glass moving toward his lips. "Why?"

"You asked me a question a few days back, and apparently you decided to find the answer out for yourself."

"What question is that, Ray?"

"You asked me if sleeping with a senator's daugher was as gratifying as sleeping with a major's wife. I still can't answer that question, but you can now. Tell me, is it?"

Jarvis's face blanched and he shook his head. "I don't know what you're talking about."

"Like hell you don't!" Gann snarled. "I don't have to remind you, my friend, that Marla is a senator's daughter."

"Marla? Hell, man you're out of your mind! I never touched her!"

"Sure, *partner*. And a pig's ass is made out of dyed wool, too. I heard you in here with her this morning, but I've got even better proof than that. That four-eyed clerk had been listening at your door the same as he had at mine. It was all written down on his little notepad—names, times, what was said, the whole damned works. 'Miss Marla Canfield and Mr. Phillip Bradley, room number thirteen,' was his last entry."

Jarvis's face trembled and he blinked his eyes compulsively. "No . . . Ray . . . that's not right. He . . . he's wrong, I swear. We were just talking and—"

"Sure, you were talking all right, or at least *she* was. I heard it all, friend, and read the rest right after I killed that clerk. I'm sure you understand. I couldn't stand having his entries falling into the senator's hands any more than you can stand having them fall into mine."

"I'm sorry, Ray. I really am. We love each other and couldn't help ourselves. That's the truth, I swear it. Let me go this time and I'll clear out of here. You can have the money, Marla, and everything else. I'll never touch her again, you have my word on that."

"I know you won't, and I don't need your word on anything," Gann said rising and advancing on Jarvis, who was back peddling toward the wall. "And the main reason you won't is that you won't be *alive* to do it again. She's my ticket to the top, and no miserable orphan bastard like you is going to get in the way. When you're found, they'll say you committed suicide, simple as that."

Gann was nearly on top of Jarvis now, and he tossed his glass onto the bed, switched his revolver to his left hand, and closed in on the terrified man before him.

"No, Ray! Please!" Jarvis pleaded, raising his hands to shield his face. "We've been friends and—"

Gann's right hand shot out and closed around Jarvis's throat with such force that it pinched his windpipe completely off and compressed his Adam's apple to a hard knot. In a matter of seconds, perhaps more from sheer pain than lack of oxygen, Jarvis slumped forward, unconscious. Gann immediately looped an arm beneath his shoulder and dragged him to the chair. He slipped the bedsheet noose over Jarvis's head, pulled it taut, then stood back and watched the unconscious man sag against the knotted sheet. After he was sure the device would hold, Gann kicked the chair out from under Jarvis's boots. Jarvis's head snapped upward and he hung there, dangling two feet off the floor. After a quick check of the hallway, Gann stepped out, closed the door behind him, and went into his room.

Forty-five minutes later he was in the hallway again, with Marla's hand on his arm, and he noticed her nervous glance toward the door of room thirteen. Gann smiled in a particularly cold way while patting her hand.

"Mr. Bradley asked me to apologize to everyone for his absence tonight. He's not feeling well, and complained of a splitting headache when I went with him to the livery stable this afternoon. I haven't seen him since, but he was quite sincere about sending his regrets for missing our wonderful dinner party." Gann smiled sweetly as they turned on the landing and started down the stairs. "Besides, it would be quite uncomfortable having one woman and two lovers all seated at the same table, wouldn't it? I don't think the senator would be understanding at all if he knew that to be the case."

Marla's lips quivered, twin tears trickled down her cheeks, and she stumbled midway down the flight of stairs. Gann steadied her and proceeded downward.

"You'll be just fine, honey," he said. "Just smile, be happy, and make your father very proud of both of us. I'm telling you that for your sake as well as mine. I merely have some money and a marriage at stake—you have your life."

thirteen _____

It was a grim-faced platoon of mounted infantrymen who arrived at Sage Creek in midafternoon on the second day after leaving Outpost Number Nine. The four privates had been generous with their recounting of the way they had been treated by the cavalrymen, and there was an ominous silence among the soldiers of Second Platoon when Lieutenant Fowler signaled for a halt just short of the headquarters tent. Once again the cavalrymen looked up from their work, which now consisted mainly of picking up scraps of lumber, driving a last nail here and there, and generally putting the finishing touches on the station.

Lieutenant Ecklehart had been standing near a group of his men, and now he moved forward apprehensively to approach the waiting platoon. He stopped before Fowler and looked up at the unsmiling officer. "I'm Lieutenant Ecklehart. I assume there is something I can do for you, Lieutenant?"

"Yes there is. I'm Lieutenant Fowler, Easy Company. I'm here to speak with Captain Raymond J. Gann."

Ecklehart smiled with a helpless shrug. "The captain isn't here just now. As a matter of fact, he never seems to be here when you people show up. I am in command until he returns from Douglas, so perhaps I can be of help to you?"

Fowler swung down with a glance toward Sergeant Olsen. "Put the men at ease, Sergeant. Have them dismount and wait in ranks."

"Yes, sir."

Fowler turned back to Ecklehart while Olsen transmitted the order, and spoke again after removing two folded maps from his saddlebags. "I would like to compare these maps with yours, Lieutenant. They are both identical with regard to this area, but each was issued by a separate army agency."

"I don't understand," Ecklehart replied, shaking his head in confusion. "We have sufficient maps already, and as you can plainly see, our work here will be done before nightfall."

"That's not the point. I'm not here to give these maps to you, I'm here to compare them with yours. Shall we step into the tent?"

"Of course. Why not? It seems to be a pointless exercise to me, but you have had a long ride, so why make it for nothing?"

The two officers stepped inside and Ecklehart immediately displayed his map, which Fowler perused carefully.

"Would you care for a brandy, Lieutenant?" Ecklehart asked, reaching for the bottle while Fowler continued his scrutiny of the map.

"I never drink on duty," Fowler replied flatly, without looking up.

A contrite expression crossed Ecklehart's face. "Oh," he said weakly as his hand slowly stopped short of the bottle.

"Come over here," Fowler said, unfolding his maps and matching up the proper sections with Ecklehart's. "You've done a fine job of building this station, Lieutenant," he offered as the cavalry officer moved over to stand beside him.

"Thank you, Lieutenant. We've done the best we could."

"There's just one small problem."

"Problem?" Ecklehart asked in surprise. "What kind of problem?"

"You built the son of a bitch in the wrong place."

"The wrong place!" Ecklehart blurted. "What the hell are you talking about?"

"Facts, mostly. Here, have a look. The map you've been using is a forgery. Everything is exactly the way it should be on yours, except that the names of these two creeks"—Fowler pointed them out with his finger—"Hat Creek and Sage Creek, have been reversed. And there's one other slight problem—the Nebraska border has been moved west about twenty miles. Your stage station was supposed to be built in Nebraska, but when you go to the latrine in the morning, you're shitting in Wyoming Territory."

"What? That's impossible! You can't do this to me! My entire future is at stake here!"

Fowler smiled for the first time since he had arrived. "*I* didn't do it to you, Lieutenant. But my CO has plenty of reason to think Captain Gann did. Here, compare these maps, the one Gann gave you and the two actually printed by the government. See where the boundary line between Wyoming Territory and Nebraska actually splits the difference between the two creeks involved, with Sage Creek to the left and Hat Creek to the right? But here on Gann's map, both creeks are on the Nebraska side, and the names of the two creeks have been reversed."

"My God! You're right!" Ecklehart gasped, reaching for the brandy bottle in earnest this time, and not caring whether he was on duty or not. "I'm ruined!"

"Not necessarily, if you actually had no part in this juggling act. But one thing is certain—you're not in command anymore."

"I'm not?" Ecklehart asked with a mixture of relief and curiosity in his voice.

"No you're not. You're under arrest, and I'm assuming command until we get this thing straightened out."

"Under arrest?" Ecklehart said numbly, slumping onto a stool. "Can you do that?"

"I certainly can, and have. Your CO will be under arrest as well, just as soon as he returns." Fowler glanced at the untouched glass trembling in Ecklehart's hand. "I'd say you can go ahead and have a drink now, Lieutenant. You aren't on duty anymore."

Lieutenant Fowler ducked out of the tent and approached the cavalrymen who were watching him warily from a distance. "Listen up!" he said. "I am your new commanding officer until otherwise notified. Lieutenant Ecklehart is under arrest, and so will Captain Gann be, when he gets back. This station was not only built on the wrong creek, it's also approximately twenty miles removed from the right state. You are now standing beside Sage Creek, Wyoming Territory, not Hat Creek, in the state of Nebraska."

Fowler paused to let the shock of what he had said wear off the men who had worked so hard on the project. "I don't hold any of you at fault, but there will be no more work done on this station until further notice. Now since we all have some time to kill until Captain Gann returns, I have an observation to make. It's not an order, a suggestion, or an indication of my approval.

"The way I understand it, there's some unfinished business to be conducted between this cavalry unit and the mounted infantry. I am also under the impression that the number of participants was not exactly equal on both sides during your last, shall we say, business meeting. Four privates and one sergeant under my command have expressed an interest in resuming that meeting, with an equal number of men of matching rank from your construction platoon. Is that proposal of any interest to you cavalrymen?"

A low grumble swept through the cavalry ranks, and a burly sergeant stepped forward. "Hell, yes, Lieutenant. We'll talk business with 'em anytime."

"Fine, Sergeant. Come over here and you'll be the spokesman for your group." Fowler turned toward the platoon behind him. "Sergeant Olsen? Front and center!"

The two sergeants came forward and stood on either side of Fowler, who glanced alternately at each man as he spoke. "There will be no guns, knives, rocks, sticks, or any other weapon used during the meeting. You will express your opinions with fists, and fists only. Each of you is responsible for his own contingent in that regard. Is that understood?"

Both Sergeants nodded.

"Fine. Now it looks like there is going to be some difficulty in determining exactly what the name of this station is supposed to be when this is all through. Therefore, I have a suggestion to make. If the cavalry comes out on top, this will be known as Sage Creek Station, to save their outfit from the embarrassment of having the world know how badly they fouled up. If the mounted infantry wins, it will be known henceforth as Hat Creek Station." Fowler smiled and looked at both men. "That's just a little added incentive. Now, I am considering myself officially off duty for the next hour. In light of that fact, I am going in to have a drink with Lieutenant Ecklehart." Fowler turned toward the headquarters tent while saying over his shoulder, "Commence, gentlemen, whenever the mood strikes you."

The first light of dawn had just touched Kincaid's window when he heard Gann pounding on the senator's door. "Time to go, Senator! We've got a lot of miles to cover today!"

Kincaid waited for Gann to pound on Jarvis's door as well, but there was no second knock. According to the arrangements he and Windy Mandalian had made the previous evening, Kincaid would wait in the hotel until all three men left, while the scout waited across the street near the livery stable. When he heard the senator's sleepy grumblings and the footsteps of two men going down the hall, he thought it odd and wondered why Jarvis would be left behind.

After waiting nearly five minutes, Kincaid eased out of his room, pressed an ear against Jarvis's door, heard nothing, and cautiously made his way down the hall to descend the stairs. He wondered if Jarvis might have slipped out of the hotel earlier in the morning, and he stopped in the lobby to peer through the window at the stable across the street. Just a few minutes later, Gann and Canfield led their horses from the building, mounted, and rode down the street in an easterly direction. Kincaid stepped onto the boardwalk at the same time that Windy emerged from an alleyway, and the two of them looked at each other and shrugged. Kincaid ducked across the street and they went into the alley again.

"What do you make of it, Windy? Jarvis isn't with them."

"Yeah, I know. I wonder what the hell he's up to."

"Hard to tell. Did your hostler friend have anything to say about that meeting between Jarvis and Gann yesterday afternoon?"

Windy grinned sheepishly and shook his head. "Must be overpayin' the help, Matt. The old bastard got drunk about noon and slept right through it. So much for spies. But he'll be huntin' me up here in an hour or two to tell me a couple of horses are gone."

"He'll be a little late, then, because we won't be here. We can't let Gann get too far away, but we know where he's going and can catch up with him. Jarvis we don't know about. I'll go back over to the hotel and check his room, and you keep an eye out here in case he tries to slip out of town."

Windy nodded and leaned back against the wall, shifting the heavy Sharps to a more comfortable position in the crook of his arm.

Kincaid had barely entered the lobby when a scream split the morning calm, and he raced up the stairs, taking them two at a time. Turning down the hall, he saw Jarvis's door standing open, with a shadow cast across the entranceway.

Drawing his sidearm, Kincaid eased down the hallway with his back to the wall, hesitated beside the doorway, then sprang inside in a crouched position, with the gun cocked and held before him. The room was silent except for the sobbing of a woman standing there with her hands clutched to her face and staring upward.

Just above her and to the left, turning slowly in the breeze created by the open door and window, Jay Jarvis hung from the bedsheet with his mouth open and blackened tongue protruding grotesquely, his half-lidded eyes staring blankly at the far wall.

"He killed him," she said over and over again in whispered disbelief. "He killed him."

Kincaid lowered the hammer on his gun, holstered the weapon, and moved forward to place his hand lightly on her shoulder. "Ma'am? I'm a friend," he offered gently. "I'm not going to hurt you. I'm here to help."

She might have been alone in the room, so little attention

did Marla pay to Kincaid's words. "He killed Jay," she said, her lips barely moving. "He killed Jay."

"Do you mean Jay Jarvis?"

Marla nodded numbly. "His real name was Jay Jarvis. And I loved him."

"I'm sorry, ma'am. Do you know who killed him?" Kincaid asked softly.

"Yes, I know. It was my husband."

"Your husband?"

"Yes, my husband. Captain Gann."

Kincaid couldn't control the shock in his voice. "Captain Gann is your husband?"

Again she nodded. "Yes. He forced me to marry him yesterday morning." Her eyes remained locked on Jarvis and her lips quivered. "Please help me. Take him down, please. I beg you."

"I will, but I don't think you should watch this." Kincaid took her shoulders in both hands and turned her around stiffly. "Just wait out in the hall while I get him down."

Marla nodded and stumbled toward the doorway. Kincaid thought he heard a door close as he stepped forward to raise the stiff body up high enough to free the noose from its neck, and just as he was lowering the corpse onto the bed, he heard the flat report of a small gun being fired nearby.

Quickly freeing himself of the dead man, he raced from the room, tried the latch on room twelve, found it locked, then stepped to room fourteen. He could smell the acrid odor of gunpowder seeping through the crack beneath the closed door. Kincaid burst into the room and stopped dead when he saw her lying there.

Marla Canfield lay sprawled on the floor, with blood from a bullet hole spreading over the left side of her chest. A small-caliber revolver was held limply in her grasp. Kincaid bent down to check her pulse, and then listened for a heartbeat, but found neither. When he rose and turned wearily toward the door, the barrel of a Sharps swung past the jamb and Windy Mandalian stepped into the doorway, prepared to fire.

"Sorry, Matt," Windy said, lowering the rifle. "I heard a shot and I thought maybe Jarvis got the drop on you."

"No. There's no fight left in Jarvis. He's dead, over there in his room. Miss Canfield said she was sure Gann did it. She found him, he had been hung, and I guess she was in love with him. It must have been too great a shock, and she came in here and shot herself."

"Is she dead too?"

"Yes she is. She said Gann forced her to marry him yesterday morning. Now, with both Jarvis and her dead, all he has to do is get rid of the senator and he's home free. No witnesses and no proof. He's only one murder away from pulling this whole thing off."

"They've got a pretty damned good lead on us now, Matt. Fifteen, maybe twenty minutes. We've gotta catch him before he pulls the trigger on Canfield."

"Yes, I know. I'll explain all this to the hotel owner when we get back."

They were riding their horses at an easy canter across the plains, but that didn't change the pained expression on Canfield's face every time saddle leather slapped against his butt.

"Do we need to ride this fast, Captain?" he asked, jowls flopping. "I have never deluded myself that I was an expert horseman, as you are well aware."

Gann grinned. "We've got a lot of ground to cover, Senator, and we want to get to the station before too late in the afternoon. We'll take a break after a few more miles."

"I think I'm already broken, son," Canfield grunted, grasping his saddlehorn and hanging on.

They had rested their mounts briefly, twice, before what Gann had been looking for came into view. Ahead and just off to the right was a deep washout, the bed of what was known as a dry creek, because it was in flow only during the rainy season. When viewed across the rolling prairie, it couldn't be seen from a distance, and a man or horse that fell into it might lie there for months before being found. Gann knew he was still an hour away from the station, which suited his needs perfectly, and he glanced across at the senator while pulling in on his own reins.

"You look like you could use another rest, Senator," he

192

said, nodding toward the dry creek. "Let's stop here for a few minutes and let you catch your breath."

"How much farther is this goddamned place anyway, Captain?" Canfield asked in dismay. "I'm beginning to think I should have settled for a description instead of actually seeing it for myself."

"That's what's wrong with you lazy, fat-assed, rich sons of bitches," Gann said flatly as their horses stopped side by side. "You want everybody else to do your work for you."

Canfield glanced across in total shock. "Now hold on a minute, Captain! I'll not be talked to—"

The senator broke off abruptly as Gann eased the Scoff from its holster and leveled it across his right thigh.

"What—what's the meaning of this?" Canfield gasped, the whites of his eyes wide in his reddening face.

"The meaning is that this charade is over. But before it is, there's one thing I want you to know. Your daughter is my wife, she's a bitch dog in heat, and you are an ignorant, bloated son of a bitch!"

"No! You can't talk about Marla that way. She's my baby and—"

"I'll talk about her any way I please," Gann snarled, his face twisted in a cruel smile of triumph. "She's my wife now, senator, and since she is, I don't need you anymore."

Gann pulled the trigger. A bullet slammed into the senator's stomach, his eyes bulged, a groan blurted from his mouth, and he tried to speak as he tilted to one side. The captain casually cocked the weapon again and fired a second time with the revolver aimed slightly higher, and the next slug crashed into Canfield's chest and sent him toppling from his mount to flop in the grass, then slowly slide into the creekbed. The senator's horse bolted away, and Gann reined his mount over close to the bank and aimed the Scoff for a third shot, which tore a gaping hole in the dead senator's neck.

When he reined his mount around again, he saw the outline of two riders coming fast, topping a distant swell. Gann studied them momentarily before lashing his horse into a hard run, jumping the creekbed and heading straight for the construction site at Sage Creek. He glanced over his shoulder several times in an attempt to determine who was behind him, and finally decided that whoever it was, they were after him.

Kincaid and Mandalian pulled their plunging horses to a stop near the bloodstained grass where Canfield had slid down the bank, and Windy leaped down to see if there was anything he could do for the senator. Seconds later he was scrambling upward and swinging onto his horse's back again.

"He's dead, Matt. We were a couple of minutes too late, but we've got Gann now. He knows we saw him kill Canfield, and now he's gonna have to go to tree when we catch him," Mandalian yelled, giving the roan its head and racing away beside Kincaid.

It was obvious that they had pushed their horses harder than Gann had pushed his, and now the cavalry officer was slowly pulling away from them.

"Let's not run them to death, Windy," Kincaid said, referring to the tiring animals. "He can't keep that pace up forever, and our mounts will be a little stronger when the time comes to call on them."

"He's headed straight for Sage Creek," the scout replied, slowing his horse to match Kincaid's gait. "If he can get to his troops and turn them against us, we still might be in for a hatful of trouble before this is over."

"Let's hope Fowler is there by now," Kincaid yelled back. "If that does happen, it might be kind of nice to have a few familiar faces around us when it does."

Gann could feel his horse start to falter in midstride as he neared the construction site, but he urged it forward mercilessly anyway. He could make out the low silhouette of the buildings, and knew he had but a quarter of a mile to go and then he would be surrounded by loyal troopers who would respond to his commands. One final glance over his shoulder revealed no sign of the riders behind him, but he continued to push on at his reckless, horse-killing pace.

When his mount pounded onto the beaten earth where the station had been built, he waved his Scoff and pulled the horse to a jolting, rock-grinding stop.

"Get to your mounts, men!" he yelled at the cavalrymen gathered off to one side in a sorrowful group. "Move, damn it! Now! There are two outlaws behind me who just killed Senator Canfield!"

Not one man moved, and Gann stared at them in wild-eyed bewilderment as he reined his sweat-drenched horse around to look at them again. "What the hell's the matter with you! That was a direct order!"

Lieutenant Fowler stepped away from the entrance to the headquarters tent and looked up at Gann. "You don't give the orders around here anymore, Captain. I do. You are under arrest."

Gann glanced frantically over his shoulder and saw his pursuers, now no more than two hundred yards away. After a moment's indecision, he lashed his heels against the flanks of his exhausted mount and raced away to the right at a ninty-degree angle from his pursuers.

"This is what we've been saving them for, Windy," Kincaid yelled. "Let's use them now!"

Both horses broke into a dead run and quickly closed the gap on the fleeing Gann. The captain tried to jerk his mount's head up as it drooped toward the ground, but the horse's heart had given out, and it stumbled over its front legs and pitched forward, throwing Gann over its head. Gann rolled several times before scrambling to his feet and snapping off two quick shots, both of which went wild. He started to run, tripped and fell, then turned on one knee and raised the weapon to fire his last shot at the two riders, who were less than fifty yards away.

The sharps came up, and Windy took but a second to aim before his finger closed on the trigger and the heavy slug slammed into Gann's chest and sent him flying backward in a crazy sprawl. Seconds later, both Kincaid and Mandalian were off their horses, and when Gann rolled onto his side and attempted to raise his revolver again, Kincaid's weapon belched flame and the right side of the captain's head seemed to disappear. He flopped over backward in the tall grass, his revolver fell from his grasp, and Captain Raymond J. Gann lay dead.

Kincaid and Mandalian advanced cautiously, leading their horses and holding weapons ready to fire. When they got close

195

enough to see that the whole right side of Gann's face had been blown away, they lowered their guns and stood in silence for several seconds.

Kincaid felt a curious sense of disappointment. Gann had died too quickly for one who had caused so much death and suffering to others.

Windy, seeming to know how Matt felt, placed a hand on his shoulder. They stood there silently for a moment; there seemed to be nothing worth saying.

Finally they turned around and headed back toward the station, leading their horses. Fowler came out to meet them as they approached.

"I'm damned glad you were here, Mr. Fowler," Kincaid said. "If Gann had been able to get his men to follow him, we'd be dead now."

"I'm glad I was here too, sir," Fowler replied. "What now? Shall I send a detail out to pick up Gann's body?"

"Yes, do that," Kincaid said. "I'm afraid we'll have to pack that garbage back to Laramie. Also send a detail to fetch Senator Canfield's body from that dry wash back there. We'll take him back to Douglas. The local undertaker can make arrangements with Washington to ship his body—and his daughter's—back home for burial."

Fowler blinked in surprise. "How many bodies did Gann leave behind, sir?"

"Too many, Mr. Fowler, entirely too many," Kincaid answered wearily. "We'll stay here tonight and head out for Douglas in the morning. While we're there, we'll pick up the payroll from the bank. With a whole platoon along, we should be able to get it back to Laramie safely."

As the two officers and the scout approached the station, Second Platoon formed ranks and stood at attention, as did the cavalry construction platoon, but there was a visible difference in the attitudes of the two units. Second Platoon stood tall and proud; even the blue of their uniforms seemed to shine more brightly than those of the cavalry detachment, who appeared somehow shrunken, as though the wind had been let out of them. In the front rank of Second Platoon stood five men with an assortment of black eyes, contusions, and split, swollen lips. They looked like they were trying to suppress wide smiles, and the effect on their broken faces was grotesque and obviously painful. Behind them, nailed to the wall of the stage station's main building, was a freshly painted, hand-lettered sign that read:

HAT CREEK STATION

Watch for
**EASY COMPANY AND
THE MYSTERY TROOPER**
Twenty-third novel in the exciting
EASY COMPANY series from Jove

Coming in December!

MORE ROUGH RIDING ACTION FROM JOHN WESLEY HOWARD